GOOD INTENTIONS

Good Intentions
By Stephen Jackley

© 2015 Stephen Jackley

ISBN: 9780993526510

First published in 2015 by Arkbound (Publishers)

Second edition published in 2018

No part of this publication may be reproduced, stored in a retrieval system, or transmitted, in any form or by any means without the prior permission of the publisher, nor be otherwise circulated in any form of binding or cover other than that in which it is published and without a similar condition being imposed on the subsequent purchaser.

Arkbound is a social enterprise that aims to promote social inclusion, community development and artistic talent. It sponsors publications by disadvantaged authors and covers issues that engage wider social concerns. Arkbound fully embraces sustainability and environmental protection. It endeavours to use material that is renewable, recyclable or sourced from sustainable forest.

Arkbound
Backfields House
Upper York Street
Bristol, BS2 8QJ
England

www.arkbound.com

GOOD INTENTIONS

STEPHEN JACKLEY

Building futures, Bridging divides

Dedication

To all those who take the road of good intentions,
hoping for the best.

No man is an Island, entire of itself; every man is a piece of the Continent, a part of the main; if a clod be washed away by the sea, Europe is the less, as well as if a promontory were, as well as if a manor of thy friends or of thine own were; any man's death diminishes me, because I am involved in Mankind; And therefore never send to know for whom the bell tolls; It tolls for thee.

– John Donne, 1572–1631

1

The present path was one he did not want to walk. The destination was as equally undesirable. And yet, grudgingly remembering *the mission,* there was no other paths for him to take. The decision he had made was one that dictated his destiny. It bound him to the domain of outcasts and drifters. *To take from the takers and give back to the taken* – it was a motto, more like a promise, which now shaped his every move.

Thunder again, so far away that it could have been the passing of a plane. *Rumblings in the sky.* That was probably how it would begin. And then?

He had no time to consider an answer. The destination was before him: The Bank, a temple to man's modern god. Its classical colonnades supported a porch where people gathered, looking out at the rain. He swept past them, barely seen, and pushed through the turning doors of the main entrance.

Brightness and warmth could not soften the hard depths that had set in his mind. Inside he had become a new animal, mutating from man to tiger, poised to explode in a blood-rushing endeavour of risk. No room for hesitation. No time for second thoughts. He reached into an inner pocket of his coat and gripped the handle of a gun.

There was one customer in the lobby, who stood before the glass screen of the first cashier. The other cashier was waving him over impatiently. He snatched a slip of paper from the elevated desk set into the wall and pretended to study it. A deposit slip.

There were no forms for what he was about to do.

Funnels of rain flowed down the creases of his hooded long-coat, water dripping onto the floor. His sports bag became an accomplice to the silent rhythm, waiting for the load it was meant to carry. Dark stains spread as blood on the navy carpet, blooming into circles that hovered on the thresh-hold of permanence and transience. And still the door to the right remained shut.

I've timed it wrong, he thought.

Heart hammering, sweat beading, he realised he was now alone in the bank lobby. To abort seemed the only option – adding failure to what had recently been an unbroken sequence of success.

Click. There was no doubt about it: the lock on the door was disengaged. Two words leapt up from his mind and echoed in the resonance of a mantra: *No Hesitation!* He quickly withdrew the gun, pointing it into the face of a silver-haired man.

'Back inside!'

Branch Manager, a platinum name-tag on his jacket declared. Bushy eyebrows rose to the fringe of his hair, but no other part of his body moved. The gunman stepped forward and pushed him back, letting the door snap shut behind.

As the manager slid against a wall, the gunman turned to

face the two cashiers. They both looked at him with ashen faces – the nearest with her mouth wide open; the other with his hands in the air.

'Get on the floor. Keep your hands where I can see them.' They immediately complied.

'Don't even *think* about pressing any alarms!'

Time was running out; he had already glimpsed another customer enter the bank. But after systematically emptying the four cash drawers of the teller stations, his sports bag was only quarter-full with notes.

He walked over to the manager, whose face had become a bleached swamp that oozed apprehension. The two cashiers flinched as he passed, their eyes locked on the gun. "No one's going to get hurt," he assured them. 'Now,' he looked at the manager, 'if you would kindly open the safe, I'll be gone.'

The silver-haired man levered himself up and made a deep, hacking cough. One of his hands rose to cover his mouth, but then he dropped it to his side, palm pressed to the wall.

'Come on, speed it up!' the gunman roared.

The safe was only a short distance away, in a separate room behind the cashiers' stations. Fingers trembling, the manager entered a code on the keypad. After two bleeps the heavy steel door swung open. There was no time lock – not after the cash had just been delivered and waited to be counted. In that respect the robbery had been timed perfectly. The gunman rushed in and quickly looked around. Within seconds he had the sports bag brimming with higher denomination notes

GOOD INTENTIONS

taken from the middle shelves.

He ran to the door that gave access to the bank lobby, not bothering to check on the cringing cashiers. With the gun flashing silver in his hand, he entered the lobby.

A young man stood there – the same customer who had entered two minutes ago. A mobile phone was pressed to the side of his face, which he dropped as the gunman lurched towards him.

'On the floor!'

With arms outstretched, the young man made a dive to the floor, making a kind of yelping sound as he hit the carpet. In other circumstances it would have made the gunman laugh.

Half-walking, half-running, he crossed the lobby and slid the gun into his pocket, glancing back to ensure that no one followed. A camera above the door winked back at him, getting the best view of a face that wasn't his. It never saw the object that fell from his hand. Even the young man, in his terror, did not see the glint of gold as it rolled across the carpet. By the time someone found what the gunman had dropped, it would be too late.

* * *

Walking to a pace that far dwarfed his racing heart, he ignored the rain watchers outside and hurried along the pavement. But it was impossible to disregard the sirens approaching from up the road. Somehow an alarm had been raised, even before the young man had entered the lobby, probably by one of the cashiers. He fought against the urge to run and instead walked *towards* the sirens, darting into an alleyway just as the first police vehicle came into sight. Blue-red efflorescence sparked off the rain as tyres screeched to a halt behind him.

At the end of the alleyway he turned again, re-joining a side road. Although no one followed him – yet – the threatening wails of the law stubbornly refused to recede. It had always been planned for the changeover location, or getaway, to be five minutes away – far enough for the car or whatever other transport option to be disassociated with a robbery. But now he just wished the getaway was closer.

Two streets away, the maroon car could have been a docked ship – nudged tightly against the curve like Noah's Ark resting upon the mountains of Ararat. Reaching it, seeing the silhouette within, filled him with relief. He climbed inside and slammed the door. One deep breath epitomised his accomplishment.

As rivulets of water traced patterns on the side mirrors, deft hands reached out to take the cash-laden sports bag. One finger, hooked into a claw, flicked through the bundles to check for any dye packs or tracing devices. That soft sound of money slapping against itself rose inexplicably above the louder volume of rain. So, too, did her voice, which was cold and clear as a glacial stream.

'A success then,' she smiled, lifting her eyes from the money and staring into his. Swirls of light green met his own chestnut gaze. Before he knew it, their bodies embraced. Her fingers traced through his auburn hair, throwing back his hood and pulling off his prosthetic mask. They kissed – just long enough for the sirens outside to grow a little more insistent.

As he turned the ignition – easing forward on the accelerator to let the wheels bite into wet tarmac – she returned to counting the money, licking her lips.

The car swept alongside rows of houses and into a twilight netherworld, disappearing as it reached the turning.

* * *

'Gone in six minutes?' the policeman queried the shocked cashier, who clutched a cup of tea and nodded to confirm her previous response.

'Although at the time it seemed much longer', she added.

A crowd had gathered outside the bank in spite of the rain, attracted by the rows of police cars and forensics vehicles. Two constables were busy taking statements, most of which would be useless and quickly discarded, yet a few might prove crucial to the ongoing investigation.

They knew the robber was a male, between 20 to 30 years old, about six-foot tall, of medium build. That was not much to go on. The description of his clothing was really too general to be of much use, especially in this weather: a dark raincoat with the hood up, dark trousers, footwear not yet ascertained. They hoped CCTV footage would reveal more details, although on the forensic front it appeared he had taken precautions. But when one of the technicians approached the chief inspector it signalled a new lead for the case.

'He left this behind,' the man said, holding up a small plastic bag. The inspector took it and stared at the golden object inside.

Mumbled words tumbled from his mouth. 'I don't believe it.'

Few could have predicted the robbers' next set of targets, spread across the whole of the country, with seemingly no aspect of connection except the hint of a similar method – and, of course, the 'calling card'. They left it behind in each robbery: a single coin, with a scratch carved crudely across the metal.

The investigators in each case were baffled as they found themselves caught up in a nationwide network of crimes: one day a bank robbery, a month later a building society, next week a cash-in- transit snatch. All highly planned and all – somehow – connected. Sometimes the robbers wore subtle disguises like wigs and probably prosthetic masks, other times balaclavas. There was often just one of them, but never more than two.

Most detectives thought it was a large group in operation, whilst others toyed with the idea that it was always the same two individuals. A minority still believed the crimes couldn't possibly be connected, but the unshakable problem with this latter view was, of course, the calling card.

GOOD INTENTIONS

'Has the whole country gone mad?!' one chief exclaimed. 'I can only think people read of these robberies and decide to copy them, leaving the same thing behind in each case!'

Yet such a scenario would mean each robber would have to be clever enough not to get caught, which, given the typical mentality of criminals, is a rarity. They *all* get caught... eventually.

Or do they?

This is the question the authorities hated to contemplate: the very idea of someone breaking the law, time and time again, yet never facing the consequences. To them it was a picture of anarchy, chaos – even hell. But they knew, deep down, that *some* would always slip from their grasp, especially the ones with enough power, wealth and – most importantly – influence. These were the most dangerous: not some idiot kid sitting in a jail cell, not even the lunatics in the asylum. No, it was those who had the 'get out of jail free cards', the 'untouchables', who got away with the foulest deeds.

Fortunately, they were pretty certain the 'coin bank robbers' were not of that calibre. Those criminals were fair game – approved by the higher echelons to be arrested no matter what the costs of apprehending them. The victims needed it; the bankers and businessmen wanted it; the papers called for it – and the law demanded it.

* * *

In the brightly lit room of the hotel they counted the loot. He sat on one side of the bed, she on the other. Neatly stacked piles bordered the sea of notes between them, totally covering the floral background of the duvet.

Day by day, week by week, their vision was nearing fruition. At the beginning it was a dream, now it was becoming a reality.

'Where next?' she asked, once the totals were added up.

He reached for a folder on the desk and flicked through the pages.

'Somewhere up north, maybe.'

The maps, routes and blueprints presented a plethora of possibilities. Each location was a siren call towards furthering their target. Looking through the list of premises, he was seeking somewhere to set them up on a new path – a platform to launch higher.

'The shop's doing well,' she said, having returned to the laptop on her pillow. Her gold-streaked hair spilled prettily onto the bed like the mane of a mythical unicorn.

'How's BlueBridge?' he asked, following the curve of her body down to her legs.

'Hmm… not so good,' she replied. 'It could use another cash injection.'

He frowned. 'So how much does it need?'

'Well, at present,' she paused, looking down. 'Another hundred k. Right now, it's overdue by half that.'

'What about increasing the donations from the portfolio and print shop?'

GOOD INTENTIONS

She shook her head. 'Yes, but that wouldn't fulfil this year's commitments – not without sacrificing operational costs.'

He looked at the list of targets in his hand, wondering. For too long they had followed the same modus operandi, taking cash that could only *sustain* their operations, rather than advance them. A new plan was called for, something they had long discussed, and he tossed the folder onto the desk in finality.

'It's time to go onto the next stage. But before that, we need a big hit, something to outweigh all our previous jobs. What do you think?'

She smiled. 'I'm ready as ever.'

They had met two years previously. She had been working as an Aid worker – a voluntary position in the heart of the African DRC. The first time he saw her, she was covered in sweat and dirt, struggling with a buffalo calf that a boy needed returning to a pen. Their meeting was quite by chance, although as with all such 'chance' events, it was part of a greater destiny. Fate's great blueprint is only glimpsed in pieces far down the line, when the events that threaded a life together have long passed. That day in Africa was still clear in his mind…

Her hair was matted and unwashed, but its golden sparkle captured his heart. So did her deep green eyes, those two emerald-coloured stars guiding a traveller to paradise. Her limbs shone bronze in the sun, glowing with youth and vitality.

He had come to Africa as part of an investigation – a study on the extent of third world poverty and what could be done to reduce it. But he had a very different solution in mind to that of his contemporaries, or indeed the woman he loved. By the time he told her his story, in all its madness, sitting alone in the African wilderness, it took her by utter surprise. He told her almost everything, which by then included admitting to a series of bank robberies. She was not impressed. The fact that poverty, inequality and oppression existed was not something she disputed: unlike most Westerners, she knew it first hand. But she wasn't convinced that crime was the answer, especially if other people were harmed in the process of 'redistributing wealth'.

Back then, he had tried in vain to convince her there were no casualties *per se* in his robberies; that the people he stole from were – directly and indirectly – responsible for the poverty she saw. His explanations of the workings of the financial system and the operations of global corporations fell on un-listening ears. She simply could not come to terms with the concept of 'charitable crime'. Nevertheless, they parted amicably, and (perhaps against his better judgement) he left her his contact details.

During the months of their separation she returned home and started a new job in an accountant's office. She did not forget Africa. She thought about everything he told her, looking at it afresh, beginning to see how it was true. Wide-spread publicity on the banking sectors' corruption helped shift her view, but it was the memories of the impoverished children that haunted her the most. Why should the many suffer and die because of the greed of a few? she questioned. She dreamt of a world that could be different if only people stood up for what they

GOOD INTENTIONS

believed in – with courage, determination and enlightenment. One night she decided what to do. All it took was a simple phone call. They met again in a completely different setting, a café in London. Within months she convinced him to let her participate in a robbery and after that they planned every future one together. She actually found herself looking forward to the next heist.

They flirted with risk after each success, continuing to leave behind a 'calling card' but varying the different methods and techniques in an attempt to baffle investigators. The papers soon caught on, calling them the 'Coin Bandits', but never realising it was the same man and women. Even the police didn't seem to realise that.

In all their robberies, they had only gone into premises together on two occasions – both times wearing a complete disguise consisting of balaclavas and long coats. She usually hung around in the background, just as a backup or getaway driver, but other times she went in by herself.

Of course, he had tried to prevent this, but she was adamant. In time he learnt to trust her as an equal partner, but he still felt uncomfortable when she insisted to do a job by herself. Her courage was without bounds. His resolve was indefatigable. Together, nothing could stop them.

2

Late that evening, blades whirled above the flashing lights of cameras. The makeshift barrier erected around the helipad could scarcely hold back the rows of journalists, and the casino manager began to wonder if letting them up was really such a good idea. He tried to justify it with the logic that publicity meant money.

The sliding doors of the helicopter opened, letting forth a stream of suits and one sparkling dress. Many of the journalists found themselves taking photographs of the long, tanned legs before quickly searching for the face of this renowned celebrity. A singer, a dancer and an icon for the new generation – she was everything the masses wanted. She was also a voracious gambler, quoted to stay up into the early hours playing poker in some luxurious club or casino.

The manager stepped forward to greet her. His usual confidence had dwindled beneath the singer's monolithic frame. Her perfect smile, contrasted with huge sunglasses, almost entrapped his carefully prepared welcoming speech. Somehow, though, he got through it – proceeding to lead her to a complimentary suite, usually charged at £950 a night. For her, as with everything else in the casino but the games, it would be free – along with all the other high-stake players. Most of these others were staying in hotels scattered across

GOOD INTENTIONS

the city, whilst she herself preferred to be as close to the action as possible.

The first game would be tomorrow – one of ten, spread over two weeks, until only two players remained. The minimum stake was £100 and the jackpot would eventually rise to over £10 million. That was enough to capture anyone's attention. To a select few, however, even that sum would be considered 'small change'.

For there are those who spend thousands of pounds on bottles of fermenting liquid; tens of millions on inanimate canvasses; the same amounts on houses and vehicles that they rarely see or use. As the wealth of entire nations is hoarded behind impenetrable steel and re- created in the digital circuitry of supercomputers, others fight daily just to eat and drink. It was a situation that had seen over seventy percent of the world's resources controlled by less than two percent of the population. These were the hidden rulers of humanity – the Kings and Queens of a globalised oligarchy founded on monopolisation and manipulation. It was a system that overlooked over ten million children dying before their fifth birthday every year. As a pandemic, the capitalist machine had gripped every city and country – spreading in spider-like patterns away from population centres, along roads and airways, to practically every corner of civilization. Its tendrils sucked out the life of the poor, using their labour to prop up an ever-slanting pyramid of disproportionate power. And with them the world itself was being systematically pillaged, polluted and destroyed. Yet no virgin forest or underwater oil well could sate the hunger of this man-made machine. It would churn on, ripping away every dream of renewal, resisting all meaningful change, with those at the top riding on a churning tsunami of destruction.

Of course, the casino manager didn't see it this way. There were few who did – and even fewer who sought to actively change it. Those who contemplated the global injustice simply resigned themselves to the 'inevitable fact' that they could do nothing about it. To most it was a matter of enjoying life whilst alive, maybe setting aside a little for the next generation; even though, tragically, it was that generation who would suffer from this ones faults.

* * *

Outside, a cold breeze shook the palm trees, creating a shadow play of shapes on the grass. Amber and cerulean floodlights made the trees seem ominous and alien, like living statues guarding the borders to another realm. Although well-tended and given special protection in the colder months, they rarely lasted more than a few years. Some were better adapted than others, but millennias of growing in the tropics made them ill-accustomed to the bitter winters. Even in early spring they longed for warmer climes. There was also the soil… something deep down in the Earth, seeming to sap

GOOD INTENTIONS

all warmth with an unrelenting thirst.

A figure sat against one of the ridged trunks. He chugged on a bottle wrapped in a brown bag, feeling the jagged heat caress his body as it trickled down. The coarse liquid might have caressed his broken body, but it was another ream of barbed wire for his soul. This was his reward after a day's begging, plus the wrapped baguette he still had in his coat.

His face was pockmarked and unshaved, red and warped by uncounted years of hardship. Wild black hair was prematurely speckled with white, obscuring a long white scar that ran across the left side of his scalp. He had no possessions but a rucksack, which held nothing of value – just an old flute he played long ago, a shirt, some strange stones he picked up by the river, a jumper, and a rolled-up sleeping bag.

He had long since given up all hope for gain and improvement, choosing drink (and drugs, when he could get them) as an escape from all the broken promises, setbacks and disappointments that had drained the best of his life. Now all he had was the amber liquid and that ounce of survival that kept a man 'keep on going on'.

The casino's gardens were one of the few places he felt safe, whether sober or drunk. Even at night the plants were akin to companions, never mocking or threatening. Occasionally he heard a bird sing, and when that happened somewhere deep inside him smiled. Maybe it was the part that kept him alive, but he needed the whiskey to numb the pain that lay adjacent to it, slowly killing both. He was just about to take another swig when he heard a voice behind him.

'Oi!'

He tried to get up but he was too slow for the security man. 'You're not allowed here. Clear off!'

'Urgh,' he slurred.

'Come on, or I'll call the police,' the man said, looming over and nudging him with a black boot.

This was the first time in a year that he was caught in the grounds – quite a notable achievement, even though he knew a secret way in. He shuffled off down a path and out the main gate, closely followed from behind. Something hit his left shoulder and bounced onto the pavement with a series of metallic clunks. In the gatehouse, the casino guards laughed. He kept on walking, thinking not of vengeance but another drink.

By the time he remembered leaving his sandwich behind, he was sitting on a bench by the river. The night was cold, but not as cold as the current that ran through his heart – something he had long become accustomed to. Was it anger, frustration, disillusion or just simple pain? Sometimes it gripped his body and called out to be heard, like a rushing torrent from a desert monsoon, sweeping across a barren land. He knew that it would just be a matter of time before he could no longer resist its call.

So cold, yet so *fresh*.

At least he had some whiskey left.

* * *

GOOD INTENTIONS

The poker tournament received attention from several national newspapers and in one dominated the seventh page – right next to a feature on 'the coin bandits'. They could not fail to notice.

'Look at this,' she said, handing the newspaper over.

He was sat by the aisle, watching a young couple who had just boarded the London-bound train. *We look just like them,* he thought, taking the paper and reading the article she indicated. The headline screamed '£10 Million Prize' and he immediately thought of what difference that amount could make – with the capacity to change hundreds, even thousands, of lives.

With a shunt the train moved forward again, as bright rays of morning sunlight peaked around the station.

'That's our next target,' she said, after he finished reading.

'You serious? Sarah, it's way above our league…'

'Why?' she protested. 'If you set barriers, you will always stay within them. You said we need something big. This is it.'

He leaned close to her and lowered his voice. 'We've got nothing on this casino apart from a newspaper article. It's not a viable option.'

'You're wrong, John,' she replied. 'I know someone who works there… someone we can trust, been there for years.'

He paused, considering this. 'Alright, but it's your project. If you can get some good background, a workable plan – great. But we really need a target that's realistic, which we already have reliable intel on.'

They had discussed such a place last night: a lavish city centre bank, where they were heading for now. John had already managed to get the blueprints for its interior as well as maps for the surrounding area. He couldn't wait to see it for himself.

As the train pulled into the next town, Sarah's attention was drawn away. 'That's fine,' she said, 'you work on your bank, and I'll work on this.'

John followed her eyes to the young couple, were now on the platform kissing – totally oblivious to the world around them. As the train moved off again, they parted.

For the rest of the journey Sarah was mostly silent, gazing inscrutably at the swiftly-passing countryside. It was inevitable they would disagree; that always happened when two strong minds had different perspectives. But somehow, in the end, they had to co-operate, choosing whichever target was the best.

John read the article on 'the coin bandits', almost chuckling when the reporter suggested that the robbers were 'an organised crime group'. He just hoped such a conclusion was shared by the police.

Upon arriving in London, they chose another cheap hotel to base their operations. He set off alone to an appointment at the bank, leaving Sarah to unpack and do some research on the casino.

In the heart of the city, Coutts was an exclusive centre for private investors, elite businessmen and corporate holdings.

GOOD INTENTIONS

Not anyone could open an account there. It was built on deals and speculations, and its foundations were the super-rich.

As John strolled through the glass doors, he was immediately approached by a smartly dressed man.

'Can I help you, Sir?'

'Yes, I've got an appointment with Mr. Wainruth. My name's John Stevens.'

'Very well, Mr. Stevens, I'll tell him you're here. If you'd like to take a seat, I'll be back in just a moment.'

John watched him walk away to an office and began his discreet surveillance of the bank's interior. He sat down, carefully noting the position of doorways, staff stations and cameras. There were no guards, but there was a heavy presence of CCTV, with complicated alarm systems being an inevitability. It was brightly lit, with marble flooring and gold-rimmed tables, making it seem more akin to the lobby of a luxurious hotel than a bank. He had little time to form a complete picture of the interior before the man returned.

'Mr. Stevens? Could you follow me please?'

He was shown into one of three small offices, located on the right side of the lobby. Only those with more established connections found themselves led up past the first floor, which was the domain of corporations and multi-millionaires.

Inside the office, a large man got up slowly from behind a desk. The carefully crafted suit seemed to mould to the huge bulge of his stomach without the slightest crease or line. It made his bronze-etched name tag stand out like a neon sign.

Shaking John's hand with a firm grip, Mr. Wainruth introduced himself informally. They soon got down to business.

'I have to say, this is an unusual investment portfolio, Mr. Stevens,' Wainruth said, after John had explained the workings of WinImplex.

'You have selected a number of small companies that are showing no dividends. At this rate you'll be having substantial losses by the end of the year.' Wainruth talked as if it was his own money, which, in a way, it would be.

Assigning the entire *WinImplex* portfolio to this one bank was a risk, but a necessary one. It meant giving the bank full access to every transaction and an unsettling level of control. 'You have to understand,' Wainruth continued, 'we will invest in businesses that have good records, which we think will give good returns. Our success rate is unmatched.'

'That's good to hear,' John replied.

'But it's a very volatile market, as I'm sure you know. Some returns may not exceed the initial investment.'

'I understand,' John nodded. 'There will be a few companies I want to keep investing in, but apart from those I'll let you decide where the rest of the money goes.' From his pocket, he withdrew a small piece of paper – a list of companies – which Wainruth read with interest.

'I'm not familiar with any of these companies on your list,' he said.

'What does this SeaCite Expo do, for instance? It's making substantial losses.'

GOOD INTENTIONS

John thought about telling Wainruth what first came to mind: that SeaCite was probably the best hope for underwater habitat technology, eventually leading to human colonies in the ocean, with applications in space as well. But he limited the description to something an accountant could understand, highlighting how it could generate profits in the long term.

He had set-up WinImplex two years ago as an umbrella investment portfolio, focusing on developing technology. There was also a print shop, originally intended as a counterfeiting operation, and a charity – 'BlueBridge'. These enterprises were organised so that one supported the other, avoiding outside suspicion and successfully 'laundering' money from robberies. It would soon reach the stage where the whole organisation was self-supporting and no longer needed cash injections. At the top was BlueBridge – the purpose on which all else was based. It had the sole aim of reducing worldwide poverty; a lofty goal that countless others had pursued and that BlueBridge aimed to push further. So far it was behind the building of four village schools in Eastern Nigeria, a scholarship programme in Bangladesh, and a hospital in Bolivia. It also gave support to fledgling businesses that employed poor families on living wages, establishing links with fair trade co-operatives. John had founded it a year before meeting Sarah in Africa. And it was just the beginning. One day, he vowed, the Organisation would become a launch pad into a new era of equality, justice and opportunity. One day, he told himself, no more robberies would be necessary, nor would any child die from hunger, or a family perish from want of basic medicine. All would be given opportunities to reach their potential, able to use it to benefit the whole of humanity.

But he could tell Wainruth none of this. They skimmed over a few other companies before finalising the portfolio. He signed the necessary forms and handed over one of his passports for Wainruth to photocopy. Despite doing this countless times before, he always felt nervous. The procedures to verify the validity of a person's identity were growing more complicated by the day. Nevertheless, if there were any issues, Wainruth didn't raise them.

As he walked out the office, he got another chance to view the teller stations. To maintain the sense of luxury and intimacy, there was no glass screen. The robbery would have to be done in surprise, as swiftly as possible given the alarms and police response time. Nevertheless, before leaving the building he noticed the same weak spot that he took advantage of in the last job – a final reassurance that it was indeed the right location.

* * *

From his office, Wainruth watched John leave. He looked through the portfolio again and frowned. The number he dialled on his mobile phone was one he long ago committed to memory.

GOOD INTENTIONS

'Yes?' a voice rumbled after one ring.

Trying to maintain his confidence, Wainruth spoke three syllables of perfidy.

'I've found one.'

3

Shortly after Wainruth put down his phone, Sarah headed to the Crown Casino on Newport Parade, having spent all afternoon researching it on her laptop. A graphic website had portrayed it as a 'palace of dreams', where 'anything is possible'. It had two floors for all varieties of gambling: roulette, baccarat, blackjack, poker, and others she never had a chance to play. There was an exclusive hotel that took up the other nine floors, rumoured to be where a President signed away a nation's fortune. Two fountains flanked the grand entrance and played through a range of patterns.

As she walked onto the gaming floor it was like some powerful psychedelic agent was being pumped into the air. A rich crimson carpet buoyed up the surging crowd, as crystal chandeliers exuded a magical luminescence. Rows of flashing slot machines surrounded her as she progressed to the Blackjack tables.

Where is he? she wondered, dazzled by the display of opulence and flow of people. Although dressed to blend in, she found it hard to believe she could ever be counted as one of them. *Perhaps John is right*, she thought, looking at all the security – cameras, guards, special alarm systems…

The man she was looking for was an uncle, but he could have been a brother, or even a father. Since childhood he had

GOOD INTENTIONS

looked after her, despite his status as a 'black sheep' of the family. His gambling and minor dabbling in the world of crime certainly didn't earn him the reputation of a good role model. But in her eyes he was solid gold. It seemed as though his employers agreed, for in the three years he had been working at the Crown Casino he had become a top croupier.

She could now see him standing at the centre of a circle of blackjack players, dealing out cards. Nothing had changed: he still had that slicked-back hair, that avid gaze. His subtle smile could have been an emblem of his thoughts, or even an extension of the dark red jacket he wore. Confident and tall, it was hard to believe that at one time in his life he was an alcoholic and addicted gambler.

She sat down in one of the empty seats and watched his eyes brighten in recognition. 'Ladies and gentleman,' he announced, 'you are now in the company of my beautiful niece!'

They all looked in her direction.

'Can I talk to you on your next break?' she said shyly. With a row of nearby slot-machines playing their raucous tunes, it was hard to hear her own voice.

He grinned, dealing out cards with a flourish, then raked in the piles of chips for the three players who didn't fold.

'Sure! Half an hour, at the bar? Why don't you play a few hands?' He looked over at another player. 'She was always good at the game of 21.'

Sarah almost laughed at this comment, remembering the outcome of their last game together. 'No thanks,' she replied,

'I'll get a drink at the bar.'

Before she could get up, one of the men offered to buy her one. She politely refused and extricated herself from the crowd, choosing a quiet corner table at the bar to sit alone, watching without being watched – by the punters, at least.

It was interesting observing the interactions of couples and groups, hearing the mix of laughter and shouting whenever they won something. There were banners everywhere advertising the poker tournament: posters on the walls, streamers hanging between the chandeliers, even special drinking mats placed on the tables. They all declared **'Winner Takes All – £10 Mill or Nil'**.

Didn't everyone know the winner *always* took it all, whilst the loser walked away unrewarded? A parallel was upheld in society, resulting in a widening gap between rich and poor – those who had it all, and those who had nothing. Due to a globalised economy, it had become possible to 'relocate' the bulk of the poor to other countries, where they could be hidden and forgotten by the middle classes of the west. Sarah knew it was these third world workers who made the opulence around her possible; they harvested the raw materials that were processed in factories and exported away, underpinning the foundations of western life. It was all about control – who owned the mine, the factory, the mill; the boat, the train, the plane. Corporations, not governments, ruled the world. Those without power and wealth were without any control, worthless pawns in a ruthless game of financial accumulation. *Me and John... together, we'll fight it,* she vowed, re-affirming an oath that was held as sacred as any secret society's membership rites.

A ringing siren rose above the casino buzz. Someone had won big. Looking up, she saw her uncle moving towards the table, carrying two drinks from the bar.

'You seem moody today,' he said, sitting opposite her and putting down the drinks. He acted as if they met regularly, when in reality the last time they saw each other was Christmas.

'No... it's just not really my scene. How've you been?'

'Oh not so bad, considering,' he replied. 'You should love it here; you *will* love it here, if you stay long enough. Just don't bet too much. Anyway, tell me how things are going?'

She spoke about her job as an 'office admin' and her travels before coming around to the crucial question. 'Are you interested in making some money in an unconventional way?'

He raised his eyebrows a little, then grinned craftily. 'You know me girl, I'm always interested in that.'

'Even if it meant robbing a casino?'

Leaning across the table, his smile was slowly – really slowly – replaced by a poker-faced expression. 'You know Sarah, if this is some kind of joke...' but looking at her, he knew it wasn't. 'Every day, I see this place robbing people – and hell, if it weren't for the tips, they'd be robbing me as well.'

A couple walked by their table, the woman carrying a purple handbag that was positively bulging with playing chips. Sarah looked back towards her uncle, whose gaze was still piercing.

'I don't know what you've gotten into, but I want to know. In fact, I *need* to know. And unless you've learned to fool this old man, you're not kidding me about this either.'

'What time do you finish work?' she asked.

'Tonight – two am. Where you staying?'

'Alworth Hotel,' she said. 'East Brunswick Street. I'll wait up.'

'You sure? I can come tomorrow afternoon, if that's better for you.'

'Two o'clock's fine,' she said, 'I'm only just getting used to this time zone anyway.'

He smiled again. 'You're a girl of mysteries, aren't you? You've got a lot to tell.'

'Yes, uncle Howie, I sure do.'

Right above their heads, the first round of the poker tournament was in progress. A special area had been cordoned off around the highest stakes table. Around a huge oval cloth, the ten celebrity players faced up to the fear of losing first. Nobody was surprised when the 'amateur' of the tournament, a young kid from Argentina, took the initial fall.

Access to the second floor was strictly controlled, with security personnel posted at the escalators and lifts. Only sponsors, selected journalists and the mega-rich were allowed up. It meant the casino had to divert some of its men away from their usual posts on the ground floor, but it would be solely for the tournament's duration. The only action over the year had been a few drunken brawls between punters, two assaults on staff, four suicides (all in the hotel – only

GOOD INTENTIONS

one formally declared as such) and a dozen petty thefts. The main thing they had to look out for was fraudsters, cheaters and card counters – all of whom were swiftly identified by cameras, active surveillance and integrated computers. Not a metre of the casino was left unwatched.

No one had been stupid enough to blatantly run away with House money, but if they were to do so they would be swiftly caught at the main entrance, which was the only access point for members of the public. At the push of a button, the casino could be sealed tight in seconds and the police would arrive within minutes.

Management had been fighting for years to get a licence for specially-armed security guards, but current laws prevented this. Not that it mattered anyway. Business was booming and nothing could harm it. Every year the profits were increasing, with this trend set to continue whilst the gambling legislation was being loosened up. Soon every major city in the country would have its little taste of Vegas.

Covering the expenses of the players and marketing the event was costing an unprecedented amount of money. But it was a worthwhile investment, for in the long term they would see more revenue. People would come with the dream of winning, of getting something for nothing, looking at the winner of the poker tournament as evidence that this can happen. No one ever remembered the losers. The winner would be showered with grandeur and heightened fame, then quickly sent packing. Others would stream in, magnetised by the allure of gambling, hoping to take the same path.

The House knew what to do, as always: let them win, make them king, then reel 'em in…

* * *

It was dark and cold outside, but Sarah needed to go for a walk. Out through the closely-watched gate of the casino, she once again couldn't imagine how such a place could be robbed. No bank or building society had such heavy security. Even so, doing the 'impossible' had always appealed to her: flying in the face of conventional thinking, daring to be a pioneer.

As she walked along the river, she watched the sparkling lights of skyscrapers glitter on the water; a thousand diamonds intertwining in a tapestry of light. The low moon joined in as well, casting a pathway of sombre silver that was broken by the shadow of a bridge. As she neared the arch, she suddenly became aware of the risk she was taking: a young woman walking alone at night in a deserted pocket of the city's heart. All her life she had taken risks. Perhaps one day she would push Fate too far, and the risk would finally be too much. But until that day came, she would flirt with fear and even death, laughing like a small warrior before an angry dragon.

A man's cough jolted her from these thoughts. Gazing ahead, she saw a shadowy figure sitting on a bench beside the path. He was wearing a heavy coat, his face dark with the growth of a beard. A glint of glass, followed by a heavy smell

GOOD INTENTIONS

of spirits, confirmed her suspicions. She increased her pace.

'Came ere darlin, I need camponeee '

Her body tensed. She hurried up the steps of the bridge, glancing round to check that she wasn't being followed.

I know what John would have done, she thought, drawing a sigh. Whenever they walked together in towns or cities, he never went by a homeless person without giving them something. She tried to convince him that doing so was 'a waste' – that the money could be better used to help others who wouldn't spend it on drink or drugs, such as those they had worked with in Africa. But he reminded her that the poor were just as deserving wherever they were. Moreover, to judge a fellow human in ignorance of their circumstances was kindred to a politician's corruption: blindly overlooking that all have their place and purpose and that all are essentially equal. She wondered if it would ever be possible to end the inequality, oppression and needless suffering that had arisen from capitalist greed. Whether it was or not, she had to try.

As she neared the hotel, she looked around again. It had become a habit in recent months, something closer to caution than paranoia. Even seeing no one in close pursuit could not quell her anxiety.

Although it was approaching eleven o'clock, the hotel lobby was still busy. A group of businessmen were apparently departing for a late flight and one was shouting orders to a baggage carrier.

Sarah collected her key from the desk after waiting ten

minutes for the group to pay their bill. She came close to compromising her position by deftly removing one of the men's wallets: this was what the sight of money in the hands of the ignorant rich did to her. But she had never succumbed to pick-pocketing, especially now that there were much bigger pockets to choose from.

Once in the room, she was careful not to disturb John, who was asleep on the bed. After quietly changing out of her dress and into a tracksuit, she went downstairs.

The city was dark, yet still swarming with activity. It would never – in the fullest sense – be able to rest. For too many moved and struggled and suffered beneath its long shadows, sending out their unheard thoughts into the heartless dark. Few rooms in the hotel shone with light, and those that did were mostly empty. A shuddering moon fell upon the slit-like windows, drawing on the hours.

By the time two am arrived, Sarah was sitting in the hotel lobby, drinking her second cup of coffee. Several circular tables were spread out before the reception desk, but there were no other guests. Although the bar and restaurant were closed, the lone receptionist was happy to make her drinks.

There was a mixture of magazines and newspapers, which Sarah perused. In one of the national tabloids she came across a short article on John's recent robbery. It seemed the bank was offering a 'substantial reward for information leading to an arrest.'

At 2:15am her uncle arrived in the lobby. He wore a suede

jacket that covered his casino uniform, although Sarah glimpsed a hint of crimson at the collar. He looked young and slim even in this shady setting, with a graceful posture that oozed confidence. But close up, his face showed signs of tiredness.

'My mystery gal!' he exclaimed, embracing her. 'It's been too long.'

'I know uncle,' Sarah said, 'things have just been so busy. Do you want a drink?'

Howie looked confused. 'You want to talk right here? Don't you have a room?'

Sarah paused and then told him about John.

'Well, we might as well talk here then,' he said, frowning a little. 'I could do with a drink, yeah.'

She nodded and went over to ask the receptionist for two more cups of coffee. A few chocolate-topped biscuits came with the saucers, as before.

As she walked back across the lobby, she saw that Howie had chosen a table further back.

'I've been thinking about what you told me at the casino,' he said, taking a sip from his cup. 'Tell me one thing. Has that boyfriend of yours got you into this? Is he some sort of criminal?'

'No,' she replied. 'Everything I've done has been by my own choice, and John is not a criminal, just as you're not a criminal. In fact, you two are very similar.' She watched her uncle pick up a biscuit and dip it into his coffee, trailing a few brown drops into the saucer before he chomped on it.

'That's just what I wanted to hear,' he said. 'Guys like me are scum, Sarah; they care only about themselves and, if you're lucky, a few 'special people'.' He picked up another biscuit and did the same as before. 'As for being a 'criminal' – I've broken the law, yeah, but so have a helluva lot of others who are in high places and never seen the inside of a jail. I just hope you're one of John's 'special people', if what you say is true.'

'I am,' she replied, 'but there's more to this than that. I'm not sure if you could understand… you will need to meet him to believe what we're doing.'

'Oh, don't worry, I will! As soon as possible. I want to know what he's got you into. I bet it's card counting.'
She shook her head
'No? Drugs then? Some kind of cannabis farm?'

'No, uncle.'

'Then what?'

She looked at a painting that was hanging on the wall behind him: a depiction of a bridge over a river. She could almost hear the water rushing by.

'Sarah?'

'It's bank robbery,' she finally answered. 'We rob banks, building societies, security vans. I've been doing it with John for over eight months. He's been doing it for years.'

Her uncle's blank expression was unchanged, so she continued.

'We're using the money to change the world – to actually make a difference; more than I could ever hope to do by

GOOD INTENTIONS

volunteering in Africa. It's for the better good, and I need your help to take it further.' She paused, expecting him to say something, but he just sat there. 'With this casino heist, you would get one third of the takings, an equal split. Just think of that, uncle: over three million!'

'Three million…' he echoed, his voice barely audible.

A heavy silence seemed to descend over the lobby. For a moment she thought the receptionist was standing behind her. But the lady was still sitting at the desk, and no one else had entered.

Howie was staring into the distance, his mien unreadable. *Has all this overwhelmed him? Was it a mistake telling him?* she wondered.

It seemed ages before he cleared his throat and spoke. 'You want me to help you… rob the casino… and you've done this kind of thing before?'

'Yes.'

'Give me your hand, Sarah,' he said, reaching across the table.

'Swear on everything you hold dear; swear on your late mother's life, my sister, that you're speaking the truth.'

'I swear it's true.'

He gripped her hand for a second, strongly but without causing pain, then let go. In his eyes a rim of moisture betrayed how strongly he felt for her. His worry was evident in his face and posture, still leaning over the table and staring at her like a concerned family doctor.

'You're a daughter to me, Sarah. I remember just before

your poor mother died; how she promised me to look after you. I've never forgotten that vow.' He sat back and pushed away his drink. 'If it was anyone else, I'd say "yes, I'm interested", but you – such a nice, caring young woman it's too much. You could end up in jail; you could even get killed. I couldn't live with that responsibility.'

This is just what she feared he would say. 'Listen uncle, that won't happen. We've – *I've* – done this kind of stuff before.'

'So you've said. But you need to get out of it. *Please*. I can't help you ruin your life. What would ,' he paused, not wishing to continue.

'Look,' she replied, letting part of her frustration show in her voice,

'If you don't want to help, fine. I understand. I'll just end up doing the same thing, but the risk of getting caught will be higher, because we won't know what you know.'

Once again, he was silent. Pondering. She had him between two impossible choices, and part of her felt guilty at putting him in this predicament.

'Alright,' he sighed. 'Let me meet John first. Then I'll make my decision.'

She nodded. At least he had not completely rebuffed her. 'Would tomorrow be okay?' she asked.

'Yes. I'll take a day off.'

'Your place, afternoon?'

He agreed. 'Call me if there's any problems.' He got up and drained his coffee in one gulp, apparently not caring that it

GOOD INTENTIONS

was cold.

She watched him rejoin the dark city outside. 'Now comes the hard bit,' she whispered.

4

By the river he lay, sleeping until bird chorus took away the clinging cold of night and dawn rays painted the water amber. Only in the winter months did he seek shelter – usually some hostel filled to the brim with trouble, run by zealous Christians. He hated being trapped behind windows and doors, for it left him feeling claustrophobic and vulnerable. Yet his dreams (when he could remember them) always seemed to be *inside*, within a place whose name he had long expunged from his thoughts.

Despite the dull throb of an alcohol-induced headache and the soreness in his body, he got up and stretched. The plastic lining and blanket that covered him during the night was put away in his backpack, after he shook the dew off. A vague feeling of hunger rose up in his empty belly and he remembered there was a restaurant nearby that threw half its food away. It was an hour or so before the garbage men collected the bins there, so he had to hurry.

On the river a brigade of ivory-hued swans sailed by, their regal heads held proud. They moved like statues in a watery mist, caught on currents outside of contemporary time and space. As he passed, one of them broke from the formation, beating its legs invisibly beneath the water. For a while it followed him as he walked along by the river bank, keeping

GOOD INTENTIONS

pace despite swimming against the current. It made one deep sound before he ascended the steps of the bridge.

He vaguely remembered one person walking this way in the night – a woman – but the details were obscure. She had looked beautiful, even in the silver sketching of moonlight and the swamp of his inebriated memories. How he wished to have a woman like that. Or even just a woman. *Perhaps she was just a swan,* he thought.

He had seen many people in his younger days – people who moved with beauty and sometimes with shimmering wrath. People who weren't there. Now he looked back on these visions as figments of his imagination; something which had led him to alleged insanity… to *the place*. The mere prospect of seeing one of these 'sightings' again made him shiver. It would be all right if he saw the woman again though, maybe even spoke to her, if for nothing else than to prove she was real.

As he reached the top of bridge he looked down. The white swan had vanished. Only a subtle swirl in the current told of its passage.

* * *

The strident notes of a ringing telephone filled the hotel room.

'Turn that thing off,' Sarah said sleepily, covering her head with the duvet.

John picked up the phone and a woman's voice greeted him, informing him it was eight o'clock in the morning.

Pushing aside the sheet, he slipped out of bed and went to open the curtains. A note on the desk caught his eye:

> Didn't get to bed until 4am last night.
> Had to meet my uncle. He works at the casino.
> Talk to you tomorrow. I'm dead tired.
> Sarah x

He took a shower, had a quick shave, and prepared for a morning of reconnaissance.

They were serving a complimentary full English breakfast in the hotel restaurant, but he was happy with a coffee and a bowl of muesli.

He asked the staff to take up lunch for Sarah, knowing she would appreciate this. Then he departed, heading for the bank.

The streets rumbled to traffic – double-decker buses, taxis and luxury cars. In the centre of it all the vertiginous crystal cages of skyscrapers rose up into the clear sky, becoming steeples of man's newest religion. Indeed, money was the aim of it all, the driving purpose of every ambition, galvanising every dream.

John blended with the crowds as a zebra blends with the Savannah. He moved with a grace that comes only to the self-assured, at the same time maintaining an underlying caution.

Coutts bank stood as it always did, impervious to the world around it. Cameras clasped the edges of buildings, staring down with circular eyes – the apertures of a digital appendix that ended in a nervous centre of intelligence.

The watchers, John thought, *whoever they are.*

A poster on a double-decker declared the answer: advertising the recruitment number of a government agency. It was fleetingly reflected in the ground floor windows of a CityGroup skyscraper. Somehow – at least to John – the reflection seemed more important than the actual object. Just so did the real watchers, or rather the controllers of the watchers, make themselves hidden, projecting layers of power and authority that were really subtle mirages.

As he proceeded along an alley – what would become the main getaway route of the robbery – the sight of two police officers made him slow down. They were standing before a slumped figure.

'Yes,' one said, 'we know that. But you can't be here.'

John passed them, glancing at the figure they were talking to. To his surprise, it was a woman. Short hair, a big coat, age about forty. She had a dog sitting by her side, a little Jack Russell.

He almost stopped, but the presence of police over-ruled that. If they searched him they would find detailed maps of the area, centred around the bank.

Another time, he vowed.

Quickly the voices of authority vanished under the surge of traffic. He had completed a circuit of the bank. The getaway routes were confirmed. All that remained was a 'dry run', which would test escape times. He estimated that it would take only three minutes from the Underground station to the bank using route one. Route two would be about six minutes. Another changeover location – a bus stop – lay approximately four minutes away. These were the alternate transit nodes of their escape. All were consolidated by the proximity of toilets, which allowed a change-over of disguises. Even so, he still felt daunted by the sheer quantity of cameras. Disguises could be made fallible with such pervasive surveillance. Dangerous connections could be made at a future date. This made it necessary to move bases immediately after the robbery, a tactic he had used many times. In this case leaving the country for a few months seemed the best option.

As he descended the escalators in the Underground station a man pushed past, holding a mobile phone to his mouth. Hot air rushed through the passage, followed by the screeching blast of an arriving train. More people pushed past, all of them wearing suits, as new faces appeared on the other escalator. None smiled. They were plugged in, connected to the umbilical cord of the system, enslaved to the age of information.

How many of them would think about people like the homeless woman? John asked himself. *Is there any amongst them who even realise the world stands on the brink of massive change?*

Walking across the platform and onto the train, listening to the electronic ding as the doors clamped shut behind him, he realised the answer lay with technology. For them, for modern society, for the western world, technology would always magic up a solution. Just as it always did.

GOOD INTENTIONS

Feint music reached John's ears. It came from the MP3 player of a boy who stood next to him.

And the next generation will think no differently, John thought. Yet a day may soon come when man curses the inventions that had advanced him so far, for technology is a double-edged sword of creation and destruction. Industrialisation, mass production, genetic modification… so much intended to improve human life has actually done the opposite. Sometimes long-term effects are only realised until it's too late to reverse the damage. What was good in theory can easily become bad in practise: the same devices intended to advance the race could end up destroying it.

In any case, technology could never be the sole solution to the world's problems. It is the wisdom and will to use it for the benefit of all – for every generation – that matters.

His thoughts went back to the organisation, to BlueBridge. At the present rate it would take a millennium to achieve his and Sarah's vision. Poverty and inequality were increasing, easily out-stepping whatever changes that charity could make. It defied their aim to resurface the contours of inequality, redistributing the entombed gold hoarded by the super-rich. So far, their robberies had barely scratched the surface. *Sarah's right,* he thought, *huge differences require massive steps.*

By the time he got back to the hotel, just after mid-day, Sarah was awake.

'Hi babe,' she said.

'Hey, sleepyhead.'

'Where you been?'

Sitting down, he told her about the bank. 'It looks a brilliant prospect. I've seen two good getaway routes, with alternate change-over locations, and the money looks big too.'

'How big?' she asked.

'I'm not certain, but probably around three hundred k. That would be our biggest heist.'

Sarah looked at him with an expression of appeal. 'But why go for three hundred k when you can go for ten million?'

He took a deep breath. 'You're not still serious about this casino thing are you?'

'I've arranged to meet my uncle at his flat this afternoon,' she replied, 'all I'd ask is you go there with me and see if something can be planned. If it can't then we'll focus on the bank.'

He paused. 'That's fair enough. I'd like to meet your uncle, anyway.

When do you want to leave?'

'As soon as you're ready.'

They arrived outside the block of flats just before 3pm. It was not exactly one of the city's ghetto estates, but it hovered on the borders. A group of sullen teenagers were gathered around a bench, cloaked in the unmistakable scent of cannabis. Crisp wrappers and other rubbish drifted half-heartedly around a stained square of grass that might have once been a communal garden. The only sounds were dogs barking, the teenagers chattering, a jumbo jet passing overhead, and the ceaseless murmur of city traffic.

Sarah pressed the buzzer to Howie's flat, careful not to touch the wad of chewing gum that had been plastered onto the button below. The front door immediately clicked open and they ascended two flights of stairs to apartment number 24. A weather-beaten face belonging to a man of about forty-five stood in the open doorway. He was smoking a cigarette and wearing a black shirt and jeans.

'Come in, come in!' he said. 'The palatial mansion's seen better days.'

John wasn't sure what to make of this remark, but they shook hands as Sarah did the introductions. There was a spacious living room with an adjourning kitchen, and they both took a seat on the sofa whilst Howie made drinks. Cigarette smoke dominated other smells, but beneath it was the trace of a strong perfume.

They all had teas: an Earl Grey for John, a Green Tea for Sarah and some kind of 'Australian Bush' tea for Howie. A vivid label of a jumping kangaroo hung idly against the side of his stained mug.

It took time, but gradually the initial current of uncertainty wore off, until all three of them talked freely. It was only then that Sarah asked the crucial question.

'Have you thought about what we talked about last night?'

He took a sip of his remaining tea. 'Yeah, I haven't decided yet.' He paused, then looked across the table. 'Tell me, John, do you have some kind of plan? Sarah tells me you've done heists in the past.'

She could feel John tense beside her, but his response was cool and smooth.

'That's true,' he said, 'and I'm pleased to say no one has got hurt – that's not how I operate. My aim – our aim – is basically a modern version of Robin Hood. We are already making a huge difference around the world.'

Howie didn't reply. Sarah could tell he was at a crucial stage in making his decision, so she continued on from what John said. 'This is for real, uncle. I've seen it myself. We've helped build schools and hospitals, and we've set up an organisation to funnel the money to where it's really needed, without drawing suspicion. We need your help to take it to the next level. You could be part of something that makes a huge difference to thousands of lives.'

They could both see the passion in her face as she spoke – the glitter in her eyes, the flame of beauty that shined so bright.

'That's all very well, Sarah,' Howie said, 'but you should know me, girl. I'm not interested unless there's something in it for *moi*: some big dosh.'

'Oh, there is,' Sarah smiled, 'that's not a problem. Like I said last night, you'd get one third of the take, over £3 million.'

Howie looked at John, seeking confirmation of this.

'Fine with me,' he said.

'So what's the plan?' Howie asked.

Before John could say anything about how there *was* no

GOOD INTENTIONS

plan, Sarah quickly answered her uncle's question.

'The tournament's for two weeks, right? They've got to keep the ten million in a safe and they've got to give it to the winner. Even if it's by wire, the cash needs to be on the premises – that's written in by law. The way I see it, robbing this casino is going to be like robbing a bank – only on a larger scale. You must have knowledge of security, floor plans?'

Howie nodded.

'So, how would *you* rob the casino?'

He twisted the cup around in his hand and sat back in his chair.

They could hear the drone of a plane passing overhead.

'Lots of ways,' he said, a crooked smile briefly uplifting his face.

'But the way you said it, that's not gonna happen. I've been working at the casino for almost three years and I've seen how screwed up the security is. But about a year ago they revamped the strong room and installed loads of cameras. Getting to that room is impossible now. It's beneath the ground floor, in the very heart of the casino, reached only by a corridor that is constantly watched and guarded. No way in from above, no way in from below. It's got the standard solid-steel tungsten door and reinforced concrete walls, fitted with a range of sensors. There's no way you can drill in there or get past security. No, it's impossible.'

Sarah could not hide her despondency, but John was pleased to hear this. Now she would focus all her attention on the bank. Meanwhile, Howie's mind still appeared to be somewhere else, prompting Sarah to lean forward.

'But you just said there are lots of ways you'd rob the casino,' she said.

'Yeah,' he said, snapping back to the present. 'The money's not just kept in the strong room – the cashiers have it, too. There's a room on the ground floor, right next to the entrance, which is the only place where punters can get their chips and cash in their winnings. It also connects to two ATMs. *That's what I'd be looking at. There's at least half a mil in there at any one time… but with this tournament, it's gotta be double that. In fact, I'd wager that it's even more than double.*'

Even John's eyes lit up at this information. 'How is this room protected?' he asked.

'Oh, strengthened glass, coded door, alarms – but there are ways around that. If you've robbed banks, you should know that. I've got the code to the door, in any case. But getting the money ain't the issue. It's getting out that will be the problem.'

He cleared his throat and continued. 'There's one entrance to the casino. You will have seen it if you've been there: a main gate, leading to the two fountains before the entrance portico. That's where security check your ID. There's a little lobby with a reception desk and lifts for the hotel. As you walk through the casino doors, you'll see the ATMs and cashiers room directly on the right, always under scrutiny. They make a point of monitoring everyone, especially with this poker tournament. You would not be able to come in,

GOOD INTENTIONS

grab the money, then get away.'

He drank the last dregs of his tea, letting out a small burp. 'But I know another way in.'

Sarah watched avidly as Howie continued, realising that her wildest hopes may be reachable.

'At the end of every week, cash from the cashiers' room is taken to the strong room. Very rarely does it get brought directly to a van at the entrance. It needs to be taken in cases, which are carried across the gaming floor to a secure door. This goes onto the corridor that leads to the strong room. Now, the corridor has a door to the outside – a special access point for deliveries. That's where I'd get away with the cash. On that side of the casino, you've got an access road for delivery vehicles, leading back to the main gate, and gardens enclosed by a wall. If you can get over that obstacle, you're sorted.'

Howie looked across at John. 'I take it you know how to open cash cases?'

'We've done it before,' John replied.

'Do you know if they have dye packs?' Sarah asked.

Howie raised an eyebrow. 'I'm not sure, to be honest. I don't think so. I know some guys last year opened one of these cases with angle grinders, taken from some casino in Reno, and they ended up with a bundle of useless, dyed cash. But over here, we're not that sussed. I'd bet these cases don't have dye packs.'

'What about the guards? How many are there?' Sarah asked.

'Depends on how many cases there are, girl. I've never seen

more than four guards – three of 'em doing the mule work.'

John had not said anything for a while; he just say there with a hand rested beneath his chin. Nevertheless, Sarah continued to question her uncle.

'What about cameras? Alarms?'

'That's where you'll have problems,' he said. 'There's a camera outside the delivery area, above the door I can give you a code for. You won't be able to wear balaclavas or anything. They'd see it immediately and the police would be there before you could get away. So I don't see how you can do it.'

Sarah could, and so could John. They would just wear one of their more subtle disguises. They had a variety of wigs, 'facial additions' and masks that had proven invaluable on complex jobs. But they would need to get the cases off several grown men. They'd still need guns.

'There's one other thing,' Howie noted, 'there's rumour that at the end of the tournament, management are planning something spectacular. I'm not sure what, exactly, but one guy says they're bringing the whole ten mil up to the second floor. If that happens, they'd need to bring it up from the strong room, via the same corridor, through the gaming area door, then onto one of the lifts or escalators. But I'd never be able to find out when they move the cash until they take it onto the gaming floor.'

A ringing noise suddenly broke into their conversation. Howie got up and went to the door.

John took the opportunity to lean over and whisper to

GOOD INTENTIONS

Sarah: 'this is all speculation.' But she was more concerned with who had rung the bell.

'Yeah, who is it?' Howie said, speaking into an intercom panel near the door.

There was no reply.

'Bloody kids,' he said, collapsing into his chair, 'always ringing that damned buzzer.'

Sarah wanted to ask if he was *sure* it was just kids; if perhaps it might be someone else. But instead she brought her attention back to the heist. 'You mentioned an elevator. Could it be accessed and brought to a halt via a maintenance room? Is it possible to get the cases from there?'

'By God, I never thought of that! It's possible, I guess. But you gotta understand, I can't go snooping around, asking questions. It would raise suspicions. I can't afford that.'

Another ringing sound filled the flat, but this time he ignored it. 'I can tell you some things with certainty: cash gets taken from the cashiers' room to the strong room, usually on weekends. I can let you know when they move it from within the casino. I can give you the code to the outside delivery door. It's up to you to plan a heist using this information. I can't do anything else.'

'We understand,' John said, 'you've already given us some very valuable details. I'd like to visit the casino sometime, get an idea of the setup.'

'We could look at the grounds as well, see if there's a way over the wall,' Sarah suggested.

The bell rang for a third time. In one frantic motion Howie *leapt* from his chair and ran over to the window.

'Oi!' he shouted. 'Yeah, you! Next time you do that I'm coming down there to shove my friggin fist into your bloody face!' For good measure, he cleared his throat and launched a wad of phlegm down below.

This is a person with issues, John thought. *Was he really the same man who had practically been Sarah's father?* He looked across at her, but she was just chuckling.

'More tea, anyone?' Howie said, moving away from the window. 'No, I'm good thanks,' John replied.

Sarah didn't want any either. She knew they had to leave before her uncle's partner returned. They began to make their exit moves, and Howie showed them to the door. He embraced Sarah, kissing her on the cheek, but wanted to speak to John alone.

'Give us a few minutes, girl,' he said.

She nodded and disappeared down the stairs.

'So it's serious then?' he asked John, once she had gone.

John wasn't sure if he meant their relationship or the robbery, but in either case the answer was 'yes'.

'I'm a good judge of character, kid. It's a knowledge that I've refined at the tables: learning who are the cheaters, the suckers, the bluffers, the good'uns and bad'uns. If you care for her – and I'm sure you do – I don't want her included in this. Talk her out of it. I know she can be stubborn, but I'm not helping if she's involved.'

GOOD INTENTIONS

John felt like saying how hard he had tried to 'talk her out' countless times; how he felt far happier if she never took part in any robbery, in the slightest way, let alone this one. *He didn't even want to rob this casino.*

'I'll give you the code to the door,' Howie said, 'I'll show you where it is, I'll even let you know when they're taking the money from the cashiers room, via my mobile. All I ask is two things: Sarah ain't involved, and one third of the money.'

John nodded, saying he had no problem with this, which wasn't exactly true. 'I've been thinking this robbery could be delayed further anyway,' he said, 'the tournament might mean more money, but even if it's half a million any other day, it's worth doing.'

Howie smiled. 'Well, it's good to know that Sarah's met someone whose neither greedy nor impatient. I'd normally agree with you, Stevo, but there's one problem with waiting.' He looked down at his watch, frowning.

'I've heard management are going to relocate the cashiers' room and build a chute direct to the strong room. That's happening soon. So if you're gonna rob the casino, now is the best time, and probably your last chance.'

This is not what John wanted to hear. 'Alright,' he said, 'I'll be in touch.'

As John descended the stairs, he wondered how he could ever dissuade Sarah from doing this heist.

5

The storm did not break until they got back to the hotel room. He had managed to dodge her questions whilst driving back in the rental car, but now he had to convince her not to proceed with what they discussed in Howie's flat.

'I can't do this, Sarah. Neither can your uncle. He told me not to get you involved, and I don't want you involved either.'

Her expression was unchanged, so he continued. 'We've got a really good job with the bank. I've spent two days working on a plan and it's faultless. With this casino, it's all risk and speculation.'

She was still silent, appearing to gaze at something outside the window. 'It's fantasy, Sarah,' he added, trying to elicit a response.

After a few minutes the first thunder unrolled. 'I don't believe this. I don't believe *you!* You call this fantasy – and yet a year ago so was building hospitals in Africa. Were you sitting there stone *deaf* in my uncle's flat? He's just given us a brilliant plan to work with, more money than we could ever dream of, yet you're turning it down?!'

Although her voice was raised in anger, John kept his cool. 'I heard what your uncle said, Sarah. A lot of it's uncertain, you've got to admit. It's too risky. Why go for something like this when there's a low-risk, high- yield job to choose from?'

'Why crawl one metre when you can jump a mile?' she

shot back.

He almost pointed out that no one could jump a mile anyway, but to annoy her further was folly. 'I'm not doing it, Sarah', he said in finality.

She turned away and headed for the bathroom. 'Fine! Then I'll do it on my own!'

Before he could respond, she slammed the door.

Somewhere else in the hotel, a vacuum cleaner was being used. Traffic noise seeped in from the streets, whilst in the bathroom all he could perceive was silence. It was fifteen minutes before she came out again. He had laid out his notes on the bank, hoping to change her mind. She came up to him and leant down to look at the notes with an obvious expression of besiegement on her face.

'Just think of it, John. Ten million pounds – surely that's worth a bit of risk?'

'You're not serious?' he asked, pushing away the notes on the bank and looking at her. 'Bloody hell, Sarah! Even the lower amount is too risky, and you're talking about the near impossible. How exactly do we get the ten mil? Drill into a safe? Take the manager hostage?'

Now it was her turn to be calm and collective, although he could see an icy undercurrent of crackling frustration hiding beneath this exterior.

'I've been thinking about the elevator,' she said, 'it's the perfect place for an ambush.'

Disbelief and consternation creased his brow as he

absorbed what she said. 'The elevator? Are you mad? You weren't injecting something in there, were you?' Even as he said this, he knew it was a mistake.

Sarah's eyes burned as she screamed in his face. 'Fuck you, John!'

In one swift movement she grabbed her coat and stormed out the room. John just stood there staring. He wanted to chase after her; to apologise for any unintentional hurt he had caused. It was too late now, though. *Let her cool,* he thought. *She'll be back soon enough.*

* * *

An amber sun sketched the skyscrapers a bloody red, each thousandth window counting down the minutes of another lost day.

Like a ship that sailed upon an azure sea, a layer of cloud hovered on the horizon, its bottom set ablaze by the fiery orb beneath.

All the workers were going home – from offices, shops, schools, and factories – countless places where an hour became another hour, on and on in unequivocal symmetry. Dreams were forgotten, replaced by the insatiable need for material acquisition: conditioned to work, produce and consume until death cut the umbilical cord of The System. Oh, how the heavy blocks of the few, at the top of the hierarchical pyramid, weighed down all those below!

GOOD INTENTIONS

As the last rays of sunlight caught the copper edging of corporate buildings, a chill wind uplifted from the east. Could it be that the answers to tomorrow's questions were blowing on its back?

The world was ever-changing and it would never cease to change. As coastlines crumbled to the tides and continents wandered, so do the constructs of man. In time's great loom, a mighty empire today will become a ruined waste tomorrow. Power, that slave driver and great destroyer, is always on the move. North to south, west to east, circling the globe from city to city and hand to hand, it was a ravenous wind that would never be detained. In the east an old empire was rising. In the west a shadow loomed. Yet both sides stood on the same foundation, perhaps as never before; a foundation that was prone to tremble – even to subside into total instability.

And the wind blew on. In the twilight of a fallen state, in the capital of an island kingdom, it curled around the glass needles of enterprise, tracing the steel thrones of crownless kings.

The city was a Janus-like creature, showing one face in the day and another at night. There were many aspects it revealed only at certain times, in certain places, from the commercial inner heart to outlying pockets of exclusion. Sometimes the streets were haunted by ghostly animal shapes: foxes seeking the discarded waste of humans; glowing eyes creeping between walled gardens. Other times the lines of vehicles changed the hot tarmac arteries into flashing, snake-like entities. For every hour the matrix of civilization intertwined and knotted, interacting above and below – dividing and uniting, fusing and fissuring. Nothing could be known for certain, nothing could be completely predicted, and nothing was ever as it seemed.

Somewhere in the labyrinthine networks of roads and buildings was a smoke-filled room occupied by three of the city's most powerful men. All were part of a worldwide organisation, which had connections in every major enterprise – legitimate and illegitimate. Some people called them the Mafiosa, but this was a word that only touched upon their influence. They were much more than a loose collection of families divided by territories and greed.

In fifty years the structure of their organisation had changed dramatically. Although its principle foci were on drugs, fraud, counterfeiting and money laundering, its operations expanded into a variety of legitimate markets – from stocks and shares to construction, contracts and tourism. The spirit of globalisation had brought a unity to the Mafiosa that had never been known before. Now these hidden rulers of cities cooperated and strengthened one another. They exchanged information as efficiently and rapidly as an elite military unit, and indeed their influence reached right into the heart of the military and police. They were another side to the 'military-industrial complex' that had been spoken of by President Eisenhower so long ago. But in this new world it was commerce that took priority and

GOOD INTENTIONS

corporations that governed. Thus it was in business that their main concerns lay.

Something had been brought to their attention, one of the many hundreds of blips that showed up on their radar, and the men in the room were discussing it. Glasses of the finest whisky were spaced between loose papers and tablets on a circular table. A shaded lamp hung overhead, providing a measure of illumination, but shadows still claimed half the room. All three men had features that were hard to discern.

The subject of their conversation was John and Sarah's organisation. They had discovered that the Printshop, WinImplex and BlueBridge were all, in fact, owned by the same person. That had become apparent when the investor at Coutt's Bank had first raised his suspicions. What they wanted to know was where the money came from.

'This guy is unknown,' one of them said. 'We don't know anything about him. No inheritance, no corporate employment, no loans or prior businesses. He doesn't even show up on the gambling databases. Where'd he get the money to start these enterprises?'

'Police and security files show nothing,' another said.

It was the peculiar nature of the businesses that had them perplexed: a small printing and stationery retail outlet, an 'investment entity' that picked out failing technology companies, and a charity, which on examination looked genuine. It made little sense. Various possibilities were briefly discussed as to the true role and origin of these businesses and the founder behind them, John Stevens.

Up to now, the third man in the room had said little on the subject. Most of his face was in shadow, which was made prominent by the lighted end of a cigar. Circles of reflected light glowed in his eyes as he breathed in.

'Send someone in,' he said, puffing out a cloud of white-blue smoke. Outside, the wind blew even stronger.

* * *

Sarah rushed through the hotel lobby and got the next available taxi to the Crown Casino.

She couldn't believe John had used her fractured history against her. She remembered telling him about her past in the second month of their relationship. She had made it clear that it was a sensitive subject, confiding in him how she had survived the temper of an alcoholic father and had watched her mother turn to drugs as an escape. Her father had abandoned them in the midst of debt and broken promises, as empty as the bottles he left behind. Part of her hoped things would get better after that, but it forced her mother to turn to stronger substances. The last time Sarah had seen her mother, she was lying dead of an overdose. She had only been twelve. After that, she was taken into care. Things would have got a lot worse if not for Uncle Howie, who stepped in, fulfilling a promise he had made to her mother. As if to prove to others that she would not take the same path as her parents, she had

GOOD INTENTIONS

battled past social exclusion and studied hard to get a place at university. Through sheer determination and willpower, she had carved out a new life of opportunity. Now she aimed to give that same chance to others.

After asking the taxi driver to drop her off just outside the casino gate, Sarah took the opportunity to walk around the perimeter. She was on full surveillance mode, noting every single detail that came to her attention. A wall, about ten feet high and peaked with barbed wire, provided effective security. There was no apparent access point apart from through the gate. The number of cameras and security personnel who guarded it were unsettling. Of course, she had no problems being through, but to get into the actual casino it required showing her driving license.

Howie's description was accurate. She took note of the cashiers' room directly to the right of the entrance, with two ATM machines by the wall. She got some chips, exchanging £50, and went to one of the Blackjack tables.

Howie had taught her this game, but she had never played it in a casino before. To her surprise, after about twenty minutes, she had doubled the money that she started with. The magnetism that turned a person into a compulsive gambler flowed in her veins, just like Howie, and she was careful not to let it take over. She had come here for one reason only.

After a few minutes of drifting around she found the door Howie had referred to. It was directly opposite the cashiers' room, separated by a huge line of flashing slot machines, with two blackjack tables on one side. Sarah identified it as the route security personnel took when they carried the cash boxes to and from the strong room. The door led onto the corridor that Howie had mentioned, which was unknown territory. Somewhere beyond that corridor was another door for deliveries. Her next step was to find where the delivery area was; before that, however, she wanted to look at the elevators.

They were located near the main entrance. A young security man was standing there, talking to an elderly couple. 'If you have a room in the hotel, you will need to use the elevators in the lobby,' Sarah heard him say.

'But we want to go to the second floor,' they protested.

'There's a Tournament up there at the moment. Only those on the approved list can go. Sorry.'

After a few mumbles the couple drifted away, leaving Sarah staring at the highly-polished elevator doors. 'Can I help you, miss?' the security man asked.

Up close, she could see he was about 25 years old, and his muscles pressed against his back shirt. 'Oh,' she said, 'I wanted to go to the second floor too, but guess I'm not allowed.' She began to walk way.

'Miss!'

'As it's early and you're going up on your own, I'll make an exception,' he said.

Sarah flashed a smile. 'You work late here?'

'Yeah, but I've got a break in an hour.'

GOOD INTENTIONS

'Then maybe I could return the favour with a drink?' she asked.

'Sure' he grinned, as the elevator doors opened.

'See you down here later then.'

The doors slid shut, to Sarah's relief. She looked at herself in one of the mirrors that were fixed to the elevator wall and ran a hand through her hair. Impossible thoughts dashed through her mind. There was no time to assess if an ambush was possible. As soon as the elevator doors slid open, she backed away from a huge camera.

'It's not him!' a voice exclaimed.

Quickly, she squeezed past a group of reporters, who seemed to be awaiting some unknown celebrity. The second floor was a swirl of glittering dresses and smart tuxedos. Some gambled at the £50-£100 minimum stake tables, others drank cocktails at the bar, whilst the majority watched the poker tournament.

By weaving her way through the crowd, Sarah eventually reached a rope barrier. Behind it a row of cameras focused on a group of people who sat around a large, elevated table. She recognised some of the faces: a movie star, a singer, a famous entrepreneur. They were all intent on the game. A large screen TV affixed to the wall gave a close-up of the table.

The singer looked to have the worst hand. If Sarah was playing, she would have folded, but the singer was not giving up. She raised with the other three. An ace of diamonds was drawn from the dealers pack. The entrepreneur folded, leaving the movie star, an old man with a beard, and the singer.

Looking at this striking woman with her straight 'poker face', Sarah had to admit she was beautiful. Her dress, her hair, her eyes…everything about her was radiant. And she was not giving anything away. She raised with her two opponents, putting the total prize money of this one game to £115,000 – the biggest amount so far. When their remaining cards were revealed, there was a gasp from the crowd. The singer, whose hand appeared the worst, had won: a Full House verses Three of a Kind. Sarah was pleased. It almost felt as if she herself had won; a triumph against the odds, bolstering her confidence for the upcoming endeavour.

She went to the bar and ordered a Martini 'on the rocks'. Crisp and fresh, just as she liked it. Then she turned her attention to the flow of people. All seemed oblivious to none but themselves and those closest to them. They felt safe, secure, protected – detached from the lower classes below. If it were not for the cameras, a skilled pickpocket could make off with thousands of pounds in jewellery and cash. So much wealth and opulence in one place was evident to anyone who had seen and experienced what Sarah had. She could eulogize what she planned just by looking at the clothes they wore. Just one of these garments could set-up a child for life. Some of the items of jewellery could supply a village with fresh drinking water for years. *Did any of them realize this?* she wondered. *Do any of them care?*

On the ground floor, the security man waited by the elevator. He hoped the woman would remember their meeting. She was one of the best-looking ones he had seen in the casino tonight. And she wasn't even wearing a proper dress! He guessed her age at around 22, and her figure had that sleek, sensuous form all red-blooded men longed for. But there was something else about her – a subtle magnetism below the surface, a deep mystery which he could not identify.

When the elevator doors opened and she stepped out alone, he could not hide his delight. The bright light shone off her tanned skin, which glistened almost as clearly as her eyes.

They wandered off to the bar and he insisted on getting the drinks, which were free to staff anyway.

'So how long have you worked here?' she asked.

'I'm pretty new to the job. Started six months ago,' he said.

'Do you like it?'

'Sure. The money's OK. I get a chance to meet some interesting people… beautiful ones, too,' he smiled. 'What do *you* do for a living, may I ask?'

She looked down at her drink and took a long sip. 'Business owner,' she said.

'Really? What sort of business?'

'A print shop. We do cards, mostly.'

'Where abouts?'

Sarah wasn't comfortable with these questions. She wanted to be the one who probed, gathering information, not him. But she continued to play along and engage in the conversation as if she enjoyed it. 'In Leicester,' she answered, 'I've had it for about two years now. One of the things we do is print playing cards, so I'm interested in the ones at this casino. I've never been to one before so it's a new experience.'

'Have you tried your hand at any games?' he asked.

She told him about her recent success at Blackjack and her observations of poker, which prompted him to recount a little story about his prowess at that game. Eventually she brought the conversation round to where she wanted it.

'I can't believe the winner of that tournament gets ten million pounds. Surely it's not given to them in cash?'

He shook his head. 'No, it's sent electronically. But in the final night there will be a few million on display, just to put on a show, encourage the punters to gamble. You know how it is, marketing the business.'

She smiled. 'Oh yes, I'm very familiar with that. So have you ever seen what a million in cash looks like?'

He was eager to impress her and fell right into the trap. 'A few times. Never seen it spread out though, just in bundles. Wouldn't you love to lie on a bed of money?'

Her eyes twinkled. 'I sure would… rolling around naked, flinging it up on the air, that's one of my dreams' she added.

He cleared his throat. 'Yeah, you can count me in on that too,' he winked.

'What time do you finish work?' she asked.

He looked at his watch. 'Not for another two hours.'

'Funny, that's around the time I go to bed.'

Before he could reply to this, Sarah felt her mobile phone vibrate.

'Not a boyfriend, I hope?' he asked.

'Err, no, just a friend,' she replied, opening her phone.

It was not a call but a picture-message from John. A series of pens had been arranged on a table to spell out the word 'Sorry'. It was a gesture so adorable that it checked her half-formed plans.

'I've got to help out my friend,' she said.

'That's too bad,' he sighed. 'Can I have your number for another time?'

After a brief hesitation, she gave it.

'My name's Matt, by the way.'

'Sarah.'

Clattering bells rang in the foreground: someone had got lucky on the slot machines.

As they parted, she cast a brief glance back in his direction, then proceeded through the crowded casino with its buzz of sound and colour. If anything came of their meeting, it was attributable to Fate alone. Fate had brought her to that elevator just at the right time, just as Fate had drawn her eyes to the £10 million poker tournament whilst on the train. In fact, Fate seemed to be behind every major turning point and event in her life. Or was it really all blind chance? Maybe some moments are picked out from others in the same way a sparkling stone is picked from sand. Ultimately, however, even the sand shines; it just depends on how the light reflects, relative to the observer. Life's moments of Fate could thus be seen as juxtapositions of multiple possibilities. Who could tell what other pathways might have been taken, what other choices may have led to different destinations?

Had Sarah looked behind as she exited the casino gate, for instance, the ensuring days would have been a lot different. Had she seen the man who entered the lobby of the hotel with her, much loss would have been avoided. Yet no sage can tell us what is for better or worse, for often *all* things seem to have a hidden purpose.

On returning to the hotel room, John was waiting up, looking remorseful. Without saying a word they both embraced, putting their arms around each other and swaying in a gentle motion.

'I'm sorry about earlier,' he said. 'I was wrong to completely dismiss the casino. I'm willing to take a look at it, maybe work something out.'

'I'm sorry too,' she said, 'I overreacted. I know it's a risky job and you were right to point that out.'

His hands slid down her flanks, drawing their bodies closer. He wanted to feel her warm skin, taste her kisses, never let her go.

'Take it easy, sailor!' she laughed. 'I need a shower. Wanna join me?'

'Yes m'am!' he said.

Hours later, as they lay exhausted, they whispered the things that only lovers could say. Theirs was a bond that was uniquely strong; her fiery passion mixing with his, making every fallout all the more intense. And yet such chemistry made every

GOOD INTENTIONS

moment of union eternal. In the privacy of their hotel room, the noise of city traffic could not be heard. Only their steady breathing and beating hearts took measure of time.

If nights could be counted as grains of sand upon an ebony shore, one facet of clear significance could be discerned: that all are linked, moving and forming as one, yet in detail not quite the same. So, too, with all in this world, though few have grasped the consequences.

6

The group best known as the Mafiosa had developed an efficient method of gathering information. In any country there was a handful of specialist 'private investigators' who worked for them alone. They could be called upon at any time. Some were ex-military, some had done time in prison, others were just well connected to the Mafiosa families and needed a way to ascend the ranks. All had proper jobs that raised no suspicions on their real livelihood, whether it was working as a bank clerk or as a police officer. These mercenary investigators had two primary tasks: to monitor and track targets via direct surveillance and, if required, to 'neutralise' them via lethal force. For more difficult targets, the latter task was dealt with by another section of the Mafiosa. Nonetheless, a person had to be highly skilled, resourceful and ruthless to achieve the role of 'investigator'. Each had an area controller who allocated the necessary resources, received regular reports, gave details on new targets, and outlined what was required.

The investigator dispatched to watch John Stevens was well known within the Mafiosa ranks. His name was Carlson. There was a time when men like him would have quickly risen through the hierarchy, but these days it was guile that came before ruthlessness. Carlson's unique style and drive

GOOD INTENTIONS

had earned him the reputation as an 'enforcer'. The nickname of 'Locker Man' had been given to him following one of his earliest assignments. On that occasion he had used a small unventilated freezer-box to trap two of his targets. It didn't take him long to obtain all the information he needed. They both went away with hypothermia and a life-long fear of confined spaces, but compared to some of Carlson's other targets they were lucky. Luckier than they would care to contemplate.

Carlson had been working for the Mafiosa for nine years, ever since he was approached in prison at 19 years of age. A member of the local crime family on Carlson's wing had noticed his skills in manipulation, fighting and planning – giving him the task of 'neutralising' another inmate. He narrowly avoided getting caught, but on release was offered a permanent job. They refined his techniques, taught him new ways to survey and kill targets, then set him loose to do their bidding.

For him, the money was great and so was the living. From the very beginning, he found the work to be satisfying, and, when given the task of 'neutralisation', immensely therapeutic. It released all his tension and anger, giving him a rush that was unparalleled by any other activity. This was a natural feeling, he told himself; an inevitability of life given what he had suffered in his early years.

But these days a restlessness and discontent followed him. He was no longer being given the assignments he enjoyed. Now a killing came once in a blue moon, when in the beginning it had seemed like every other week. Carlson increasingly found himself surveying some moronic target, following them around and sitting in the same place for hours on end, waiting for their next move. It was frustrating, annoying work. Last time he was required to monitor some minor drug dealer without being noticed by the police detectives who were doing the same. It went on for two weeks, and when the dealer started leaking delicate information Carlson expected to get a neutralisation order. But no! They sent others in to do it.

Now he found himself watching a man they suspected of money laundering: target #10112, John Stevens, who appeared to be of the same calibre as the dead drug dealer. So far he had learnt that Stevens was staying at an inner city budget hotel with an attractive young woman. They didn't appear to be married, so he wasn't particularly interested in her role within Stevens's enterprise. Still worth checking out, he thought, and she may be able to provide him with some vital information.

He just hoped there was more to this assignment than just money laundering. Every day the desire to practise his true God-given art called out to be fulfilled, like a song that can never quite be forgotten.

So, in the background, 'The Locker Man' watched. And waited.

* * *

GOOD INTENTIONS

The next day John agreed to look at the casino, on condition that Sarah would look at the bank. Afterwards they met at a busy café.

'So what do you think?' he asked.

She really wanted to find faults in his plan, but couldn't think of any. From the hour or so she had spent in and around the bank, all his notes looked accurate. The digital printouts of the area provided an ideal getaway. 'Yeah, it looks good. What do you think of the casino?'

Like Sarah, he wanted to point out the bad points, without looking as if he totally dismissed it as a potential job. 'I'd need to see this delivery door that Howie talked about,' he said, 'but even after walking around the perimeter, I saw no way over the wall.'

Sarah admitted that she hadn't seen one either. The wall surrounded busy roads and was watched by cameras, so climbing over it was not feasible, especially if they had to carry back the cash cases. Both of them realised they could not go ahead with the robbery if they had to use the main gate. Having just one entry/exit point was a negative for any job, and was particularly applicable for this one. The gate was constantly monitored, could be remotely shut, and was linked up with other security systems.

After John agreed, she contacted her uncle and arranged a meeting outside the casino. Howie's condition was that she would 'keep out of it', although he agreed to meet John alone just before 9pm. She didn't argue with this. After all, it was enough that Howie hadn't changed his mind about the robbery altogether.

As John prepared to leave, she insisted that he would not overlook anything, even if it appeared risky. He tried reminding her that some risks just weren't worth taking; if there was no way over the casino wall, then robbing it was an impossible prospect.

'Perhaps,' she said. 'But whenever there's a will…' John did not have to be reminded of their motto.

He parked the car a short distance from the casino and immediately saw Howie. The night was cold, and a series of thin clouds passed across the moon. Even without the veil of vapour, its silvery light was dominated by the glaring modernity of man. Lights from cars, streetlamps and signs forced the darkness into unnatural life.

'I'm not happy meeting you like this,' Howie said. 'I'm taking a big risk being seen with you.' John tried to reassure him that during the robbery he would wear something to disguise his appearance, but Howie just grunted.

A limousine cruised past them, heading for the VIP parking area. 'Come on, this way,' Howie said, taking a small path that led through some gardens. Floodlights lit most of the shrubs and trees, painting them in eerie shades of red and blue. A flowered walkway led up to an archway of plants, the sort of thing one might expect to see in a garden competition or in the grounds of some famous manor house. Palm trees lay between the wall that surrounded the casino grounds and a large delivery door. Howie drew John's attention to it.

'You see that small door next to the big one – that's the one I was talking about.'

'Yes,' John replied. Even from a distance, he could see the camera that loomed above it. There was also the occupants of the casino hotel to consider, who were able to look down from their rooms on the delivery area below. Even now, he felt as if he was being watched.

'That leads onto the corridor where security carry cash to the strong room. Get in there, at the right time, and you're sorted. Bear in mind there's usually three or four guards, along with cameras. But how you deal with that is your problem.'

To John, this was not the biggest dilemma. Getting over the wall was. He mentioned this to Howie.

'Yeah, I've thought about that as well. But, as my grandma used to say, if you can't go over, go around.' He looked at his watch. 'Well, I better get going. You've got my number.'

'But what if I can't go around?' John asked.

'There's three dimensions in this world, kid.' With that, he walked away.

John stood there watching him disappear through the archway. His shadow flickered and crawled like an elongated ghost, lingering on the stone, until it finally jumped away. Yet the feeling of being watched remained. It was more of a subconscious impression than an abject understanding, but this did not diminish its intensity. *It's nothing,* he thought. *At least I can convince Sarah that there's no way to rob the casino.*

A light breeze stirred the uppermost branches of a palm tree, partially masking a stealthy movement elsewhere. It sounded like a rustle of leaves, intermixed with an unidentifiable *trickling*. It seemed to be coming from some bushes, but when John paused to listen there was just silence. So he turned and began walking down the path.

Again, a noise. This time it was the unmistakable sound of a cough. Barely metres away. John veered around, quickly confirming that nobody was on the path. They were somewhere else….

* * *

In the hotel room Sarah flicked through a range of channels, finding all were meaningless. She was in a of mind that finds one sick of life – or rather, of society – where the primary question was *'what's the point?'* There was no point, really. But there was always a purpose. Thinking back over her life, she marvelled at how much she had accomplished. From an impoverished, traumatic upbringing, to exotic world travels working with the poorest people; seeing in their struggles part of her own. She had come to realise that there was always someone else who had it worse, which had led her to strive to help them. Then she had met John and fallen in love, finding a new purpose in life without forgetting the old one.

But do the means justify the end? It was too late to think about this question. The path had already been taken, and there

GOOD INTENTIONS

was no going back. She saw ahead a bright horizon, a sparkling future where inequality no longer took precedence. To live, to struggle, to die for such a dream... all this she could do.

Her ringing phone interrupted these thoughts. The screen read '**Unknown Caller**'. She tapped the green icon.

'Hi Sarah,' a male voice said on the other end. 'It's Matt'.

So, she thought, *you've finally called.*

'You busy tonight?' he asked.

The last thing she wanted was to go and see him, but she really had no choice. A purpose and dream were more insistent than any duty, even if that duty was one of love. She arranged to meet him at a popular pub a short distance away. Before leaving, she wrote a quick note to John telling him that she was 'following up on a lead'.

The bar was noisy and crowded, mostly filled with young students.

She did not have to search for Matt because he found her.

'How'd you find me in this crowd?' she shouted above the blasting music.

He smiled and said smoothly 'You'd stand out from any crowd.'

He brought the drinks and they sat by a relatively quiet table. Looking at him, she found herself a little surprised. He was younger than she remembered, and even in the dim light she could see his hair was frosted with bronze-blonde strands. Instead of the characterless casino uniform, he wore an open-necked shirt, which matched the blue colour of her own dress. Initially, she found it hard to bring the conversation round to where she wanted it. The beating music, pumped up by a hidden DJ, kept breaking into her carefully planned questions. There was a disco at the back, and she did not refuse when he asked her to dance.

They joined with the group of young couples who moved their bodies to the music's beat, gyrating and swinging in tandem. It was the type of music that necessitated bodily contact, and soon they were both pressing against one another. She was caught up in the moment, pushed onwards by the need to fulfil her purpose and gather more information on the casino.

She had to make a choice: either totally betray John, who was one of her purposes for living, or take an opportunity at furthering her other purpose – robbing the casino. It was one of those crossroads in life which had dual consequences, leading to totally different destinations. A moment of Fate, perhaps.

* * *

Peering into bushes, John glimpsed the shadowy form of a tramp, sitting down like a Buddha in a leafy cave. The stench of alcohol and unwashed clothes were more distinct than the actual shape of him. At first John was fearful, but this soon resided into caution, and then curiosity. *How had this drunken tramp managed to get into the casino grounds, past security at the entrance? And what did he hear a few minutes ago?*

GOOD INTENTIONS

'Hi there,' he said.

The tramp shifted and coughed, unable to get out of his little den because John was blocking the way in. 'What kind of whiskey's that?' John asked, looking at the amber fluid in the bottle clutched closely to the tramp's chest.

'It's mine!' a broken, croaky voice shouted back.

'That's OK. I don't want any. I usually only drink JD anyway.'

It had been a while since the tramp had drunk Jack Daniels. 'I can't afford that,' he said.

John reached into his pocket and handed over a £20 note. 'Here you go -courtesy of the casino.'

The tramp tentatively reached out to take the money, then smiled and said 'thank you' when he had it within his coat. 'You win big then?' he asked.

'I will do, one night,' John replied.

The tramp took another swig of his whiskey and shuffled out of the bushes, forcing John to stand aside. When he stood up, he presented a daunting sight; face all pock-marked, hair and beard untrimmed, eyes glowing with an untamed wildness. John did not feel threatened – not because he was bigger and stronger, but because in his experience the destitute were very different from the dangerous.

'What's your name?' he asked the man, who croaked out a word that sounded like Nail. 'Nice to meet you, Nail, I'm John,' he said.

'Forgive me seeming rude, but how did someone in your state get in here?'

'I used to be able to come here without hiding, but now they've got guards which go round,' Nail said, launching into a coughing fit.

John waited for him to finish. 'Look, I can see you need help. And I need help too. I want to know how to get out of here without being noticed by security. Do you know a way?'

Nail began moving his body like an agitated meerkat. 'Why?' he asked, his question barely audible.

'Because there are people looking for me there,' John replied, 'I need to find another way out.'

Nail coughed. He was about to say something, then he stopped. Heavy fumes of half-digested alcohol wafted out with each exhalation.

'I'll show you… if you give me half your winnings,' he said testily.

'Alright, deal', John replied, extending his arm to shake Nail's hand. At first there was hesitation, but eventually his grip met John's and they shook cordially to re-affirm an agreement.

Nail led him along the wall of the casino's perimeter, constantly pausing and looking around as if another person was watching. It made John feel uneasy and, despite his past experiences, he wished he brought the gun tonight, just in case. Amidst the floodlit undergrowth of the casino gardens, shapes moved. The palm trees whispered, as if conspiring to fall upon an unsuspecting foe.

Nail stopped and bent down to the ground. There was a storm drain, the sort of metal culvert that one can find in any city street, only this one was much larger.

'You need a hand with that?' John asked, as the tramp groaned to lift the metal cover up. It appeared to be completely loose, but it was still obviously heavy. However, before John could go round to help, Nail had already heaved it aside. He descended into the hole and began climbing down a ladder that was shrouded in complete darkness.

So this is it, John thought. Howie was right: if you can't go over, go around, and if you can't go around, *go under*.

Standing there, looking into the darkness, he paused. *Was this really such a good idea?* Nail could turn at any time and attack him in the unknown of whatever lay below, when he was disorientated and defenceless. It was not an enticing possibility.

Before John could hesitate further, Nail switched on a torch.

'Down here,' he called, as if John was too blind to see the torchlight. He made a choice, deciding to put caution aside, and lowered himself onto the ladder. The rungs were slippery and cold. They consumed the heat in his hands like ravenous teeth. Nail was shining the torchlight onto the metal, reassuring John and helping him to see where he was going. It took seven steps to reach the bottom.

A few inches of water trickled along a tunnel, and Nail began to follow its flow. Every footfall echoed off the stone walls, which John could barely see in the torchlight. Behind him there was only blackness – a total absence of light. As they moved forward, he began to think there was someone else back there, a presence as unavoidable and unrelenting as his own shadow, only far more sinister and alien. It was like walking the deepest catacombs below the Roman Coliseum, where the ghosts of slaughtered gladiators moved in bloodless pain. Footfall by ominous footfall, he moved forward.

When a faint glow of light appeared ahead, distinct from the torch beam, John moved faster. But he could not pass Nail, whose pace was maddeningly slow.

Eventually the tunnel opened into a wider space, with shallow alcoves embedded into the walls. There was a kind of grate, which had a series of metal bars that looked out on a silvery sparkle of moonlight. Nail squeezed through a place where some of the bars were bent sideways, forming a large gap. John followed.

He could now see where they were: the tunnel had brought them to the river bank. They stood near a bridge, with the water flowing serenely past. By scrambling up some rough steps and hopping over a banister, John could reach the pathway that led along the river. It was a perfect getaway route.

Nail watched him with those eerie, wild eyes, keeping silent but looking almost deadly. John walked up to him. 'Thank you,' he said quietly, reaching into his pocket and handing over some notes.

Nail stretched out a shaky hand to take them.

'Is there anywhere you can go?' John asked, 'A hostel? Family?'

Nail simply shook his head and went back to the grate, ducking through the gap faster than John expected. Within

GOOD INTENTIONS

seconds he vanished.

'Goodbye, friend,' John called into the darkness.

Maybe his ears deceived him, but a thin sound seemed to carry on the abysmal breeze. '*Goodbye...*'

As he walked to the steps, he noticed that some shapes had gathered on the river – a dozen swans, the same number of notes he had given the tramp. For a while they followed him as he walked along the path.

He thought of Sarah, whose plan of robbing the casino was vindicated. Now he was as committed to this as her.

Or so he imagined.

7

Back at the hotel, John read Sarah's note and called her mobile. There was no response. He called Howie's, but that just resulted in a few grunts and expletives. He even considered trying to contact some friends of theirs, but it was getting too late for that. Reluctantly, he resigned himself to a sleepless night spent waiting for Sarah to get back.

It was not until morning when she did.

'Where the hell have you been?! I've been really worried.'

She came to the bed and sat beside him. 'I'm sorry. Something came up.'

He looked into her eyes, able to see past their radiant depths to a hidden secret. 'Well? Are you going to tell me?'

'A friend… she got taken to the hospital. I had no choice but to go.'

'Your note said you were following up on a lead,' John pointed out.

'I was. Outside the casino, trying to find a way in. That's when I got called.'

'You were outside the casino even though you knew I was there too? You agreed not to go!'

'Oh, for God's sake! You haven't even asked how my friend is and you're trying to dictate where I'm allowed to go!' She stepped away from the bed and stormed to the bathroom.

GOOD INTENTIONS

'Sarah! Wait!' John cried, getting out of bed. But she had shut and locked the door.

'I'm sorry about your friend,' he called. 'I just love you so much, and care for you like nothing else.'

There was silence in the bathroom. After a few seconds, broken words floated out in a voice that John barely recognised. 'I know… just give me a few minutes.'

In the bathroom, the full impact of what she had done stung her badly. The cross-roads had been taken, Fate had decreed its supremacy, and there was never any going back. She had betrayed John – the one person she had loved as a soul mate. She had sacrificed one purpose in life for another. Perhaps subconsciously she knew what the outcome would be when she planned to meet the security guy at the casino, but until last night she had never seen it as 'set'.

The resolution to fulfil the mission had been too strong to disregard. To throw away an opportunity in successfully robbing the casino would have been akin to letting others die, with millions of pounds at stake. Matt had been the ticket to those millions.

Now everything she had learnt last night about the casino counted as nothing in the face of John's devotion. She had been able to extract some of the information she needed from Matt: that the money was going to be taken up in the elevator in 'several' cases, one day before the end of the tournament. But nothing else he told her was useful.

She had to face up to the guilt of her actions, which at the time seemed innocent and for the greater good. *Does every goal have complications?* she wondered. *Can one sweeping benefit justify a little harm?*

Gazing at her reflection in the bathroom mirror, Sarah thought so. Actions in the here and now, every second of every day, may define 'good' from 'bad', even 'heaven' from 'hell'. Yet they could never overrule the salvation of every man, woman and child. What is one second's drastic choice compared to a millennia of prosperity? What is one betrayal when it has the potential to benefit thousands?

Despite all this, Sarah could not expel her regrets. Like the tear trickling down her left cheek, they trickled down to her heart.

And so, as the sun rose to herald another day, perhaps only one man in the city was truly happy. Awaking in a warm bed and taking a hot shower had done wonders for Nail. He shaved and sang, moving his feet to the rhythm of radio music. Only one thought restrained his euphoria: *how long will this last?*

Last night, in the dark tunnel hidden below the city streets, he had gone back to move the storm cover in the casino grounds. Somehow, whilst climbing up the ladder, his most prized possession dropped to the ground. The bottle had smashed into uncounted pieces, spilling the golden liquid within and leaving him totally bereft. For a time he searched for an off-license, but a deep tiredness stopped him in his tracks. Without the numbing effect of alcohol, the night's coldness clung tightly to his body. After two hours of wandering, he managed to find a hostel – one of the rare ones which were clean and free of trouble. The cash from John had got him a single, en-suite room.

Now he was feeling the first urging to drink. This time, however, he resolved not to heed them. The money he had was enough to buy some new clothes and a week's accommodation with decent food. Wrestling with his demons, he was determined to subdue them and take a new path in life. It wasn't going to be easy. Nothing worth obtaining in life came without struggle – for the majority of people, anyway.

His thoughts went once again to the woman he had glimpsed by the river. He had decided that she wasn't a swan, nor one of those figures who existed in his imagination. She was real. The need to see her again was inexplicably strong; perhaps even stronger than the need to have another drink. The shattered dream fragments that he could still remember all revolved around her. To Nail she had become an emblem of beauty, wonder, and desire – all the things he had been missing, and all that he was determined to regain.

* * *

When Sarah emerged from the bathroom, John had made some coffee and ordered some breakfast from room service. She sat down at the table and nibbled at a croissant.

'You okay?' he said.

'Yeah, I'm just tired from last night.'

He nodded. 'Look, I think you might be right about the casino. It's definitely a possibility.'

Her eyes lit up.

He proceeded to tell her about the 'secret passage' that went under the wall. Her appetite seemed to become more voracious with each revelation. Soon all that remained of the continental breakfast was a plate of crumbs and two empty glasses. 'You were right,' he said. 'There's always a way, if you look hard enough, and this old sewer tunnel is just what we need.'

He began to outline the plan he had been formulating. He would find a place to park near the bridge and walk with a backpack to the river. Once he reached the grate, he would change into a disguise: different clothing, a mask, and a large sports bag to put the money in. He would leave the backpack in the tunnel, ready to change-over when he returned. Once through the tunnel, Sarah would text him from the casino, letting him know when the cash was being moved. He would then walk through the gardens to the delivery door, entering the access code which Howie would provide, and surprise the security guards as they entered from the casino gaming floor. The corridor would be a perfect ambush. It wouldn't take long to get the cash, and by the time an alarm was raised he would be in the tunnel. When the casino was locked down and police were arriving at the main gate he'd be walking back along the river.

GOOD INTENTIONS

Sarah had many objections to this plan. She pointed out that there could be problems with the guards; that it would be far better to have two people ambushing them rather than one. She raised the possibility that the cases couldn't be opened by the guards, in which case John would have to carry them alone. That was another reason to have a second person.

It was obvious who that second person would be: her. She argued that Howie should be the one who texted them from within the casino. But she also wanted to go for a far larger sum: the full £10 million that they originally saw in the newspaper. She proposed that they could get into the casino via the same route, find the maintenance room to the lift, then plan an ambush from there.

Looking imploringly at John, she ignored his frown and continued to outline the plan. 'We could find a way to stop the lift with the cash inside, access it from a safety hatch, and get the guards to handover the cases. If we were disguised as a maintenance crew we could get back to the tunnel without being noticed, before the alarm could be raised. Even if we showed up on the cameras, security would assume that we were cleared by the main gate. And the loot would be much higher.'

'So would the risk,' John said. He argued that her plan was full of holes, such as finding a way to stop the lift and fooling security with their disguises. 'How exactly would we get into the lift anyway?' he asked.

'One of us would be on the roof of the lift waiting, whilst the other would be in the maintenance room, able to bring the lift to a halt as it ascended. But I realise the details need to be worked out beforehand.'

'There's one thing you haven't remembered,' John said.

'What's that?'

'Your uncle Howie doesn't want you involved. He made me promise that.'

She sighed. 'Well, you don't have to tell him.'

He knew, from past jobs, that she was both competent and eager to take part. He also knew that keeping her out of this job would be like trying to keep a cat away from a mouse. She would argue it was her idea to start with, anyway. His only hope was for a compromise.

'I'm not buying it, Sarah. You can't plan this elevator heist by yourself if Howie won't help.'

She paused, looking down at the duvet. 'You will have to go to Howie yourself.'

'We *already have* a decent plan worked out!' John protested. 'OK… if you go with my plan, you can take a bigger role. We'll work side by side, taking the cash together. But in no circumstances am I going with this elevator crap. Sorry.'

To his surprise, she didn't continue to argue. Instead, she kicked off her shoes and slipped into the bed. For a moment he thought she had fallen asleep, but then she reached behind her head to plump up the pillow.

'I guess you've been sitting up at the hospital all night?' he said, sitting down next to her.

'Yes… really tired.'

GOOD INTENTIONS

He nodded. 'Do you want anything before I go?' he asked.

She reached over and grabbed his shoulder, pulling him down onto the bed. 'Yes…you.'

They laughed and kissed, but he still held back. 'I thought you said you were tired.'

'Never be tired of you, babe,' she whispered, lifting up his shirt.

By the time they finished it was almost midday. Sarah looked half- way between two states of unconsciousness, yet she had seemed all-to- ready to please him in their love-making.

'Will you at least ask Howie about the elevator?' she said as he got dressed.

He looked at her lying on the bed, clearly exhausted and yet still obsessed with the casino job. 'Alright,' he sighed.

'Promise?' she replied.

He came closer and looked into her eyes. 'That wasn't a bribe, was it?'

Her response was a kiss. 'No. Just promise me you'll ask Howie.'

'OK. I'll call him in the afternoon and arrange to meet him.' He was about to say '*I need him to tell me the code to the delivery door, anyway.*' Instead he asked her if she wanted anything to eat.

She smiled and pulled the duvet up. 'Thanks,' she said dreamily, before falling asleep.

He walked to the riverside, stopping off at a DIY store. Only the heavy-duty flashlights caught his eye, and he chose the biggest available. The batteries alone were the size of Maglites.

'Going mining, son?' the guy behind the counter winked.

'Oh yes,' John replied, 'I'm hoping to strike gold.'

Walking back along the river, he noticed the water was flowing higher, even though it had not rained for a while. It reminded him of the connectivity between distant things, with rain clouds over mountains flooding rivers in plains, just as what happened in distant cities reached out and affected an entire nation's towns. So it was that the web of cause and effect spread to all things, even those that seemed separated from one another.

There were no swans about this afternoon – just a few floating branches that sailed by in the murky water. Nor was the tramp anywhere to be seen. John could not imagine him lurking in the pitch black of the tunnel, but he supposed it was a remote possibility.

He entered the darkness, shining the light around warily. Like before, it was damp, chilly, and silent. On this occasion, he timed the walk to the casino's storm drain, which turned out to be only eight minutes. It had seemed much longer the previous night. Part of him contemplated going further, delving deeper into the tunnel, trying to see what other parts of the city it led to. The faint sound of running trains echoed in the distance. And there was something else, as well – something he couldn't describe – at the root of a tremble in the dark, a shiver of the skin.

GOOD INTENTIONS

He climbed up the metal ladder and pushed on the drain cover, which lifted with surprising ease. That's all he needed to know, and he contented himself with a fleeting peak of the casino's gardens. Leaving the tunnel here would be pointless, and it wasn't worth the risk.

As he descended the ladder, he looked down.

Two pale eyes shimmered in the darkness. He wasted no time in directing the torchlight down, even though he partly feared what would be revealed.

It could have been a guardian gargoyle of a Gothic cathedral, or a sentinel spirit of the underworld: a giant black rat, skin so oily that it appeared luminescent, ears pointed into ratty steeples. At least, it *looked* like a rat. Even facing the bright light, it neither moved nor blinked.

'Boo!' he shouted.

Making one serpentine blink, the plump creature casually waddled off.

Since when did rats get so big? he wondered.

A persistent ringing awoke Sarah from her slumber. There was no doubt about it: she *had* to get out of bed to retrieve the mobile phone. 'Damn it,' she mumbled, flicking open the phone without bothering to see who was calling.

'Hi Sarah,' a male voice reverberated from the speaker. For a moment she was shocked, even worried. Then she realised it was Matt.

'Hello.' *Could he help me?* she fleetingly wondered.

'I can't stop thinking about you. Where are you?'

Listening to his voice, she felt a mixture of emotions. She even briefly considered meeting up with him again, despite the guilt she had felt only a few hours ago.

'Sorry,' she replied, quickly turning the phone off.

It was harder than she thought. Knowing that she needed to get a new phone was the least of her worries.

After eating the sandwiches that John had left by the bed, she still felt zombified. In sleep she could find a measure of serenity and rejuvenation. Perhaps she could even forget.

Can time be counted by the actions of our thoughts or by the change that follows them? Some things in life are not meant to be forgotten. For Sarah, this lesson would be learned the hard way. It would return to her later, riding on a dune of retribution.

* * *

The next step was to visit Howie. John did not have his number, so called Sarah. Her phone was switched off – *again.* He decided to drive straight to Howie's flat rather than call him beforehand. Going back to the hotel to get Howie's number from Sarah would mean waking her up and, despite it being almost two o'clock, he thought that she needed a good rest. So he drove to the block of flats and saw the same old scenery: the group of sullen teenagers grouped around the bench, smoking weed; the bits of rubbish left discarded on the grass (a few squashed lager cans had been added to

GOOD INTENTIONS

the collection), and the same dogs barking out their brains. The only real difference was the weather.

He pressed the buzzer to Howie's flat, noticing the chewing gum on the one below had been removed. *Well,* he thought, *that's three points for this 'Spot the Difference' estate.*

'Who is it?' a woman's voice shouted on the intercom.

'Is Howie there?' he asked.

There was a brief pause before she screamed back 'Who are you?'

After telling her his name and that he was Sarah's boyfriend, he heard Howie's name being shouted. The woman's voice was loud enough to be heard from one of the windows above. He turned around and noticed the kids by the bench looking in his direction, talking together conspiringly.

Abruptly the door to the apartment block clicked open. He went inside and ascended the stairs, trying not to breathe too much of the vomit-stenched air. When he reached Howie's door and knocked, it was a woman who greeted him. For a minute he was taken aback. She looked older than Sarah's uncle, with curled hair that was died a deep red. It looked unkempt and wild, reflecting the stare in her eyes.

'Come in!' she shouted, hustling John into the flat and slamming the door.

Howie was sitting on the sofa wearing a dressing gown, his hair uncombed and his eyes surrounded by purple ellipses. Immediately John regretted not calling first. 'Sorry to catch you at such short notice,' he said.

Before Howie could reply, the women shouted 'Can I get you a drink?' from the kitchen area, following this question up with 'Aren't you going to introduce him, Bo?'

Howie groaned and mumbled something about a painkiller. 'Yes,' he said, 'this is John... a friend of my niece.' The woman came over and smiled. 'Nice to meet you, John. I'm Harriett. What was it you said you wanted to drink?'

He smiled back and asked for tea.

When Harriett went back to the kitchen, Howie leaned over and frowned. 'Why the hell didn't you ring first?'

John was about to answer when Harriett shouted 'Do you take milk?'

'Oh, yes please,' he called back.

'Don't you have my number?' Howie asked impatiently.

'Yes... Sarah has it. But I didn't want to wake her up.'

Howie looked at his watch. 'Sleeping? At this time? What the hell have you two been doing? Wait, don't te -'

Harriett's voice interrupted him, asking John how many sugars he took. 'One, two, or three?' she called.

'Oh, none thanks,' John replied.

Just as Howie began to speak again, Harriett asked 'You sure you don't want any sugar?'

'No thanks,' John confirmed.

Howie leaned back on the sofa with his head tilted up in the air as Harriett brought over two cups of tea – one for her, one for John – and a glass of unknown red liquid that vaguely resembled tomato juice.

GOOD INTENTIONS

The ensuring interrogation lasted for an hour. Howie got up half- way through, after taking a tentative sip of the red juice, claiming to need to 'freshen up'. He left John alone with Harriett's endless questions. She asked him about everything – from John's relationship with Sarah and his preferred vintage to his opinion of the US President.

Finally, Howie came to the rescue. He emerged from the bathroom, dressed in one of the casino's uniforms. 'Me and John need to go buy a car for Sarah,' he announced.

Harriett looked at him. Her expression changed from a motherly aunt to a disciplinarian headmistress. 'A *car*?' she said. She pronounced it like it was the strangest thing in the world. 'Now?'

'Yes,' John said, knowing an escape route when he saw one. 'I wanted Howie's opinion on what she would prefer… it's for our engagement.'

Harriett smiled, but only slightly. 'Well, it's been nice meeting you, John. And don't let Bo go drinking at the pub. He's got work in an hour.'

Already Howie was standing at the door, holding a jacket and looking anxious to get out. 'See you later' he said, shutting the door.

As soon as they left the flat, John apologised again and explained why he had come. Howie just grunted.

Stepping outside, John was hit by a mixture of anger and trepidation when he looked towards his car. The group of teenagers had chosen to migrate there, with the oldest two leaning back on the bonnet, grinning. Before John could say anything, Howie lurched forward, fists clenched.

'Oi! Get the hell off them wheels!'

The group scattered as feral dogs obeying the command of a master. As they drove away, Howie launched into a monologue about how times were changing with regard to the next generation. He then started giving instructions on where to go.

'No, turn right,' he said, pointing to a pub at the end of a junction. John pulled into a parking lot. 'Harriett said...' he began.

Howie wasn't listening. 'You've got a lot to learn about women, kid,' he said, getting out the car.

It was a typical working men's pub: old, but not ancient; unhygienic, but not dirty. At this time there was hardly anyone there. A few men in their fifties sat around talking at the bar and two lads of twenty-ish were watching a football match on a small, overhead TV.
'Pint of Fosters with nuts,' Howie said to the landlord, a large bald man who was leaning over the counter.

'How! How's it going, mate?'

'Not bad,' he replied, then turned to John. 'What ya drinking?' John asked for an orange juice, but Howie didn't seem to hear.

'Make that two pints,' he said to the landlord, who began to discuss the latest football results. They talked for a while, completely ignoring John, and then Howie went over to a quiet table by one of the windows.

'That's better,' he said, after taking a big gulp of his drink. The froth at the top made a temporary moustache around the top of his upper lip.

'Where were we? Oh yes, women...'

John listened patiently as Howie began to describe his troubles with Harriett, before concluding with how much he loved her. He asked about Sarah and then brought the conversation around to the casino.

'You've found a way over the wall, then?'

'Well, not exactly "over", but it's no longer an obstacle,' John replied.

'Good. Then why do you want to know about this bloody elevator?' John began to tell him Sarah's idea of 'ambushing' the lift as the guards took money to the second floor, remembering the promise he had made. He emphasised it was just an idea, but Howie still looked incredulous.

'Just when I thought you were a smart bloke who wasn't greedy! Do you expect me to find out when they're taking the cash up? Show you around the maintenance area like a bloody VIP? Anyway, the cash is probably going up the escalators anyway, not the lift.'

John nodded. 'It was just an idea.'

Howie finished his pint and burped. 'You should be thinking about getting into that corridor. I'm not going to ask how you're getting the cash cases off three or four grown men. You've done robberies before, apparently, so I guess you know the risks. As long as Sarah's not involved, I'm happy.' He looked around the pub, then asked John if he had a pen.

There was one in John's pocket, which he put on the table. Howie turned a small beer-mat upside down and began writing on it. Then he looked up and frowned.

'I want one third of the money, like we agreed. In cash, of course. I'll meet you outside this pub, a day after you've done it. Bring the money with you. Is that acceptable?'

'Yes,' John replied.

Howie reached across the table and they shook hands. It was a firm, direct handshake – a sealing of honour between two men. He slid the mat across the table and walked out the pub, leaving John staring at what he wrote. It was just three numbers and three letters in one line:

923xyu

The code to the delivery door.

8

Carlson watched the exchange with loathing. Ignorance had to be the worst state of mind. His job, after all, was to know what the target was up to. So far all he had been able to glean was that the target was planning something. A drug deal, perhaps. But there was no evidence that he was involved in the nefarious world of drugs. Nor was there any indication that he was associated with other criminals.

It didn't take long to get a picture of the target's friend, which Carlson sent to his handler. Within minutes he had a detailed profile: Howard Emery, 45, casino croupier, no prior convictions.

Just great. There were times in life when one had to forge one's own way; times when the best course of action was done at the spur of the moment. Part of him felt like withdrawing the 9mm and setting it on fully automatic, then spraying a deadly barrage into the dingy pub. Rattle, rattle, rattle…

And he'd laugh. Carlson hadn't laughed for a long time.

But instead he just sat there, feeling the flames of wrath waft across his restraint. *Another time, another place*, he told himself.

* * *

When John left the pub (he was tempted to have another pint, but decided against it) and arrived back at the hotel, Sarah was typing on the laptop.

'Hey you', she said, 'how did it go with Howie?'

He sat down and took off his shoes. 'Well, I tried finding out more about the elevator, but he thought I was crazy even thinking about it.'

Sarah put her head in her hands and sighed. 'I'm going to go there myself.'

He lay back on the bed and said nothing. Arguing with her would achieve nothing, and he knew how stubborn she could be. *Let her go to the casino,* he thought, *that way she will see how stupid her idea is.*

A faint rumbling in his stomach redirected his thoughts to more pressing needs. 'You want to have dinner in the restaurant?' he asked.

She smiled. 'Why not?'

They went down together and sat near a window. Evening crowds surged on the pavement outside, most of them already having finished work. No rain fell from the overcast sky, but neither did the sun pour down its rays. Both John and Sarah were completely oblivious to one nondescript man, who watched them from the hotel's bar, barely twenty metres away.

As they waited for their food, John discussed the casino getaway route. 'I can't fault it,' he said. 'The tunnel goes right from the riverside to the casino gardens. No one else seems to know about it.'

'Apart from this tramp,' Sarah said.

'Well, yes. And maybe a few sewer rats.' He remembered the giant rat at the bottom of the ladder… and the other feelings that had inexplicably overcome him whilst he was down there.

'Are you sure we're not going to have to wade through sewage?' Sarah asked.

He shook his head. 'No. There's just a trickle of stale water. I guess the worst part is the drain in the casino grounds. If someone's around when we lift it up, we'll have to abort."

Sarah just blinked. 'Uncertainty, risk – it's all part of our occupation though, isn't it? Anyway, what did Howie think of the plan?'

John was pleased to move away from talking about the tunnel. When he mentioned Howie and Harriett, Sarah laughed. Seeing this cheered him too, and he felt even hungrier.

By the time the food arrived, he was ravenous. An aromatic scent of spice rose up with the steam of basmati rice. They split the pitta bread together and dipped it into a tray of different sauces, each one unique both in taste and colour. The chicken from the curry melted in his mouth. As he bit into its creamy texture, the various problems with the casino heist momentarily evaporated.

'There's one thing I forgot to mention,' Sarah said, after they finished the main course. 'Lucy sent an email from the print shop. She needs to see us about the new range of products and renewing old contracts. Do you want to go down?'

John paused, weighing out what to do. It was always good to have a 'layoff' – the period between planning a heist and actually doing it. 'Sure,' he agreed, 'when do you want to leave?'

A waiter brought over their desserts before she could answer: an ice cream sundae topped with cherry sauce for him, and a 'fruits of the forest' option for her, with a scoop of chocolate ice cream on the side.

'I was planning to pay another visit to the casino,' she continued, after the waiter had gone. 'Also… my friend expects me to visit her in hospital.'

He nodded, annoyed with the first reason but understanding of the other. 'Just be careful, Sarah. Don't take any risks. If someone sees you acting suspiciously it could jeopardise our whole operation. Then there's your uncle, who would flip if he thought you're still taking part in this. Remember that I promised him I wouldn't get you involved.'

'Don't worry, I'll be careful.'

As he tasted the cooling rouge peak of the vanilla ice cream, John relaxed. His concerns about leaving her alone were, for the present, forgotten.

They slept together that night, oblivious to the dark city outside, with all its chaos and contracts. Several robberies, many assaults, three rapes, and one murder would take place before the sun rose again.

GOOD INTENTIONS

* * *

At the casino, another round of poker saw the fourth person knocked out of the tournament. He happened to be a running favourite, which drew wide surprise and monetary losses for all those who wagered on him winning. That night he was driven to the airport and caught a Lear Jet to his home halfway round the world.

The tournament had just under two weeks to go. Management were looking at a turnover of over a million *a night,* and that was set to increase in the coming weeks. Part of it could be attributed to the extra numbers of 'high-rollers', who bet big and spent big. The average visitor bet in the region of a few hundred, but for the high rollers it was tens of thousands. These were the people that the casino loved. Sure, there were a few winners, and sometimes – inexplicably – a night of massive profits could be followed by one of marginal losses. Whether it was someone winning the grand jackpot on the slot machines or a high- roller staking his entire fortune on one mad bet – and winning – the casino was prepared. In the long term, each win served the purpose of encouraging more bets, and hence more losses, until The House emerged as champion. In this business time really did equal money.

In addition to this, management had taken the unprecedented step of making tickets necessary just to enter the casino on the last three nights of the tournament. This meant only the richest could get in, which would ensure unparalleled profits. All the tickets had already been sold out, and in some places they were being resold at up to treble the original price. There was a large shipment of cash from the regional processing centre due to arrive tomorrow morning, in preparation for any big wins. Everything was ready, set, and waiting to go. Management were looking forward to the biggest bonuses of their lifetime. Nothing could go wrong…

~ ~ ~

When Carlson was certain that the target and his girlfriend wouldn't budge for the rest of the night, he called someone else to keep tabs on them. However, there was absolutely no way he would wait around to be relieved. The watcher was someone he detested – some incompetent fat lump who only got designated as a support to investigators because of his family connections. Each time Carlson saw his face he wanted to wipe off the greasy grin that always seemed to linger.

He drove away from the hotel in his Audi convertible and went to the house he rented in the suburbs. It was a detached, two bedroom modern building with a garage and garden. There was also a basement, which he had outfitted as a gym. He went straight down there and began pummelling his fists into a boxing bag. One time he had taken someone down here to extract information. *That was a good night,* he thought. The corpse was probably still at the bottom of the river, being chewed by fish and eels or whatever else could survive in that polluted muck.

After finishing with the boxing bag, he took a shower and read one of his favourite books: The Art of Being at Peace, by Randolph Zanier. The first time he read it was whilst in prison. It had become his only true companion in those three years he had spent in a six by nine cell. He still woke up some days thinking he was lying on the concrete slab which they called a bed. From childhood to adulthood he had been in and out of care homes, progressing to the borstal and then to the jailhouse. It was only a road, really – a path where he had been able to find his true vocation with the Mafiosa. He had come a long way. But he wanted to go further. Having the money wasn't enough – he needed the Power. And what greater thing on Earth is there than the power to choose life or death?

9

John awoke early in the morning and left the car with Sarah. He got a taxi to the station and waited for the next departing train to Bath. There were many commuters, but most were coming into the city centre rather than going out. Leaden clouds hovered above the streets, precipitating the need for umbrellas and raincoats. Only a few other passengers got on the carriage with him: a student, a mother with two kids, and a middle-aged man wearing a suit.

As the train tore through the countryside he phoned ahead to notify staff at the print shop that he was visiting. They had a lot to discuss. None of them had a clue to the extent of his operations, let alone that he was what the law called a 'criminal'. It was best kept that way. The print shop was doing well as a legitimate business and he could now begin implementing the new product. It was to be the next step for The Organisation, another strand in his rainbow-like vision of global equality and opportunity.

When the train arrived in Bath the sky was the same leaden grey as in London, only this time it let down intermittent curtains of rain, forming little streams along the pavement. People's faces were concave mirrors to the grey horizons, every mouth drawn down by an invisible gravity of tedium. A taxi waited outside the station, and as John got in he caught

GOOD INTENTIONS

a glance of the middle-aged man who had sat in the same carriage. It was too late to offer him a ride, and he seemed to be waiting for someone anyway.

The print shop had a prime inner-city location. After being dropped off outside, John took note of the new window decoration. He walked through the front door, feeling the buzz of pride. The shop, after all, was his... and it was making fine business. It sold a variety of greetings cards, posters, stationery items, certificates – anything that anyone could want printed. They had a service that allowed people to customize what they wanted, from specific logos and icons to text and item size. There was also the recent print-on-demand (POD) utility, which allowed aspiring authors to arrange for their books to be printed according to how many people placed an order on their website.

John went up to the sales counter and spoke to a young university student whom he had never seen before. 'Where's Lucy?' he asked.

'Oh,' she said, a little surprised. 'Are you Mr Stevens?' 'Yes,' he confirmed.

'She's, erm, in the back.'

He smiled and thanked her, then proceeded to walk up one of the aisles, squeezing past a bag-carrying customer who was verging into the hinterlands of obesity. He reached the door at the back of the shop and knocked.

'Come in,' a voice called.

Before he could turn the handle, the door opened for him.

'Oh, hello!' Lucy said, standing before him. She was tall, slim, in her 30's. With long ginger hair and eyes that flashed green, it was hard to tell which of her features was the most remarkable. She dressed conservatively, as always, wearing trousers and a white shirt which only revealed an inch or two of cleavage. It was enough, however, for John to re-direct his gaze to her eyes, briefly considering how emerald earrings could heighten their beauty. In the past, he had been tempted to push their strictly-business relationship into something else, but Sarah had changed that.

Shaking hands, they sat down and talked. Soon she was updating him on everything that had happened since his last visit – projects, sales, new staff. Although she was the shop's manager, she could have been its owner. After a year in his employment he had been able to leave the daily workings of the business in her capable hands. Apparently having two children to look after (by herself) was not a barrier to commitment, drive and dependability. She had even found ways to expand the business, with little input from himself.

Before long they got onto the real reason why he was here.

* * *

Carlson knew that John owned the print shop. He had been provided with detailed information on its cash flow and connections, given to the Mafiosa via the informant at

GOOD INTENTIONS

Coutts bank. It was showing healthy net profits of £40,000 a year – not bad for a business that had only been going for eighteen months. Most of this, however, was being redirected to BlueBridge and WinImplex, the charity and pseudo-investment portfolio that the target owned as well. Carlson knew that the print shop was a legitimate business, but his instructions were that it could also be a front to something else. It needed to be investigated.

For this reason he walked in and started to wander around, pretending to browse the shelves and taking the opportunity to purchase a birthday card for his mother. The girl at the cashiers desk said something about a 'custom card', but he politely refused. He didn't want to stay in the shop too long in case the target saw him. After leaving he walked across the street to a cafe, which fulfilled the criteria as an observation post.

* * *

The shop only took up half the ground floor space – the other half was for storage and printers. John also owned the second floor, currently vacant. His original idea was to use the shop as a means to produce counterfeit currency, but getting the right equipment and finding someone with the necessary skills had proven too difficult. Admittedly, trustworthiness was the most contentious issue. Those graduates he interviewed who did have the necessary skills would clearly balk at the idea of being involved in a criminal enterprise. Now he was going to begin the next best thing to making fake money: casino chips. Lucy already knew this and thought it was part of a legitimate order with casinos.

In the office he discussed the details. He kept a handful of samples from various casinos, and these would be used as the blueprints for replicas. They had ordered the necessary moulds from a manufacturer and only needed to imprint the designs. Once finished, the 'orders' would be sent to a premises he rented in a nearby industrial park – a small unit which he used occasionally to plan operations. It was rented in a different name, from ID he had made whilst using the equipment at the back of the shop. Everything from driving licences and ID cards to bank statements and utility bills could be made there. The man who had taught him to do this had gone back to his home country, but John soon learnt enough to do it alone. He had spent many a long night producing near-perfect identity documents for himself and Sarah. The only thing they lacked was modern passports. The idea was to start another printing business in Mumbai, which would address the passport problem whilst also paving the way for his original goal of printing currency.

Currently a man worked alone in the printing room, a migrant from India whose name was Alf. The knowledge and skills he had acquired were almost as impressive as his predecessor. Many times John had been tempted to tell him 'the truth', but it was simply too risky. Alf was also an

GOOD INTENTIONS

expert holographist, able to reproduce complex holograms or make them up from scratch, which is what he was most enthusiastic about. The equipment at his disposal allowed him to do both.

When John went into the print room with Lucy, Alf was busy making some posters for an upcoming local event. A batch of specially ordered certificates with unique holograms were lying on a table, ready to be packaged and sent out to a school.

'How's it going, Alf?' John said, raising his voice above the churning of machinery.

Alf got up and shook his hand. 'Not bad, Mr. Stevens.'

They talked for a while about the casino chip holograms. Then Lucy took John back to the shop to show him some of the new products they had on sale.

* * *

From the café across the street, Carlson watched the target drift around like some kind of Don, picking up stuff and asking the woman questions. It irritated him. The gloating grin of the target's face was enough to compromise his reinforced-steel resolve.

He took a sip from his coffee, relishing the bitter taste. It was always the little things, Carlson found, which annoyed him the most. Or perhaps it was the sheer quantity of these inanities that got to him.

When the target eventually left the shop and walked to a bus stop, Carlson almost spilt the coffee on his suit. The black liquid swilled around and left little droplets on the tablecloth; as if it was a psychic beacon, drawing stares from two old ladies who were sitting on an adjacent table. He exited the cafe as quickly as possible, and proceeded to a bus stop further down the road.

Fortunately, it was only five minutes before the next bus arrived, and of course the target boarded it at the next stop, choosing to sit a few rows in front of Carlson's position at the back. Such predictions came naturally: it was part of that intuition that his mentor called *assassin's instinct* – a kind of sharpened common sense.

The noisy vehicle made repeated stops in residential areas, travelling at an unnecessarily slow pace that was made even slower by the rain. From the back of the bus, Carlson was poised for when the target would get off. *Where the hell is he going?* he asked himself.

His concerns started shifting to annoyance when two kids sat next to him, who constantly moved about and shouted. Then a musty- smelling old man, wearing a wide-brimmed hat, sat directly in front of him. The old bastard succeeded in blocking his view of the target, which forced him to sit closer to the kids. One of them had a cold and kept coughing in his direction. This was a classic example of those little irritations that made him want to explode.

Finally, the mother came along and took the kids off at the

next stop. They left with a cacophony of manic shouts and coughing. The old man was the next to go.

As the bus entered an industrial park, two passengers remained with him and the target. Just when Carlson was certain that his position had been compromised, and that he was being led on a classic surveillance counter-measure, the target got off.

* * *

John walked a short distance to a block of storage units. He entered a code to get in the main door, briefly greeting the cleaner inside. Drumming metallic raindrops mixed with the cleaner's buffer, drowning out John's voice.

A staircase led downstairs, where the smallest storage units were located. The one John rented was the third door down on the left,unmarked except for a number above it. He entered another code and walked in.

The room was small but functional. Filing cabinets, cupboards, and a desk with an ISP connection fit snugly against the walls. There was also a safe that stored maps and firearms. Only one gun was in there at the moment: a Sig Saur semi-automatic for Sarah. He had left his Glock with her at the hotel. The maps were for old jobs, but there was also paperwork relating to future ones.

From one of the cabinets he removed a sports bag, which contained various electrical equipment. He put back everything apart from a cordless angle grinder – the perfect tool to open cash cases. Then he went to the cupboard, where a series of disguises were hanging on racks. He chose two generic 'maintenance crew' uniforms, dark blue boiler suits. The drawers below had various facial disguises: wigs, beards, cosmetics and even some specially made prosthetic masks. He took everything which was needed and put it all in the bag.

Rather than wait for the next bus, he decided to call a taxi. He locked the storage room's door and returned to the hallway, surprised to feel the weight of the sports bag. Last time it had seemed practically empty, even though he had carried the same items across a mile of woodland.
In the hallway the cleaner was still buffing the floor and the rain was still falling. Looking out, it was hard to believe that it was still day time.

* * *

Carlson cursed as he stood outside the building, foregoing the archway of an adjacent doorway in order to get a clear view for when the target left. *How long is this bastard going to be in there?* he wondered.

He decided to walk back down the road and stand under the shelter of the bus stop. *The target has to come back this way*, he reasoned. The only problem was that Carlson would let himself be seen, but some things couldn't be avoided. Whilst waiting there he texted the details of the industrial building to his handler. Others would decide if it was worth breaking into.

A taxi suddenly caught his attention as it cruised by, its speed declaring that it already had a fare. His suspicion proved correct when the same taxi drove past a minute later, with the unmistakable silhouette of the target sitting in the back.

Carlson clenched his fists and took four deep breaths. He had no choice but to inform his handler what happened. At least he had the taxi's number. It could be tracked to wherever the target was heading and, with a bit of luck, Carlson would pick up the trail.

An hour later, following two text messages, the target's position had been re-acquired: he was staying at a guesthouse. Now Carlson had the unenviable position of watching the little B&B for his next movement. It would mean calling in for a relief, who happened to be slightly better than the last one… in the sense a slice of mouldy Stilton stunk better than a dog turd.

There were few people Carlson liked. Those he did usually died. Standing there waiting for his relief, he reflected on this. He felt that all his friends, lovers and most of his family had betrayed him. He would rather kill than see that 'rat of betrayal' resurface in a potential ally, to nibble away at his soul. This rat character lay at the heart of humanity, he believed – ready to cheat and cause pain at the slightest opportunity. Survival, for him, was about *getting them before they got you.*

A woman passed him on the pavement. She smiled at him, and he smiled back.

Looking at her walk away, he felt a brief pang of regret. Times had changed. These days he only felt comfortable with someone else if he had total control, and that meant the power to take away *(or give?)* life. He resented only being allowed to do this when given the order.

One day, he told himself, *it will be different.*

10

It was a dilemma. A rigmarole. An inescapable quandary. She had to choose whether to go to the casino or not; whether to accept her betrayal of John was in vain, or risk getting into further trouble. Being seen by either Matt or Howie or indeed anyone else could ruin the chances of pulling off the casino heist. But not trying, simply giving up on a plan that could yield an unimaginable sum – that was something Sarah could *not* do.

She would go to the casino tonight. She would find out how to stop the elevator and get in from the maintenance room. Success would be as certain as the rising tide. *Where there's a will...* no boundaries could stand.

When she left the hotel the rain had stopped. There was a sense of impending transition; the kind of feeling one gets at the beginning of a storm, when the air is abuzz with latent tension. Time seemed to be running on a different level, objects connecting to a different dimension. The rushing cars and busy crowds gave the impression of delusion, division, even madness.

What is this world? Where am I really going? She asked herself, as she stepped out into the city.

The Mind and The World are strange, incomprehensible things, raising questions that can never – truly – be answered.

Like some wild casino, life's thousand lights and sounds often send the senses crashing into chaos. What to see and what to hear, what to do and what to feel; it was the subconscious that made the first selections.

Gun hidden, dress sparkling, eyes obscured by shades, she entered the casino once again. It hummed with an interflexing choreography of monetary acquisition, surging with ageless need. There was not a metre – not even a millimetre – that was left untouched by the bright shadows of promises that would never come true. For every King, Queen and Jack there were ten faceless numbers. The Ace, that alpha-one of ten, had the power to over-rule them all. But it could also be counted as lowest. That was an etching of the paradox of all human history: those with the highest potential were not always valued for their greatest attributes.

In the casino, money oozed from every corner and every chair, flowing up to the richest, who waited invisibly like vultures above a corpse. That corpse was society: the masses, the world itself, slowly being exploited and eaten away until it was consumed completely.

Once again, she found herself wondering... Are there others the same as us? People who stand up against the tide of oppression, inequality and injustice, fighting for the poorest and most vulnerable? People who took that extra step of risking their own life and liberty, who broke the law of the present for the sake of the law of all time: that **all are created equal**. No one should die of hunger, malnutrition or thirst

GOOD INTENTIONS

whilst others live in plenty and waste what they have. No man, woman or child should have to suffer simply because of where they were born. Equality of opportunity belonged to all. But in a limited world, with resources ever-dwindling, how could this golden principle be fully met?

The elevator could not be accessed. Security were only letting those with tickets, whose name were on the list, up to the higher floor. She would have to find another way. The hotel presented the only other option. Although it had a lift separate from the casino, they were both close together and therefore must have the same maintenance infrastructure. Get access to one and it should be possible to access the other.

She left the casino and went back into the red-carpeted hotel lobby, where a couple had just pressed the 'call' button. The hotel's lift didn't take long to arrive. When the couple got off at the third floor, Sarah pressed the lowest button marked *Underground Parking*. The whine and whirr of hidden motors brought the lift to a smooth stop within twenty seconds. An electronic bell dinged out one high-pitched note. As the doors slid open, the aroma of petrol and oil wafted through on a stale draft. Lines of fluorescent strips made shadows from beneath the scattered vehicles, with half the parking spaces appearing empty.

At first, Sarah thought that there would be no way to proceed with her mission. There would be a camera somewhere, watching the area around the lifts. But after looking around she couldn't see one.

To the left, the door to the lift maintenance area was clearly marked and just as clearly locked. This did not mean that she couldn't get in. It was the sort of lock that could be picked (a skill she had learnt as a child from Howie) but it would take a few minutes. Presently it was just her in the parking area; time was short. She withdrew the set of picks from her wallet and began to deftly wriggle them about in the lock, feeling for that tell-tale click of metal sliding into metal. Twice she had to stop this procedure – once, when a car drove in, and then again when a man got off the elevator. It took eight minutes before she managed to get the door open. The habit of timing herself in a lock-picking exercise still hadn't disappeared.

Stepping through the thresh-hold, she flicked on a light just before closing the door. The crackling cacophony of whirring gears and creaking cables made her cringe. All the lift machinery was before her. It was like looking upon the crypt of an oblong Frankenstein, filled with the tangled placenta of electricity and iron.

A ladder ran along the side of the shaft and there was a small control panel that could manually stop the lift. All this was useless to her. She needed access to the lift of the *casino*, not the hotel.

There was only one possibility: a second door, directly opposite the one she entered by. She walked up to it and pressed her ears against the cold metal. Nothing, only the relentless churning of the hotel's lift mechanism. Moreover, a padlock secured the door, and it had a Kaba – oh, how she hated those unpickable locks!

She kicked the door in frustration, sending a jolt of pain up her right leg. Above, the hotel's lift was descending, increasing the volume of noise and masking the sound of her cry.

Then she had an idea. It was something she had never tried before. Withdrawing her gun and releasing the safety, she backed away and took aim at the heavy padlocked bolt.

BANG!

The sound spiralled up the lift shaft and sent a series of echoes from wall to wall. Sarah removed the now pulverised Kaba and nudged the door open, peering into the gloom beyond.

Along with her lock-picking kit, she had brought a small flashlight. This provided enough illumination to see it was another maintenance room, with a lift shaft that was much smaller in height. There was another ladder on the side of the shaft and a duplicate of the previous control panel. There was also another door, and beside it was a light switch. Sarah paused before switching it on, just in case it was linked to an alarm. If she were to open the door, she would enter the casino itself. She could even hear the faint buzz of Pokie machines and a croupier stridently calling "vien de la jau".

Finally deciding to take the risk, she flicked the switch. A row of lamp-size bulbs immediately snapped on, illuminating the lift shaft from bottom to top. It was amber-coloured now

– an eerie shade of red that somehow seemed appropriate. The shadows fled and hunkered in the corners, bending around the square megalith of metal that was the casino's lift. The next step was to find a way inside.

Sarah looked at the ladder. *I can climb up there,* she thought, *then jump onto the lift's roof once it comes to a stop.* Her assumption was that there would be an escape hatch.

She only needed to go as far as the first floor of the casino. The gap from the lift to the ladder was only about one metre, albeit ninety centimetres too much. She had to put her back to the wall, then launch off the ladder, aiming to land on the centre of the roof. She timed it perfectly, when the lift was stationary, and did the jump without any problems.

It was the landing that went wrong. Her right foot – the same one she had used to kick the padlocked door – twisted inwards, sending another rush of pain down her leg. She cried and fell down onto the roof just as it began another ascent. Curled up, she reached down and clasped her hands round her ankle, trying to press away the pulses of pain. She worried that the people inside the lift had heard her fall, but it soon became apparent that another threat was looming. She was heading ever-closer to the ceiling of the shaft and there was no way to get off the lift. Gears churning, the heavy mass of metal would be pressed to the concrete ceiling – with her in-between.

It loomed like the roof of some Indiana Jones' torture chamber. There was no way to go, no way to stop it. All the

GOOD INTENTIONS

pain in her ankle had vanished with the impending mass, throbbing away to a dull cry of emptiness that might have been the last thing she knew.

If she reached up, she would have touched the ceiling. It was less than a metre away, half a metre. And then...

The highest lamp became a deep blood-red. The lift had stopped.

Sarah realised that her eyes were tightly closed.

Pausing, the lift began to descend.

Part of her expected to be crippled, to be forever pinned to the top of the lift. Sitting up, she defeated this expectation.

Now her concern was how to get off. She could not step onto the ladder, even when the lift was stationary, because of her injury. Nor could she remain here all night, going up and down until someone found her. And the prospect of going to the top of the lift shaft again filled her with terror.

The only option was to get into the lift itself.

* * *

With the flashlight, she examined the hatch at the centre of the roof, discovering that a handle could open it from the outside. She waited for the lift to stop moving and tried to ascertain if there was anyone inside. Then she took a deep breath and lifted the handle.

Beneath her, a man and woman looked up in surprise. The

elevator doors had shut and they had just pressed the button for their floor when Sarah appeared from above. She had little time to lose. Using her hands to grab the sides of the hatch opening, she lowered herself down. The couple did not help her and she almost cried out again when her right foot hit the carpet.

'What's going on?!' the woman screamed in her face.

Sarah immediately thought of something to allay their suspicions.

'There's a fire in the floor above… this is the only way I could get out.' Before they could reply, the doors had opened and she hopped out, leaving them staring after her.

There was no avoiding drawing attention to herself. Several faces turned in her direction as she hopped like a mad kangaroo to the escalators.

One man spilt drinks over his tuxedo as she jumped accidentally into his path. 'Watch out, stupid cow!' he called as she reached the top of the escalators. It looked as if she would get past the security men who were standing at the bottom of the escalators – they were only interested in checking people going up, not down. In another situation she might have drawn a parallel with 'social mobility', but the irony of this unformed connection was lost on her.

If Matt was among the security men then there would be no going back. Sarah's sunglasses wouldn't be enough to disguise her. It appeared, however, that he was somewhere else, for she couldn't see the distinctive shape and straw-brown hair of the man she had slept with.

'Good night, miss,' one of the security men said when she reached the bottom.

She did her best smile and walked past him. There was still the main entrance and then the gate, so she didn't allow herself to feel any relief.

Rather than hop her way from the bottom of the escalators to the entrance of the casino, which would invariably bring her a lot of attention, she opted for a slow, painful walk. It was hard. People rushed by her in a blur of colour, seeming not to notice her until they were a second away from a collision. She walked towards one of the blackjack tables, quickly turning round as she noticed Howie working at the one above. One look from him would stop the casino heist even before it began.

From the blackjack table, she looked at the main entrance, doing a double-check on the security personnel stationed there to check that Matt was not with them. Satisfied that he wasn't, she did a slow walk towards the entrance, getting out her mobile phone to pretend she was having a conversation. From beneath her shades she saw that the security men were watching her closely. They knew something wasn't right.

'Are you okay, miss?' one of them asked her.

She nodded and continued walking, still saying meaningless words to an imaginary friend on her phone.

By now the couple had told security. It was quickly confirmed that there was no fire on the third floor, which was devoted to a 'members only club' and managers' offices.

A 'stop and detain' order had been issued over the radio to all security units for anyone matching Sarah's description: 20-30, roughly 5'9, blue sequinned dress, blonde-streaky hair, sunglasses.

The array of cameras easily picked her out in the hotel lobby. Matt was one of the first to see her from the surveillance room at the rear of the casino. Quickly recognising her, he rushed to the front of the casino to be part of the arrest.

As Sarah finally stepped outside through the main entrance, she allowed herself that long-awaited relief. A sigh like the first breeze of a desert monsoon left her lips. But deliverance suddenly turned to panic when she heard shouting behind her.

'Stop!' a man's voice commanded.

She didn't know what to do. There was no conceivable way that she could allow herself to be captured – not like this, carrying a handgun, with no alibi. A part of her that she kept for the most urgent, life-threatening situations asserted itself. She broke into a run down the steps, trying to ignore the blasts of pain in her leg that put her on the threshold of unconsciousness, running until the certainty of getting away was no longer a half-hearted promise.

'Taxi!' she screamed, aiming for the first available vehicle in the rank outside.

They were closing on her too fast. Before she could get the door open, a man had shut it. 'Hold it there,' he said, reaching

GOOD INTENTIONS

for the radio on his waist. Heavy footfalls echoed behind him as more black-suited men spewed from the casino's grand entrance.

Jungle panthers might have claimed kin with the lithe movement she displayed. It happened too swiftly for the security man, perhaps even for her. In one movement she withdrew the gun and squeezed the trigger.

The wake of the bullet split the air in a sudden crack and flash of power, rendering a trail of smoke in its wake. A look of utter shock came into the security man's face. He stumbled away, allowing Sarah to open the taxi door.

'Drive!'

The driver just sat there.

Security personnel clustered outside around their shocked, yet uninjured colleague.

'Now!' she shouted, pressing the weapon to the glass right behind the taxi driver's head.

Bulletproof, she thought.

Apparently the driver wasn't *that* confident. He put his foot to the accelerator.

As they drove away, she glanced through the rear window and noticed a familiar face running after the car. Yes, there was no doubt about it. Matt was there – leading the others in the chase.

The words of Howie resounded in her head with gruesome recollection. *'There's one entrance to the casino you would not be able to come in then get away.'* No doubt about it: security had put out an immediate order to lockdown the casino, which meant the entrance gate would be sealed shut. And police would surely be en-route.

As they drove up to it, Sarah saw the steel rollers in action, drawing in each side of the barrier. The taxi could not drive through.

'Faster! Go!' she shouted to the driver, who broke into a cry of horror as the gate met the sides of the vehicle.

They shot through the ever-smaller gap in a screeching wail of metal, sparks flying up on both sides. The taxi, minus its side mirrors, flew out the other side like a runt bat from the depths of Hades, narrowly avoiding colliding with a red mini.

'Keep driving!' she shouted, totally unsure how she was going to make it out of this one alive.

Behind them, the manic sound of police sirens declared the chase had only just begun. They were drawing closer every second.

If only John was here, she thought, thinking of how Bonnie and Clyde went out in a blaze of glory. After all that happened, it seemed she would have to go out blazing alone…

11

The first order of moulds arrived at the print shop the next day. John watched as Alf began replicating the holograms from the original chips onto the new ones. It could be completed by the end of next week. Then all he would have to do was collect the chips from the industrial unit and begin implementing Stage Two: going from casino to casino, cashing in the chips for money. With a little caution and subterfuge, he could rake in over £1 million before being forced to close the operation. And when it reached that stage, there were always other countries…

BlueBridge would flourish and begin to fulfil every purpose it was created for: eradicating exploitation, inequality and poverty. Work, education, housing and healthcare initiatives would arise in every third world country, providing the same opportunities that people in the West enjoyed – albeit a diminishing number.

There would be no more high-risk robberies. The Organisation would no longer need continual injections of cash. Eventually, through the expansion of the printing business and returns from the WinImplex portfolio, it would be self-supporting and completely legitimate. But, until that day came, a few last heists were needed to keep things moving forward. If the casino job yielded as much as Howie and Sarah predicted, it could very well be their penultimate robbery, with the bank being the finale. He was very aware of the dangers in this line of work: the longer one did it, the greater the chances of getting caught. The secret to success was to quit while you were ahead. In gambling, the House always wins; in crime, the system always eventually triumphed. Its resources and wealth were limitless. But from David and Goliath to the American War of Independence, even the most powerful could be toppled from their positions through strength of will. In that view he had found the perfect partner.

In the afternoon he called Sarah on her phone. There was no response. He called the hotel and they said she still had her room key but had not been in the room since last night.

When he eventually got through to Howie, it was swiftly apparent that something bad had happened.

'Don't you ever watch the news?' Howie snapped.

'Of course. What's happened?

'Watch the bloody news and call me back.'

John immediately went to an internet café to find out what was going on. He logged onto a media website but saw nothing that would have concerned Howie – just the usual headlines about the latest sporting event (*surely he doesn't take his football that seriously?*), a flood overseas, and the publication of a government report. Then he looked at news specific to the London area, and his heartbeat rocketed.

'*Shootout at the Crown Casino*' one headline read.

GOOD INTENTIONS

'Woman sought by police in Casino incident' read another. He could barely believe his eyes as he scrolled down:

At 9:30 hours last night police were called to the Crown Casino on Newport Parade after an unidentified woman fired a weapon at a security guard. She fled in a taxi, forcing the driver at gunpoint to drive at dangerous speeds through heavy traffic. Police have released a description of the woman and urge members of the public not to approach her, but to contact them in the first instance.

As John saw the woman's description, there was no doubt in his mind that it was Sarah. He sat back in the chair and took one gigantic breath. There it was: still on the screen. Thoughts rushed and wheeled in tumultuous chaos. It's happened… *now deal with it!*

He tried finding out more information, but the best he got was 'the woman is still at large'. Another said 'a suspect is in custody'. The consequences of this were too huge to comprehend; there was the very real possibility that the police, even now, were closing in on both of them.

As he walked out the internet café, heading back to the B&B to call Howie, he was alert to everything and everyone around him.

There, right behind him, was a face he saw before. He was sure of it. The man wore a suit, pretending to browse a shop window. John couldn't be certain where he had seen him before. After taking a few random turnings in different directions, his worst fears were confirmed. He was being followed.

* * *

Carlson realised something was wrong as soon as the target came out of the internet café. He could tell a man's state of mind just by glancing at their posture. He could ascertain feelings just by looking at body language. When the target first stopped, supposedly to 're-tie' his shoelaces, Carlson knew he had been spotted. This was further confirmed by all the backtracking and looking in shop windows that followed. A professional would never let on he knew he was being watched.

Carlson dropped back and let him think his tactics had worked. He slipped out his phone and dialled the number of his handler.

'Woodstock' a voice answered on the other end.

Carlson gave him the green code in response. 'Stevens knows he's being watched.'

The voice on the other end paused, then asked, 'Have you found anything?'

'Nothing useful,' Carlson replied. 'The print shop looks legit. He's been there most of the time. Must've seen something on the computer that told him he's being watched.

GOOD INTENTIONS

An email, maybe.'

'Confirmed,' the voice answered. 'Back off... we will transfer to secondary surveillance as soon as we can get someone in to tag him. Until then, monitor his position and maintain hourly updates.'

Carlson acknowledged this and broke the connection. He was very pleased to have this assignment over soon. His specialisation was in 'direct' surveillance and 'low level' neutralisation. 'Secondary surveillance' was done by the techno wizards – phone monitors, hackers, electronic monitoring. Once the target was given a few discrete electronic gadgets to monitor his position and movement ('tagged') they could take over. But before that Carlson had to keep as much distance as possible without losing the target completely.

Tagging teams were normally only requested for the more serious cases. No doubt they had a bigger plan for John Stevens, as well as his female accomplice; it would already be set in motion.

Smiling, Carlson remembered part of the other reason that kept him in this line of work.

* * *

For the casino management it was an incident unparalleled by any other: a mad woman with a gun breaking into a lift and then literally hopping away. The police wanted to conduct a full investigation, with comprehensive questioning of every witness, forensic analysis and close scrutiny of CCTV. Management wanted the woman caught, but they also needed profits to be undamaged. They could not allow bureaucracy and an ongoing police investigation to interfere with the poker tournament. Their first priority was to reinforce the image of the casino as a safe place to be. They told reporters of the fast-track instalment of metal detectors at the main entrance. They emphasised the efficiency of their security systems and safety procedures. Although the incident was bad for the casino, it also had some positives. The publicity meant the casino's name was spread across a broad range of media, with many reporters mentioning the Poker Tournament. This could create wider public interest, attract more visitors, and increase revenues... so in many ways, the mad woman did them a favour: pointing their attention to a problem that could have led to worse incidents (the lack of metal detectors) and also helping profits.

Police investigators had put out an All Parties Bulletin (APB) for anyone matching the woman's description. They provided details to all registered hotels and transit centres in the city. The criminal database came up with nobody matching her description and neither did forensics after they collected her DNA and fingerprints in the lift area. Ballistics were still working on identifying the gun she fired, but they had no doubt it was a semi-automatic handgun, which in itself carries a minimum five year sentence for possession. By firing a live round at a security guard, or to prevent lawful arrest, she was easily looking at double figures – if not life.

What puzzled investigators the most was why someone would want to break into a lift shaft, then into the lift itself. It was clear this was not just some lunatic who decided to take a trip on the wild side; not only did she have a handgun, but she was able to pick locks. Her appearance and determination to escape further suggested this was part of something bigger. Nevertheless, their warnings that this seemingly rare, unpredictable incident could be part of some bigger operation fell on deaf ears.

* * *

When John got back to the B&B, satisfied that the man no longer followed him, he packed his stuff and prepared to leave. Then he changed his mind and phoned Howie.

'I've seen it.'

'And you don't know where Sarah is?' Howie replied.

'No, that's why I called you.'

Howie launched into a stream of profanities, demanding to know why John wasn't with her and how he could let her get involved in 'the job'.

It took several minutes before John could calm him down enough to progress further. 'We know she hasn't got caught... so she must be hiding somewhere. Have you no idea where?'

'You're the one whose been sleeping with her the last two years!' Howie shouted back.

'She had mentioned visiting a friend in hospital. Do you know who she meant?'

'No bloody idea. I've called all the friends I heard of, and they know nothing.'

'All right, if you hear anything else, let me know… I'll do the same, of course.'

Howie grunted and hung up.

John began going over his fears: that police had traced her to the hotel and now everything he had built up and planned was under threat, not to mention his freedom. Yet all these were secondary fears compared to his worry for Sarah. He could gather together enough cash and relocate the foundations of the Organisation to another country (something they jokingly called 'the emergency plan') before the police could pounce, but he could not leave without her.

As the sun set he left the B&B, carrying the sports bag which contained the stuff from the industrial unit as well as the briefcase he had brought from London. There was no sign that he was being watched or followed. The man he saw earlier had vanished. He walked the short distance to the train station and got a ticket to London, intending to pick up Sarah's trail from there. She might have left something in the hotel room – if the authorities had not already found it, that is.

When the London train finally arrived, John waited

GOOD INTENTIONS

until the last possible moment before getting on, choosing a carriage right at the front so he could observe everyone who boarded. There was no sign of the man. As the train inched forward, in the wake of tannoy announcements and the unique station *ding-dong-ding* departure tune, he shut the door.

He was certain no one was following him.

* * *

Carlson stood back from his vantage point on the platform, somewhat impressed by the progression of the target's counter- surveillance techniques. But John Stevens was still not good enough to beat someone of Carlson's calibre.

He sprung from his hiding place and leapt onto the rear carriage as the train shunted forward, easily getting the door open and finding a discrete place to sit. With each stop, Carlson would monitor who alighted, although he had no doubt where the target was heading. He texted the hourly update to his handler: *'trgt en-rt 2 london on 10:10 train frm bath. Eta 12:30 padd.'*

A few minutes later he got a reply: *'ack. Tag in pl upon arr.'*

'Ticket, please.'

The uniformed man standing in the aisle looked at him suspiciously, conveying a thought of *I know what you're up to*. For one brief tantalising moment Carlson could feel the pulse of his vocation – the cold malevolent touch of his gun – almost like the shard of a glacial god.

'Ah, yes,' he said, withdrawing the stripy-orange card from his jacket pocket. The guard took it, scrutinised it, then stamped it in his pathetic machine.

'Thank you, sir,' he smiled. Carlson knew this wasn't genuine: it was a mocking grin.

That *urge,* that overpowering flame of righteous release, threatened to flood across his thoughts, surging to the tips of his fingers, connecting with the trigger of the gun. But no. *Control...*

Onwards rushing the train passed station after station, town after town, never stopping except in a few. The skeletal silhouettes of trees were briefly sketched by a reticent moon as they passed into nothingness, silver light sketching an ever-moving grey landscape. Houses sent forth jumping spots of light before dropping back like the flaming torch of some marathon passed from runner to runner. Occasionally a sudden explosion of sound and light shot out of the ether as another train passed in the opposite direction. Not one person upon the 10:10 to Paddington gave a second's consideration to these marvellous sights.

Even Carlson, who had endured the sensual deprivation of imprisonment, had no concern for the moon in its reticence, the trees in their obscurity, the houses in their transience, or the passing trains in their haste. He was thinking about what he would do when he got back. There would be no more

GOOD INTENTIONS

standing around in the rain, no more waiting for hours on end for some rat to come out of its hole, no more being treated like an insignificant pawn. He was thinking it was time to leave the Mafiosa, to take the money he had earned and use it to live a life of his own choosing. Go anywhere, do anything, be anyone…yes, it would be perfect. Just a few more assignments, a bit more money, and that could all happen.

***

Halfway through the journey John got a phone call. The reception was terrible, but he almost cried with joy when he heard the garbled voice.
Sarah!
He was unable to hear what she said clearly and it seemed as if she was having the same problem. But one thing came through reasonably clear: the name of a place, just two elusive words.

Before he could find out more information, the train entered a tunnel and the connection broke completely. 'Damn it!' he shouted. She had not called on her mobile and she had left no number. For the rest of the journey he just sat there, waiting for her to call again.

When the train drew into Paddington station, John was the first passenger to get off, and his unknown pursuer was one of the next. Despite being so late, the station was still busy, although for experienced commuters it would be considered practically empty.

The bronze head of Paddington Bear watched them pass by, reflecting the fleeting shadows of coats and bags and shoes. None paused to gaze at the emblem of a lost generation. It was all about business, business, business. Even the pigeons seemed to pursue the ever-encouraging prospect of bigger crumbs.

A team of 'taggers' waited outside. One of them would discreetly place a tracking device on John. The others would follow and find ways to bug where he lived, worked, and stayed: what vehicles he drove, along with any close friends and family. But there was also someone else waiting at the entrance, whose actions would impact the future far more dramatically than the tagging team. He stood unassumingly outside, wearing a heavy coat and holding a few magazines.

12

'*One World!*' the tramp declared to the late-night commuters, holding up a magazine with a picture of planet Earth on its cover. Everyone continued in their haste with scarcely a glance in his direction. Earlier one had said to him 'get a job!' in a venomous tone of voice, but he was used to that by now. So many judged in ignorance, at a mere glance, never bothering to consider that each human being was a unique individual passing through life. Every person had a story, but few cared to read past the first few lines.

Over the last week he had tried hard to get a job. The few employers that overlooked his lack of a permanent address could not ignore his lack of experience. Even a window-cleaning job required 'experience', on top of qualifications that he had never even heard of. It was the same as before, with every expectation meeting with disappointment. It seemed once you fell down in the gutter, there was no way of getting back up again. To climb out always required money, or contacts – preferably both. But this time he knew it was a last chance: if he should fail and succumb once again to alcohol, it would kill him. If he couldn't get a job, then he would make one, supplementing income from selling magazines with being a street musician. The old flute that had lain disused at the bottom of his rucksack now played tunes that brought a little more light to the streets. And all the time he was on the lookout for something better – a proper wage-paying job in some shop or factory.

Yesterday he was looking at the vacancies in the window of a newsagent's when he noticed a poster. It advertised two exclusive tickets to the final night of the £10 Million poker tournament at the Crown Casino. He was reminded of the young man he had met in the casino gardens, the person who had unintentionally set him on another path and probably saved his life. He felt a need to meet this person again and was mindful to look carefully at people's faces as they passed by. Gradually, however, he resigned himself to the inevitability that the man would never be seen again. Nor would the woman… hat strange figure who floated in his dreams, just as she had drifted along by the river.

The clocks were nearing half-past twelve. He decided to call it a night. As he prepared to pack away his remaining magazines and walk back to the hostel, a familiar face passed him.

Recognition swiftly dawned. He shouted to the man, who was moving quickly away. When the man looked over his shoulder, the tramp's certainty was cemented. His benefactor was finally found.

* * *

Carlson kept within viewing distance of the target until the tagging team could take over. As he came out of the station,

GOOD INTENTIONS

something unusual happened. A beggar started shouting at the target and began running after him. Initially, Carlson thought the beggar was part of the tagging team, but that didn't make sense – they wouldn't make themselves so obvious. In any case, the target completely ignored the beggar and continued walking at the same brisk pace, even after walking straight into the path of a woman. Shortly after this he got into a taxi and Carlson's phone vibrated.

It confirmed what he hoped for, with a message that read 'trgt acq. Assn compl.' The woman had been the one, after all.

Buoyant with relief, he began walking back to the train station. The beggar, he noticed, was heading in the same direction.

Curious, sensing something larger, he went up to him. 'Excuse me, did you know that man?'

Bewilderment spread across the pockmarked face. 'Yes... or at least I thought I did.'

'You look like you could do with a drink,' Carlson replied.

* * *

As the tramp stood there, two voices raged through his head. One told him to accept the stranger's offer, the other said to refuse. Eventually he opted for the latter.

The man, however, was insistent. 'Go on... it's no problem, really! You must be hungry, if not thirsty.'

The tramp was both. He had eaten only a ham baguette and a packet of crisps, plus a few cups of tea he kept in a thermos in his rucksack (*not* laced with the usual gin). Although the man looked 'normal', dressed smartly and spoke in a kind tone, the tramp was all too aware that it could be a mask to something else.

He had yet to meet a person who showed their true self and had long since reached the conclusion that such an individual is a myth. Everyone went around wearing masks, in some form or another; some plain and permeable as veils, some hard and unbreakable as armour, most multi-layered and complex. For him, it was a question of *what lay beneath* the superficial social masks of mankind, which in his experience was rarely pleasant. Nevertheless, the tramp's rumbling stomach made a decision for him, and he grudgingly accepted the man's offer.

They walked together into the nearest pub, which buzzed to a late night crowd. Two bouncers guarded the doorway, and they only let him pass after a brief word from the man. As he walked inside, the smell of

alcohol gripped him as a vice: the frothy beers, bubbling ales, rows of bottles glowing amber and white. His grating hunger had suddenly given way to a burning thirst. A few faces turned and scrutinised him, projecting the familiar gaze of disdain which he had seen for most of his life. His companion in the suit exuded a confidence and self-assertion that soon had them turning away. The man chose the quietest

GOOD INTENTIONS

seats possible, right at the back of the pub.

'What do you want?' he asked considerately.

Resisting the stronger calling within, the tramp asked for an orange juice and a sandwich. His mind flicked back to the young man – his benefactor – who had ignored his calls outside the station. *Why didn't he stop?* the tramp wondered. *It was as though he wanted to run away from me...*

The suited man re-appeared suddenly, placing an orange juice on the table along with a pint of beer for himself.

'Thank you.'

'No problem. My name's Tony by the way. What's yours?'

After finishing his orange juice in one big gulp, the tramp replied with something that sounded like 'Nail', which was more appropriately interpreted as 'Neil'. The fact is that he didn't really know his own name. All his childhood memories had been wiped blank and he had no idea who his parents were. "Nail" was the first name he could remember being called by others, and it was the one he now used.

To him names were just another aspect of the masks people wore. He had once heard that the Native Americans had names which reflected a unique aspect of a person's character, or some insight that was seen by an elder of the tribe. *Wind Hawk, Crying Wolf, Sitting Bull...* they seemed somehow *better* to him – more natural, more true. *What would my name be?* He wondered. *Amber River? Bottled Fire?*

Craving Spirit? There was no irony or humour in these thoughts; they were as bitter as his first memories.

'So,' the man who called himself Tony said, 'how did you come to know the person outside the train station?'

'Who?' Neil asked, still caught up with other thoughts.

'The one you called to – young guy, brown hair, carrying two bags.' 'Oh. He was an old friend. I mean, he looked like an old friend.'

Tony smiled and took a sip of his drink. Neil tried not to look at the frothy liquid by biting into his sandwich.

All the time, Tony's gaze was undeviating. His eyes appeared to be rimmed by a yellow gleam, which Neil found unsettling. Something was wrong about this stranger, something he had encountered before. Nevertheless, the smell and sight of alcohol forced itself upon his thoughts, casting out all elements of caution for the sake of resisting the calling of 'The Al'.

'Do you mind me asking what made you end up selling magazines outside the train station?'

It wasn't a subject that Neil really wanted to talk about. Over the years he had refined an abbreviated life story that was nowhere near the truth. He began relating this to Tony, who, against Neil's past experiences, seemed profoundly interested. Even so, Neil couldn't take his eyes off the glass before him – the pint of beer that wasn't his. As if knowing his secret desire, Tony seemed to play with it, tracing his fingers along the handle, sighing whenever he took a sip, and smiling in the joy of the liquid's coolness.

The sandwiches were gone, and Neil thought it would be a

good time to leave. But he couldn't. Tony held him to his seat with that compelling gaze, emanating a warm re-assurance.

The glass before him could have been an ingot of gold. No, it was more enticing than the most beautiful of women. How Neil wanted it!

All the need that he had for so long managed to repress welled up from his deepest subconscious, telling him that it was *right*. What was the harm in one drink? What damage could it really do?

A man's life was nothing without a few pleasures. What's the point of living if he couldn't enjoy life? And so, when Tony asked 'you sure you won't have a pint on me?' Neil finally gave in to his demons.

'Go on then,' he replied, practically ready to grab Tony's glass and drain what was left of it.

Minutes later, his own drink appeared like a tanned woman emerging from the Pacific sea, translucently running with waterdrops, calling out to be touched. He brought it to his lips and felt the ambrosial smoothness of what had been so long denied.

An amalgamation of emotions swirled in his heart. Part of him felt a hollow well of regret, whilst the other part rejoiced… and also screamed out *'MORE!'*

After a few moments the former emotions were completely disregarded. He found himself drifting into a strange, unnatural state of mind. Everything began to happen faster. Too fast. Worse, there was a *looming threat* outside, something imprecise and growing larger. It made this man called Tony, sitting opposite him, who he had only just met, seem like a genuine friend... like someone he needed.

* * *

Carlson grinned as the beggar drank. He had ensnared him with more drugs than just alcohol. When he had carried the glass back to the table, he discreetly slipped a pill into the liquid. It briefly fizzed but didn't change the colour or taste of the beer. It was one of the drugs supplied to him to extract information from targets – this particular one induced a state of fear and compliance. Its side effects were similar to a hangover, but the beggar wouldn't have to worry about that.

Carlson had decided to kill him. His anger, frustration and longing for power *had* to be satisfied. He had never killed a person before without being ordered to do so, and he anticipated the *release* of the act to be more intense than any neutralisation order could ever be. No one would find out, of course. His superiors were busy elsewhere, thinking he had gone home after completing the last assignment. For now, he would have to bide his time just a little longer.

The beggar had knowledge of something, maybe dangerous or important. Carlson knew he was holding it back – he had gleaned that from his first question. It could possibly be significant to the Mafiosa, or it could even be part of a bigger plot that threatened Carlson's life. Such plots were always hanging in the air, ready to fall like a revolutionaries guillotine. And afterwards, when he had obtained the information he needed, the beggar would be his much-anticipated Release.

It didn't take long for the pill to start working. The beggar's eyes were already glazing over, his pupils widening with latent fear. His glass was empty. No-one else in the bar knew what was going on, of course. They were all intent on one another; flirting, dancing, conspiring…

'So why did you chase after that man at the train station?' Carlson asked.

'I'm not sure… I saw him before.'

'Where?'

'At a casino, in the gardens.'

There was something about the mention of a casino that clicked in Carlson's mind, but he could not presently remember it. 'When?' he asked.

'About a week ago.'

'What was he doing at the casino?'

Neil looked at the empty glass for a while. The flames of compulsion were swimming in his eyes – an overpowering need to answer questions; to form a friendship, or rather to find a protector. Because, somewhere in his mind, a demon was loose. The drug had simply melted the bars of its confinement. Thinking back to the night at the Crown Casino, he described the two men and what he recalled of their mysterious conversation; the mention of a delivery door, a code, cash…

Carlson sat back in his chair. 'What happened next?'

A noisy couple blundered their way towards the toilets, but Neil's eyes were fixed on a distant point, his pupils reduced to pin heads. 'I showed him… my secret way in… an old sewer that leads to the river.'

'Is this John Stevens, the man you saw outside the station?'

'I don't know his name, but yes… he was the same person.'

The pieces of a puzzle were finally slotting together in Carlson's mind. 'What did he do after you showed him?'

'He gave me money, almost three hundred. Then I… ran off, back into the sewer. I thought maybe he'd try… to get it back.'

Carlson chuckled at the beggar's foolishness, but his mind reeled with what he had been told. It was a puzzle of promises, of riches, of gold. And he could be the one who completed it. This guy, his previous target, was planning something big – massive, in fact.

'Show me the sewer,' he told the beggar.

Neil hesitated at this request, clearly not wanting to leave the safety of the bar, but eager nonetheless to please his new protector. 'Can't we stay longer?' he pleaded.

'No,' Carlson said firmly. 'We *must* leave now. You *must* show me what you showed the man.'

The beggar's eyes wavered, catching a splinter of light from his beer glass. 'Alright,' he said, lips quivering.

Carlson shepherded him through the bar as quickly as

possible. No one would ever see the beggar again, but there was a chance someone here might know him. Carlson did not want to be connected to his disappearance. With the proximity of a transit centre and the presence of cameras, he calculated the chances of him being identified as around five percent. Not good, but a risk he would have to take.

'Do you know the way from here?' he asked, once they were outside.

Neil looked around and muttered. Something about 'the river'.

'Need a taxi, mate?' a mocking voice called behind them.

Jaw clenched, Carlson swung around. He had forgotten about the door-men. 'No thanks,' he said politely.

The risk levels had just gone up by another five percent. Meanwhile, the beggar had begun drifting towards a bus stop.

Carlson caught up with him and said 'No, we must walk.'

'It's long,' Neil replied, 'maybe thirty minutes away... I'm scared.'

Carlson was tempted to laugh again. Instead, he spoke his best tone of reassurance. 'Don't worry, I will protect you.' He put a hand on the beggar's hunched-up shoulder. 'Just show me the way.'

13

Rushing away from the train station, John had ignored what he thought was an over-enthusiastic (and possibly drug addled) *'One World'* seller. The taxi waiting at the corner was just about to move off when he jumped in the back. He told the driver what Sarah had said.

'Nuacorn Health Clinic, you mean?' the bronze-skinned man replied.

'Yeah! As quickly as possible.' 'Alrighty.'

Moving through the city, John looked outside the windows, watching but not really seeing. The thought of Sarah being hurt was as bad as her being captured.

Had he been concentrating, there were several scenes that might have formed the right adjuncts in his mind. They could have even alerted him to the dangers that were swiftly gathering: a group of homeless people lying beneath a neon-lighted doorway... a policeman arresting a drunk... the flashing paroxysm of cameras outside a club. And somewhere amidst this miasma, walking together on the cold streets, there were two men. One of whom would shortly die.

Nuacorn turned out to be a two-storey building just outside the central business district. He quickly gave the taxi driver two notes, not bothering with the change, and rushed up to the lighted doorway. After pressing the buzzer, he just had enough time to notice the camera in a corner of the porch before the door opened.

'This is an emergency,' he told the startled woman. 'I'm here to see Sarah Dufrey.'

After an infuriating wait, he was shown inside and asked to take a seat in a dimly-lit lobby area. The woman vanished down a corridor, leaving him alone.

'Hello, hello, hello!'

He leapt up. The voice emanated from a corner of the room, the only part shrouded in shadow, and his immediate reaction was to unzip the sports bag for the Sig Saur.

Then he paused. 'Ya, ya, ya!'

Drawing its talons down the bars of its cage, the huge parrot stared at him with glaring eyes.

'Mr. Stevens?'

The woman had returned. 'Don't mind Harry,' she said. 'Sarah's room is this way.'

He followed her into the corridor, this time leaving both his bags in the lobby. They turned a corner and went through a pair of double doors. That was when the smell of antiseptic and Lysol hit him. With rhythmic clicks the woman's shoes tapped a synchrony on the polished white floor, almost matching the beats of his heart. The long strips of luminescent lights banished their shadows, making their solitude even more defined. It seemed that the entire clinic was empty.

Finally they came to a door. It was already ajar, and it let forth a spike of amber-tinted light into the corridor.

He entered, holding his breath.

* * *

A man can be moved by the smallest of things. He can quake in terror at the shadow of a harmless insect, or cry with the sight of a strand of hair. For that is what brought John to tears – the sight of Sarah's hair. It fell like dawn-stroked water on the white pillow, cascading from the side of the bed in a lock of glistening glory. There she was: the emblem of his Love, his life's desire, his living dream… lying with one leg raised and her foot in a cast.

They hugged and kissed, a thousand questions rising simultaneously to their lips. Seeing that all was well, the woman left the room.

'What happened?' John finally managed to ask, looking down at Sarah's leg.

She held his hand, linking their pulsing blood with each other's palms. 'It wasn't supposed to be like this,' she sighed. 'I went to the casino and tried to find out more to help us with the heist, but I got injured in the lift shaft.'

He was about to ask what made her go on such a crazy mission, but decided to let her finish the story.

'From there, it just went from bad to worse.' She told him about the confrontation outside the casino and the taxi. 'I had to threaten the driver, get him to take me away, and police were chasing right behind. We were driving along at about seventy, dodging traffic, almost getting crushed by oncoming cars, when I remembered that park at the end of Newport Parade. Do you know? The one which borders the so-called 'red light' district? Anyway, I got out and ran to the other side of the park. I managed to swap my dress with a hooker's, throwing away the sunglasses but keeping the gun. By then police were everywhere. I could see their flashing lights and hear their sirens in all directions. There was even a helicopter. But I kept moving. The pain in my foot and leg was unbelievable, John! Several times I almost passed out. Somehow, I managed to get in a car that was parked on the curb. The fat driver must have been looking to pick up a girl, and his eyes almost popped when he saw me. 'Take me away, baby,' I said, and he does just that. I remembered this health clinic and got him to drop me off a few streets away. It wasn't easy, believe me!'

'He didn't do anything to you, did he?'

Sarah grimaced. 'Yuck! The guy must have lived off burgers and fast food, and you know I only let the fit ones touch me. Joke! Anyway, yes, where was I? So I got out and walked the rest of the way here, in case he tells the police where I got out. I threw away the prostitute's clothes and came here practically naked – if it wasn't for a nurse about to leave then it would have turned out a lot worse. She was really, really nice and gave me this bed. They think it's domestic violence, by the way, and have agreed not to report it.'

John took all this in and hugged her. 'Sarah, you're a lucky angel, but are you sure these people haven't connected you to the casino? It's all over the news, you know. No doubt the hotel have already reported you.'

She shook her head and pursed her lips. 'No, I don't think so. They never saw me wearing my blue dress. I wore a coat and sling-over bag when I left that night, and before I got through the casino gate I threw them into a skip.'

John nodded.

'Don't worry,' she winked, 'they didn't cost much. Once I got into the casino, I wore sunglasses. You taught me that – the importance of having many disguises, even when planning.'

'And the ID you used to get in?'

'Different name, of course,' she confirmed.

'OK, we're probably safe… for now.' He didn't mention the man in Bath who had been following him. Sarah had been through enough without having unknown men to worry about. 'Can you remember where you put the gun?'

'Yes… it's to the left of the front door as you come in, near a bush with yellowy leaves. I wrapped it in a piece of black bin liner and covered it with soil.'

'What about your mobile?'

She paused. Lines of concentration fringed her brow. 'Oh! It's in our hotel room. Yes, definitely. I know… I'm a stupid gal sometimes.'

He laughed and told her otherwise. 'The important thing

is that you're well. In time, your leg will get better. I'll call Howie to let him know you're OK and I'll sort out paying these people for your treatment.'

Half an hour later these two tasks were completed and he retrieved the Glock from under the bushes. He was *really* tired, but one more thing still urgently needed doing: going back to the hotel. There was too much incriminating evidence there to risk delaying it. Police may be inefficient and slow, but they also kept going. The huge tortoise had an uncanny ability to catch up with the speedy hare. If everything was clear, he'd relocate to another hotel in the morning.

The whole thing was too risky for his liking – riskier than crossing a tundra inhabited by polar bears – but it was also unavoidable.

14

As Neil walked through the streets with his new-found friend and protector, a strong undercurrent of unidentifiable fear soon submerged all caution. His body told him that he had to listen and obey in order to survive, so he stuck as close to Tony as possible, doing everything that was asked.

The streets were eerily quiet and dark. Every alcove seemed to be the den of some un-named creature, with creepy eyes dancing in the shadows. All the shops were empty. All the doors stayed shut. Colour was vanquished with each step into the surging grey. Cars passed like wheel-less wagons, moving along on invisible garrote's. The jagged horizon was bordered by high-rise flats, and from each window the sickly moon imprinted its gaze. No stars. No sun. Only fear.

When they reached the riverside, Neil led Tony along the footpath. *The place* didn't take long to reach. 'It's down there,' he pointed, averse to going any further. The shadowy embankment was mirrored by the dark water, presenting an impasse of malevolent depth.

'You first,' Tony said, giving Neil a little shove of his hand.

The action jolted his thoughts to a new level, like the first breath of a man who emerges from a deep dive. His head cleared momentarily – the inexplicable fear began to dissipate – and then, as a wave draws in upon the shore, it crashed back down with renewed vengeance. He felt, once again, that Tony was his only friend in the world. Doing as requested, he climbed over the banister and descended the embankment, with moonlight sketching the dim outline of the worn steps below. Somewhere across the spectral murk of the river, a strange haunting cry was uplifted.

'AH-reeek!'

He jumped and almost slipped, but Tony caught his arm.

'Just a bird, keep going.'

Was it a bird? Was it really?

When they both stood before the metal grate, Tony peered into the impenetrable shadows. 'Is this the sewer you talked about?'

Neil was reluctant to tell him it was, but there was still a pressing need to tell the truth and to answer every question. 'Yes,' he mumbled.

Something moved in the darkness beyond – Neil could *feel* it. 'I need a torch,' Tony said.

Neil nodded and rummaged around to find the one at the bottom of his rucksack. Once found, he held it up as if it was a religious idol or trophy, feeling inexplicably proud.

Tony snatched it. 'You go first.'

Shivering with trepidation, yet unable to defy the command, Neil slid through the gap in the metal bars of the grate, drawing confidence from the light that shone behind him. Twisting shadows made it seem as if an elongated alien was passing through a cage into the realms of the underworld. *Something is here tonight,* he thought, *something sleepless and hungry.* Its aura grew with every step, gathering itself for an assault on the light and growing in the penumbra of blackness.

Through that interminable darkness of unending worlds, he walked towards the heart of the tunnel, as well as the heart of his fear. 'This is it,' he whispered, standing below the ladder which led up to the casino storm drain.

'Climb up and show me,' Tony said.

No choice, no alternative, but Neil was pleased to be leaving.

As he ascended the rungs, a metallic ice dug into his palms. Strangely, its touch felt warmer than the darkness below, and he almost felt as if he was rising out of a slimy, worm-riddled pit.

On reaching the top of the ladder, he shoved the storm drain aside and looked down. The resulting illumination framed Tony in an eclipse of silver light, with the torch shining golden in the middle. When he crawled out onto the grass, the night was crisp, fresh, open… but still threatening. He still needed Tony for protection.

Abruptly a thought leapt into his mind. *From what? Run, while you have the chance!*

He couldn't. The urge was submerged by anxiety. Like a dog waiting obediently for its master, he watched his protector climb the ladder and rise up from the ground.

* * *

GOOD INTENTIONS

Carlson looked around, surprised at the new surroundings. A wall was nearby, as well as some trees, shrubs and flowers. Some multi- coloured floodlights lit up parts of a garden, and in the distance he could see the side of a building. It could only be the casino.

So the beggar was telling the truth, he thought, *this really is a secret way in.* Earlier he had planned to kill Neil whether he was lying or not; the only difference being he would endeavour to make the latter death quicker than the former. By telling the truth, Neil had earned himself a quick, merciful ending. Carlson didn't want to shoot him in the gardens, since the gun was not fitted with a silencer; nor did he want the body to be found. It would be far better to kill him in the sewer, leaving the rats a tasty meal.

'Alright, Neil, good friend,' he said, 'we can go back down now.' Neil just stood there.

'You *must* take me back,' Carlson repeated, raising his voice in a command.

Still the beggar ignored him.

He withdrew the gun and held it up, the nozzle glistening obsidian in the moonlight. 'This is to protect you', he said, 'but if necessary, I'll use it against you. Now, let's go!'

Neil nodded quickly, as if emerging from a trance, and went to climb back down.

Carlson followed. It no longer mattered that the drug had loosened its grip. He had both the gun and the torch. There were only two ways his quarry could go, and both lay in pitch black. If Neil tried to run, Carlson would be able to locate and shoot him in seconds.

* * *

Forced back down into the sewers, Neil could do nothing but stand in the gloom, watching as Tony jumped nimbly off the ladder's last few rungs. A peculiar draft wafted along the passage, carrying the scent of many things – waste, stale water, limescale. Amongst them all was the epitome of finality, transuding from the mouldy walls, trickling like blood in the passing water: death.

He had never gone further into the sewers apart from one occasion. What he had seen then was enough to deter him from returning again. The oldest, darkest, most deserted part of the city was its underground network of passages, built by long dead people over centuries of change. Many died in the construction of these underground passages. They had become abodes, passing places and tombs – domains traversed by the homeless and hopeless. Each had a utilitarian purpose, whether for gas, water, sewage or general maintenance for the underground trains. In some parts, however, there were purposes that went beyond contemporary goals…fearful secrets, things that should stay lost and forgotten, whilst others that cried out to be found.

'Alright, walk!' Tony roared, pointing the gun at him.

Neil turned hastily towards the tunnel's entrance.

GOOD INTENTIONS

'Not that way, the other one!'

Tony's angry voice echoed off the walls and joined with the shadows, making them move and grow, seemingly giving them fuel.

It was only then that Neil finally accepted he had been tricked, but he did not so much dread a bullet as where he would have to go – both in this life and the next. There was a feeling that was deeply unsettling: to be left dead here was to be never, ever found again.

The ground sloped downwards, and a few times they passed smaller passages that branched off like the pitch intestines of a cavernous beast. Sudden rushes of sound drowned out their footsteps, which Neil attributed to the trains. When this happened the torch dimmed and wavered, as if it was a flame affected by air currents. An ugly silence hung ahead, seeming to suck away their breathing into a relentless void. Within that silence, coating itself with the very essence of horror, was what Neil feared the most.

'It's not there, Neil, it's not real,' a voice said in his memories.

As he looked into the flickering darkness, he tried to find comfort in that cold psychotherapist's logic. *Yes,* he thought, *of course you're right.*

But beyond his vision, *something* moved nonetheless.

'That's far enough,' Tony said.

Neil turned around. The brightness of the flashlight momentarily blinded him. It took him a few seconds to see the gun that was aimed at his face.

* * *

Carlson did not plan on walking too far, just enough to cover the stench of the beggar's decaying body. One hundred metres seemed an adequate distance, but he ended up reducing this by half.

Now he had Neil facing the gun and the safety catch was released in preparation to fire. One quick bullet in the head – a clean, compassionate ending for a pitiful life.

And then the torch went dead.

Darkness caught Carlson like the claws of a lion dragging down an infant buffalo; tearing through his confidence and shattering his plans. He didn't hesitate for long.

A series of flashes illuminated the tunnel in lightning and thunder as he fired the gun. It crashed and boomed in stuttering echolalic bursts, rattling with glorious power. Bullets danced off the walls and struck the floor with long wailing *piiiings*.

Neil had vanished into Hades, never to be seen again.

Yet there was an inexplicable feeling of *wrongness* that emanated in front of Carlson. No longer did it feel like he was in an old sewer, more in the emptiness of deepest space. He was alone… and yet not alone. The nothingness before him echoed in formless contradiction.

Caressing the trigger of his tool, he sprayed new fire into the tunnel. He knew it was unnecessary, really – a waste of ammunition, but he deserved it. This was his Release.

GOOD INTENTIONS

That was how, in the wake of one of the gun flashes, he saw something.

A *face*.

Pale, translucent, sickly.

Click, click, click. There were no more bullets. Suddenly, he was standing naked on a desolate moor, with a fanged beast creeping inexorably closer. Beetle-like goosebumps crept along his entire body as a feeling, which he had not experienced since childhood, enveloped him....

Fear. Deep, throbbing fear.

The face was not the beggar's. It was unlike any man or woman he had ever seen. It was the visage of a *creature*. And he knew it was real.

The torch was still useless. He wanted to smash it to pieces, bringing down curses on its makers, smashing and shouting until nothing was left. Anger shook the fear from his shivering limbs and he reached for a new magazine to reload the gun. Then he heard... a voice, a papery whisper, almost like the purr of a cat – its pitch high and low – hard to define.

It seemed to be originating before him, right where the face had been. It coiled through the darkness, strangling his limbs and freezing his bones.

Searing fright swept over him as something cold touched his arm: the touch of a corpse, a wraith... a *thing*.

Only then did his body take control, asserting itself with a rush of adrenalin, guiding his body where sight could not.

He dropped both the gun and torch and frantically fled in the opposite direction – knowing, from some deep instinctual level, that the thing was in pursuit.

A dim glow lay ahead: the ladder. Framed in silvery light, it could have been lowered by some guardian angel – or a devil trying to taunt him. He gripped the sides and *leapt* up the rungs; taking them two at a time, up to the light, cat quick, not caring what or who was above.

Once out, he heaved the cover back over, sealing it tight. Panting for air. The metal rang out a note of solid reassurance: *Clonk!*

Standing up, he looked around. Then he heard it – down below, an eerie sound. Too close, too familiar. He stood there, his breath heaving, staring at the drain cover. He wanted so badly to run, to keep on running until the very sky was within his reach, until the stars were his companions. But he resisted it. *Control…*

A chill wind plastered back his sweat-soaked shirt. He mopped his brow. Over and over again, the question arose: *what the hell was that?* Impossibilities of imagination threaded their way to his awareness, reinforcing his deepest fears. The face… the voice…

What was it? What did it say?

Unable to embrace an answer to these questions, not even wanting to, he left the casino grounds by the main gate and hailed a taxi to take him home.

Once through his front door, Carlson used both locks and

GOOD INTENTIONS

went from room to room rechecking the windows. Simply shutting the bedroom door was not enough: he went so far as to place a chair under the knob, telling himself it was a natural enough precaution given his occupation.

Sleep proved difficult. A host of thoughts and feelings gyrated through his head, refusing to settle. Most of all was that of frustration – realizing that the gun he dropped had his prints on it. He knew the beggar was lying dead a short distance away, cut down by the gunfire, which meant he could be linked to the murder. But the very thought of going back down there to collect the incriminating evidence made him shiver.

It was a daunting prospect. There was something in those sewers which he could not attribute solely to his imagination. He tried hard to think what the 'voice' had said…

Line? Bind? Thine?

The need to understand its meaning was insistent, almost compulsive. As he slipped into shrouded dreams, his mind struggled to understand what had happened.

Not even subconscious imagery could offer an answer.

PART 2

And lo to the mist,
falling...

15

Every game has an ending, but some games begin where they end. Such is the same with life and all things within it; going round and round, cycling on until the trumpet calls of eternity say otherwise. Could one life drift like a sycamore seed on winds of change, floating and twirling till it moves no more? Could one trace the droplets of a river to the vapour of clouds, and see the burning hearts of stars in the deepest ocean canyons? Such questions lie on the rim of awareness, plaguing the penumbra of dreams. They are, perhaps, a growing branch of subliminal knowledge; an apotheosis of understanding.

Time passed, and that thing which is rarely acknowledged wove its patterns. Above and below, within and beyond, there was nothing that could undermine it: Fate; God's Right Hand; Deterministic Blindness. Ever knowing, ever moving, ever Being.

Under the splenetic city, hidden in shadowless dark, the rats chose their paths. They ran with instinctive sight, knowing that a new force was gathering. Like all things, it cycled – sleeping and waking, waxing and waning, singing and sighing, fasting and eating. A crumbling mountain might have claimed kin with its spirit, if such peaks were capable of *becoming*.

Above, in a city that might have claimed kin with Babylon, people cycled on the anonymous conveyor belt of consumption. Some falling, some rising, but all moving towards an outstretched ocean of unknown. Even the Stratos Dwellers, those purveyors of broken promises, would taste its cold embrace.

A swan glided along the river. Moonlight dimmed behind the robes of clouds.

Time passed.

Facing their biggest challenge yet, John and Sarah looked to the future, with eyes half on the past. It seemed they had escaped detection, despite all the covert warnings that whispered doom. There had been no apparent problems when moving to a new base of operations – no police had been waiting to pounce when John returned to the hotel room. Sarah's casino debacle was a close call, but it was not a premature ending. For her, there would be no going back. Her secret betrayal was an insinuating reminder that *The Heist* needed to be done, regardless of the risks and her injuries. As the days passed she got into a punishing training regime, using a variety of weights and leg machines to prepare for the end of the poker tournament. This was despite a nurse telling her that she couldn't use the leg for at least two weeks.

She went from walking on crutches to managing without them at all. It was an almost miraculous recovery. On Thursday she moved out of the health clinic and went to stay with John at the new hotel he had checked into, which was a

GOOD INTENTIONS

short drive away from the casino.

John was tired of arguing with her about the robbery. She had gone to so much effort to train, and was so obviously compelled to go ahead with it that he really had no choice – not if he still wanted them to stay together.

A fire burned in their hearts, an unremitting flame of freedom and an indefatigable will that could sweep away all obstacles. His mission to lift up the poor and oppressed had become hers. The Organisation he had started alone was now nothing without her. In fact, so too was his life. He knew she felt the same way, but he could not overcome the feeling that something had changed. It was as if a tectonic plate had shifted, leaving the landscape of their relationship practically untouched but dramatically changing its foundations. *After the heist*, he told himself, *it will be different.*

There was also the matter of the bank job. He managed to persuade her to help him do it, if not before the casino heist then after. She agreed, which left only one problem: Howie. A meeting was arranged, and Sarah went by herself.

She came back an hour later, her face beaming. 'It's on,' she said, 'he will text you when they move the cash from within the casino.'

He asked her how she managed to re-enlist Howie's help, but she was cryptic.

'Oh, I have my ways,' she replied, sliding a hand under his shirt.

'In two days, we'll be running as millionaires,' she smiled, 'and our Organisation… will reach for the stars.'

Could anyone be happier? he wondered, feeling like a soldier just before a mighty victory or an explorer about to set foot on a new land.

Sitting there, with her in his arms, he truly felt… alive.

* * *

Parked a few streets away, the Theta secondary surveillance team monitored the couple through a variety of gadgets. They had kept target #10112 and his girlfriend tagged for a week now. The unmarked white van in which they were currently based had the usual transponder locator, sound-direction analysis equipment and computers linked to a network of super-fast surveillance data processors. The team were all trained on the technical side of surveillance and their role was 'monitoring at a distance' – never 'neutralisation'. Their organisation, the Mafiosa, was foremost a business, which rented out its services to other enterprises and wealthy individuals. Everything from protection and money laundering to skilled assassination could be bought. Only around twenty percent of its operations in Europe were on direct order within the higher echelons. Target #10112 was one of those rare cases.

Compared to their other targets, which were on two senior politicians ordered by clients, it was a low level operation. But the fact that it was ordered internally by the Mafiosa

GOOD INTENTIONS

elevated its importance.

From the button-sized transponder they had placed on his bag a week ago to the listening devices they had recently planted in his hotel room, they kept target #10112 under constant surveillance. References to a casino, a bank, a 'heist' and various people had all been overheard, although no real details had been gleaned on what he was planning. Nevertheless, they forwarded all new information to the regional controller.

In the smoke-filled room at the heart of the city, the same three men had gathered. This time there was a laptop and a pile of paperwork strewn on the desk, with the main light hanging overhead illuminating their faces. They all wore tailored suits and were in the latter-part of middle-age. Their faces were hard and their eyes were cold, with the exception of the third man, who was wearing dark glasses. One man lent over the laptop, frowning at the screen, as the other two sat by smoking.

'We can't contact him,' he said.

'You've sent someone to his house?' the man sitting next to him, wearing a grey-striped suit, asked.

'Yes. It looks like he's left. All his belongings are gone.'

'When was the last communication?'

After a few clicks on the laptop, the man turned and said 'at the end of the Stevens assignment, a week ago.'

The mention of Mr. Stevens, target #10112, drew the third man's attention. He had just been discussing this case with the Theta secondary surveillance team. It was intriguing, perhaps one of the most enigmatic cases he had encountered in a catalogue of criminal endeavours. Behind the shades his eyes scanned the other two men, seeking signs that they recognised what he had. He listened as they droned on about a deserting employee, a man called Carlson, then decided it was time to cut the conversation short.

'Find him and neutralise him,' he interjected.

'Is that really necessary?' The man in the grey suit questioned.

A heavy silence descended on the room after this, which the third man let hover like a scavenging condor.

'Yes,' he finally said. 'This investigator has deliberately cut contact with us. There's no excuse for that. He knows the rules.' Pausing, he took a long drag from his cigar before letting out a thick spreading cloud. 'Let the rest know about it as well. Our dogs need to learn to respect a leash.'

Nothing further was said on the matter as new mechanisms of the Mafiosa swung efficiently into action.

* * *

Dark was the tunnel by the river, even with the torch shining. Carlson had been there the whole morning, setting up hidden motion sensors to alert him when anyone entered.

From now on he'd have to watch his back, because he knew *they* would be looking for him. He had managed to relocate to a 'safe house' in the inner city, one of the few

GOOD INTENTIONS

places the Mafiosa didn't know about. Not yet, anyway. He really needed to get out of the city, but not until he'd finished the business with his previous target.

From what the beggar had told him, he inferred that Stevens would be coming this way again. If his suspicions were correct – and they were rarely wrong – it was to rob the casino. He strongly anticipated that it would be on the night of the much-publicised poker tournament final. Once he killed Stevens, he'd take the money. The loot would make a valuable addition to his retirement fund, giving him the much- needed boost he needed to start a new life elsewhere – uncontrolled, anonymous, and free.

Sometime past mid-day he forced himself to go back to *The Place*. This time he carried a huge flashlight and a Uzi pistol, one of the two remaining firearms in his supply. He found the other gun where he had dropped it, lying near the broken parts of the beggar's flashlight. There were no strange incidents – although his heart jarred when he saw no signs of the beggar's body. Looking down, he saw just a scattering of spent shells… no festering limbs, no rotting clothes, no smell, not a drop of blood.

Beyond the beam of his powerful torch, the darkness mocked him, laughing in silent subterranean tones of mirth. For a split second he lost control, shouting curses and letting forth a crackling burst of automatic fire. The tunnel simply ate it up with a long groan.

Laughing nervously at the silence, he hurried back to the

river. The equipment he had placed at the tunnel's entrance was functioning perfectly. He leaned against the wall outside, clenching and unclenching his fists as he watched the traffic move along the other embankment.

A hatred for every vehicle and its occupants inflamed his heart, warming him from within. His loathing for mankind may have been great, but he did not despise life or living things in general. In fact, he often saw himself as a 'caretaker', eradicating a species that had become parasitic – overpopulating and polluting the world, hurting and betraying each other. Whilst he would kill a man with pleasure, it was a different case for other animals. He treasured them like they were family, for never once in his entire life had they hurt him. He remembered back to his childhood when his mother brought him a dog... Bengie. A spaniel with golden ears. He recalled how he cuddled him when his father got violent, how they ran away and slept out in the wilderness, how they survived as brothers. Old Bengie...

Carlson could almost hear his pet's barks echo across the ravaged wastes of his memory; calling him back to the days that should have been better, yet at the same time were the best. When all else had deserted him, there was Bengie. When the house was a thundering warzone and the streets were cold traps, Bengie remained by his side.

And then some bastard Rat had run him down in a car.

Sitting by the river, Carlson looked at the water. Emotionlessly. He had stopped crying a long time ago.

GOOD INTENTIONS

Perhaps Bengie's death didn't empty the reservoir of his soul, but the events afterwards performed that job with brutal efficiency. First 'the home', the loss of all those who called themselves 'family', then the raping of body and mind, and finally a ruthless bout of punishments for rebelling against the system. But what hurt him most of all was the betrayals. Father, mother, carer, friend – the list was endless. All had come to him as angels and departed as devils. All had fooled him. And secretly he blamed the resulting pain on his own vulnerabilities.

'Never again,' he whispered.

Carlson's darkness did not arose from some black seed within his heart; it had come upon him as a looming shadow, passed on by others.

Movement on the river re-directed his thoughts to the present. Three white swans were sailing by. One of them, with a speckled-black tail, paddled right up to him. Its black eyes met his own. In the ebony mirrors of those twin orbs he could distinctly hear a voice, a whispering reassurance of all things lost.

'O Brother, I am here.'

The bird glided gracefully away, leaving Carlson alone again. Impossibly, almost miraculously, a single drop of saltine water trickled down his cheek, defying the emptiness of a decade.

16

Sunlight skimmed water flowing east, receding colours transfusing from red to violet. Dusk fell upon the city like a bird of prey, night as a heavy cloak. Roads became trails of flashing lights, buildings became pinnacles of participation. The distinctiveness of minutes merged in some places to hours, whilst in others they compacted to seconds.

Along Newport Parade, traffic crawled along slowly. The sirens of special police escort motorcycles made way for a cruising limousine, one of many heading into the casino.

The last night of the grand poker tournament had finally arrived. Only two players remained: the singer who had reached number one in the charts for two consecutive years, and an entrepreneur whose riches passed the billion-dollar mark. This game was the talk of every gambler across the world – from Vegas to Rio, from Monte Carlo to Perth. It was broadcast in countless casinos, premiered on television channels across all time zones.

The Crown Casino was packed as never before, heaving with an eye-watering crowd of the modern glitterati. Up on the second floor, some of the world's richest and most famous people stood to watch the final first-hand. They were drunk on expectations, inebriated with the limelight. Cameras rolled and flashed in a constant trickle of sparkling praise. At the

GOOD INTENTIONS

main gate security carefully checked every visitor, allowing only those who stayed at the hotel or who had tickets for the tournament to pass. The floodlights which illuminated the fountains changed from blue to red, moving through a rainbow. Behind the leaping water a line of reporters waited at the main entrance, eager to capture a star. Tonight the Crown Casino really did live up to its name, for there were more kings and queens from far away nations than in any grand palace or remote castle. Had there been a courtroom and a prison it might have qualified as its own little country.

Management had arranged a culmination of entertainment, from tribal dancing to a magic show. And of course, the dealers were working the tables furiously. No seat was empty, no chip was low. Even the slot machines hummed crazily to the scores of newcomers eager to ride the gambling train. Over by the teller stations, there was a perpetual cue of people waiting to exchange notes for playing chips. A hustler who worked the city streets could smell the money, feeling it like mercury mist hanging in the air. In this night alone, a million would pass in a few seconds, flowing almost invisibly from one hand to another. No-one looked to where the money was heading; to where it would sit with the idle luxury that embodied the spirit of its owners. They only played. But up on the second floor, as soon as the poker tournament started, all gambling came to a temporary halt.

The singer sat opposite her opponent, wearing a stunning violet dress, her face glowing in the height of youth and the epitome of good fortune. Sapphire earrings sparkled beneath three huge chandeliers. A streak of golden hair obscured part of her left eyebrow, which frowned at her opponent. He was scrutinising her, an idol of masculine power, his smile both enigmatic and captivating. Apparently in his late thirties, he carried with him years of practiced experience, cunning and strength. On his right hand, a huge black-diamond ring stood out proudly, rumoured to be the largest of its kind in the world. Thick black hair almost matched its hue. His deeply tanned skin seemed pale in comparison to that priceless gem.

The match was equal. Neither side could be fooled or intimidated; neither side could be read. They wore closed-book expressions whose bindings were locked together with iron and gold, gazes undeviating to none but the cards.

As the dealer drew the first hand, the singer almost hinted at a smile, but checked herself when realising that any gesture whatsoever could be read by *this* opponent. She knew from her aides that he was notorious for looking past a ruse, seeing it for what it was. Moreover, this was *her* money that she was playing with. The winner would walk away with £10 million; the loser with Zip. That was not the most important thing, though. Her pride and reputation were on the line. She had never lost a game, at least not publicly. And for that matter, neither had he...

The money was nothing. It represented less than three percent of his total wealth. To win was about confirming the status as undisputed World Poker Champion. To lose would mean risking being seen as inferior. If it was another opponent, he would have bribed them to let him win, which he had done twice before in crucial games.

This one could not be bought off. Looking into her icy eyes, he was dismayed to see a blanket of strength and determination. Even after successfully bluffing her with an eight-pair, she remained unwavering.

On the seventh game his luck temporarily departed. He had kept rising in cockiness, hoping to convince her that his hand was better. It wasn't. His Three of a Kind was nothing to her Flush. He lost over £3 million then, which almost covered her losses for the preceding games. His eyes could not hide the anger within.

That bitch is beating me, he thought, into the tenth game. He had over-run her for the first set of hands… now she was doing the same to him. It was time to raise the ante. There was a break due and he was going to ask the casino to allow him to raise the jackpot to £20 million. It would be an unprecedented step, but he was certain a little cash "present" would smooth the process over.

As it turned out, management seemed only a little reluctant to agree to the proposal, since they had planned to unveil the £10 million brought up from the vault in order to give the media "a spectacle". He pointed out that nobody could really tell £10 million from £20 million from their TV screens. He persuaded them that it would make an interesting twist to the event, making the game a true battle between determined individuals.

Obviously, the singer would have to agree...

'Where am I going to get £10 million from at such short notice?' she protested to the casino manager. '*He* might be able to transfer it from some bulk account – it would take days for me.'

The entrepreneur came over from his corner to speak to her. 'Oh, I have no problem waiting for the prize money, darling.'

Such blatant confidence of winning fuelled an ever-growing keenness in her. She wanted to teach him a lesson, and ignored the voice inside to be careful. 'Alright – you're on, mister. £20 million.'

The news quickly swept through the casino, and it was made into a full feature story. By the time that the final leg of the tournament was ready to commence, an intricate tale had been woven, presenting her and him as literal adversaries whose battle of wits went beyond mere monetary gain. It wasn't far from the truth.

From childhood she had fought against patronising, demeaning individuals. She had made it her mission to prove them wrong – from the secondary school teacher who said she would 'go nowhere', to short-sighted, greedy music managers, and now this cocky entrepreneur.

Yes, she'd show them all.

17

Far away from the casino, two figures moved in undirected stealth. They were outcasts and rebels of a broken society, cruising the city at night to spray their mark on its entrails. From the estate where they lived, they got a bus to the city centre and searched the streets for something to destroy. Like seeds from a plant whose fruit was only ruin, they sought to show others what life was really about. Destruction, sorrow and angst were all they knew. The 2 16-year-olds had little experience of love, compassion or accomplishment. Yet within their human hearts they *did* find fellowship, artistic expression and even a measure of honour.

'Yo, Paul! Look at this!' one of the boys said to his companion. He was pointing at a picture of a bikini-clad woman in a clothing store. He had a strong impulse to kick the glass and run away.

'Let's go, Ben, I can see pig lights down the road,' his friend said.

Blue flashing lights always unnerved him.

They headed away from the city centre towards the river, kicking over a few bins in dark alleys and using spray cans to scrawl graffiti on barren walls. To others, their writing would be an indecipherable mess. To them, however, it resounded with colour and meaning. It was the only way for them to tell the world who they were, what they were about. Every other avenue was blocked. Years hence they could advance into the arenas of drug dealing and robbery, of which they had already placed a few tentative steps.

Getting a job was out of the question. They knew their dreams could not be reached that way. Role models in their neighbourhood and popular films had proven that what society called 'crime' was the only shortcut to riches. In a 'dog eat dog' world of materialistic, selfish goals, they saw no other way to advance forward or to 'be someone'. Despite this, they were still more akin to children than men, their behaviour governed more by impulse than by reason.

Towards the river they went, taking a secret joy in the sparkle of lights on the tranquil water. Shadowy darkness still held the embers of fear within their hearts, but they did not dare let this show. All weakness and vulnerability had to be stamped out; for, to them, it was their own past weaknesses that had caused their suffering.

Under the bridge they withdrew their spray cans and began painting a picture of anger, strength and hope. Letters merged with numerals, icons merged with shapes. It was a flowing portrait of sentience, inseparable from metamorphic renewal. Feelings were frozen in razor- edged lines, pointing away from the present but stuck there nonetheless. If modern music could be written without quavers or crochets then it could be found under that dark bridge. Rap rhyming swirled across the blackened bricks, spray-painted in colours alike to the blood that was yet to be shed.

'Come on, Paul, let's go down to the river,' Ben said.

They scrambled over the metal banister and chucked the empty spray cans at a solitary swan that had been drifting sedately in the current. Howling at their wavering reflections, they ran along the embankment, looking for anything that could be remotely valuable. Occasionally, floating items coated in slime washed up with bits of wood. One time Ben had found a pair of brand new trainers which he cleaned, dried out and sold to a younger kid.

They reached one of the old tunnels that had once spewed out raw sewage. Now only trickles of water crept under the metal grill, which had a gap on one side large enough to squeeze through. In the darkness it looked like the giant mouth of a monster with jagged, broken teeth.

Other kids' graffiti covered the walls either side – fading faces, words, symbols. To Ben and Paul, it was all out of fashion. They shook their remaining cans vigorously and began the process of replacing the world's old marks with the new.

Click-spray, rattle… whoosh….

'What was that?' Paul asked.

They both paused and listened. Traffic droned on the far bank of the river, a police siren wailed in the distance, and the trickling murmur of water continued beneath the grate. 'You're hearing things,' Ben said tauntingly, going back to finishing the edging of a big 'E'.

A few seconds later, Paul heard it again: the same unidentifiable sound, coming from the tunnel. It was similar to the rush of wind through power lines, with a note that trembled at the end, disappearing as quickly as it came.

He moved towards the entrance and shone his torch through the bars. Total silence partnered the dark beyond.

'What ya doing?' Ben called from his work-in-progress.

'Nothing,' Paul replied, 'just checking something.'

He ventured into the tunnel entrance, fitting past the gap in the bars with plenty of room to spare.

Swinging the torch beam slowly from left to right, he revealed an open space with a series of little alcoves. A deeper patch of darkness lay where the tunnel continued further. Paul did not like what he sensed in that direction.

A wrongness.

That faint sound radiated down the tunnel again, this time ending in a kind of deep snarl which echoed from wall to wall.

'Paul!'

Ben's voice made him jump. 'What?' he said angrily, trying to disguise his fear.

'Come on man, let's finish this.'

Backing away from the tunnel, Paul retreated through the bars and re-joined his friend. He wanted to leave the river side, but Ben insisted that they 'cover up all the other shit' and use up their remaining spray cans.

GOOD INTENTIONS

No further sounds issued from the tunnel, yet the silence did not allay his fears.

Ben was just finishing the last touches of his graffiti section when Paul asked him again, 'did you hear that?'

He was starting to get annoyed. For the past five minutes, Paul had been pressing him to hurry up, and now he was claiming to hear noises again.

'What's wrong with you…' he began.

But then he heard it too: *footsteps*, coming from above, where steps led back up to the embankment.

'Quick,' he said, nudging Paul, 'someone's coming.'

They slipped through the bars of the tunnel entrance, turning off their torches and finding a shadowy alcove to hide in. Shoulder to shoulder, hearts rushing, they listened intently and strained their eyes to pierce the darkness before them. Ben could feel Paul shivering. He knew it wasn't due to being cold – they both wore coats and hoodies.

He could hear the unknown person creeping around outside, drawing closer. *I'll stab him,* he thought, feeling for his knife.

The dim obelisk of silver moonlight was fractured by the bars of the metal grate. Suddenly it was eclipsed by a shadow. A lance of torchlight slashed into the tunnel, almost touching one of Paul's trainers as it swept from right to left.

Now the cold metal handle of the Stanley knife felt reassuring and comforting – stronger and more reliable than any adult hand. But as the dark figure came into view he found his confidence had vanished. The man was older, taller, more imposing.

Nudging Paul to signal his intention, he sprinted off into the tunnel, ignoring the shouts from behind.

'Hey!' Carlson shouted. 'Come back!'

As he watched the two boys run into the tunnel, he found himself taking out his gun and going into a shooting stance. The torch beam easily picked them out, although it wouldn't be that way for long.

Restraining himself, he lifted his finger from the trigger. Then he pressed it sharply.

The two kids vanished. Of course, he knew the safety on the gun was on. Somehow, shooting two kids in cold blood didn't feel right. He knew they were a potential threat to his mission (which in his eyes warranted death), but sometimes exceptions had to be made.

What if Stevens comes here later and sees those two brats? the colder side of him questioned. It would make no difference. Stevens would be mad to abandon a planned robbery just because of two random kids. In any case, Carlson reasoned they would be long gone by the time the target got here. *Assassin's instinct.* The problem was if they returned this way it would re-trigger the motion sensors at the entrance. The battery-operated devices, obtained through the Mafiosa's military connections, would send another remote signal to his alarm. It had already interrupted him as he sat watching a crucial point of the poker tournament on television.

GOOD INTENTIONS

So he decided to wait. Unfortunately, it meant having to sit in the dark, hiding in one of the larger alcoves near the entrance. Memories of what happened last time resurfaced: the 'face'; the strange voice that had echoed in the darkest recesses of his mind. Such haunting recollections chilled him to the core.

Then, in the deep silence beyond, he heard a scream.

Once they got away from the man, Ben and Paul switched on their torches and fled through the tunnel like greyhounds trapped in a drainpipe. After about three metres, realising the man was not in pursuit, they stopped beneath a ladder.

'Who was that?' Ben asked breathlessly.

'How the hell do I know? I just 'wanna get 'outta here!' Paul exclaimed. It was what lay *within* the tunnel that raised his skin in goosebumps, not so much the man outside. *Something is here*, he thought, *if only I could see it*.

On second thoughts, he was glad he couldn't.

'Alright, calm down!' Ben replied. 'My little sister would be better down here than you.'

'Shut up! You don't know wh -'

He was suddenly interrupted by a noise – the same sound as before, only louder, *closer*, mere metres away. It was a shuddering wail of pain and hunger, neither animal nor human.

'Err, yeah,' Ben said quietly, 'I think I agree with you now.'

Looking up at the ladder before them, he whispered, 'Let's get out this way!'

Climbing up a few rungs, Ben noticed that his torch started to flicker. He turned around and saw Paul holding onto the ladder, waiting for him to go higher. *Both* their torches were flickering.

'Come on!' Paul shouted. Then there was pitch darkness.

Ben banged his torch on the metal rungs, but it was no use. The cold metal seeped into his fingertips, touching his very bones. Abruptly, the ladder vibrated, as if a great weight had been slammed into it.

'You alright, Paul?' he asked shakily. No response.

'Paul?'

Sweat trickled down his neck and broke out along his brow. There was still no answer. Slowly his eyes were adjusting to the dark, able to see a faint ring of light that was coming from the drain cover. He tentatively reached up for the next rung of the ladder and began climbing up.

'Bennn…'

A voice. Ben paused. There was a dragging sound below, like the pushing of clothes on stone, as if a body was…

No! It's my imagination! He wanted to shout but couldn't. The drain was inches away; the portal to another world – safe, warm, bright.

Reaching up, he put his feet on the last rung… and slipped.

* * *

GOOD INTENTIONS

Carlson sat there wondering what happened. Thoughts rushed through his head like rising bubbles in a boiling kettle. *Was it Stevens? No, it was a kid's voice... there was no gunfire, it can't have been that...what about the other one?*

He considered switching his torch on and going to investigate, but the thought of returning to *that place* again was not appealing. Millipedes made a home of his skin whenever he thought about it: the face, the voice...

'Come on,' he whispered, urging the kids to come back so he could re-set the alarm. A part of him – a part he refused to acknowledge – knew he would never see them again. It was the same part that screamed in his head GET OUT, every minute growing in volume. He released the safety on the Uzi. He checked the extra magazines in his pocket. In the dark, he waited.

In... out... in... out... slowly he breathed, remembering the necessity of serenity for survival.

Ten minutes passed and there was still no sign of movement. His body was cold and stiff from waiting so long. *Whatever's happened*, he inferred, *the kids have gone.*

Finally accepting this logic, he got up and crept to the grate, resetting the shoulder-high motion sensors before making a final glance into the tunnel. It maintained its aura of uncertainty.

Once outside he listened intently for the sounds of anyone approaching. Only here did he realise how 'heavy' the atmosphere had been in the tunnel; in there it had been like inhaling a necrotic gas. That it used to be an old sewer and the walls were still lined with dubious strands of green could not explain the putrid stink of decay, which was mixed with a gassy draft of rejected flesh.

As he walked away Carlson once again contemplated the meaning of the scream. A myriad of 'what ifs' crossed his mind as he ascended the steps back to the embankment and re-joined the pathway. He moved with utmost stealth, all too conscious that the target could soon be approaching.

18

Drums beat in synchrony to resounding trumpets as two trolleys were wheeled in from behind a red curtain. The chief manager of the casino stepped forward and faced the row of cameras. Beneath the huge chandelier, prized centre-piece of the high-stakes floor, his bald head almost glowed. Some of the cameramen even found themselves adjusting the contrast options of their devices as they zoomed in on his face. The manager smiled, wide and generous, and began his speech.

'Ladies and gentlemen, welcome back. This is the last night of the best poker tournament of the century. We have seen giants crash and stars tumble since these two weeks of spellbinding entertainment began. Now you're going to witness the final two opponents going head to head. There will be no breaks, no intermissions. We're going right to the very end.'

He glanced behind him, briefly drawing the audience's attention to the two trolleys of cash. 'You will be aware the stakes have been raised, doubling from ten million to a massive twenty million. This was never planned or anticipated, I can assure you. For *these* two opponents, it's more than a game.'

He began mentioning the main sponsors who had funded the event, then pointed to the money. 'Now behold the jackpot, ladies and gentlemen. This is what the winner will get.'

Turning to the singer and entrepreneur, he dipped his head. 'Best of luck to the both of you!'

A chorus of claps followed him as he walked away.

Silence descended again throughout the whole casino as people on both floors were drawn to the television screens that presented the game. The two opponents were sat in frozen postures, their mutual concentration obvious.

It seemed like a repetition of the last round as the entrepreneur smashed the singer in the first few hands. Increasingly the beating looked sure to drain her of her last million. Not once had the entrepreneur bluffed; not once had he given anything away. In some hands, she clawed back a little of her losses, but they were minor victories. He was always staking big, raising on hand after hand – and winning.

Then came a miracle: an unheard of Straight Flush (odds of 72,193 to one), which won her a massive £5 million, drawing gasps from the crowd and a thin crocodile smile from the entrepreneur.

She could feel it in the air: the buzz of being a champion, the glory of winning.

The entrepreneur sat there as one of those dragons that flanked the entrance of an upmarket Chinese restaurant: a granite statue with the deadliest gaze. His palms were starting to sweat. He could feel a drop tracing the under-rim of his black diamond ring. It appeared the singer was doing what she did last time – swinging the odds on her side, drawing on some powerful source of adamantine luck. He

GOOD INTENTIONS

hung on, refusing to fold except when it was hopeless. He even restrained the wish to throw in his cards and walk away in disgust when *she* bluffed *him!*

The undisputed champion, 'Mr. Big', the ruler of an empire, was finally falling. Some stations were already playing 'Another One Bites the Dust'. He was down to only a few hundred thousand. Collar now soaked with sweat, countenance in a perpetual frown, he faced her with a look of undisguised hatred.

* * *

Two hours later, at five minutes past midnight, the singer boarded her helicopter on the roof of the casino. A few fireworks were being let off below, and she could still hear the roar of applause ringing in her ears. She could not believe what had happened. It was hard not to hide her tears when she thought of the reversal. Somehow he had won. Every cent of the £20 million was his.

They had played until the casino became a mausoleum for its silence and suspense, right into the third watch of the night, when somehow it had all gone wrong. A series of devastating hands left the singer with only a thread of hope. As fickle as a dice, luck made its sly retreat. Sweat, money, alcohol, perfume – all vanished beneath the fumes of defeat. To the singer, the casino had become a dungeon, and at the last fateful hand the air became rendolent of total despair.

She was pleased to get away. She would have to work hard over the next few years, signing many undesirable contracts, in order to pay for her present style of living. For him – the bastard with the black ring and smirking grin – the money was nothing. Victory was all about dominance, pride, boasting. As she thought back to his gloating laugh, she repressed a fleeting wish for vengeance.

The winner takes it all, the loser stands to fall she thought, looking down on the city lights below, thinking only briefly that there were people worse off than her.

19

Slowly twilight crept upon the pitch night as daylight conquered the shadows. Rain had fallen before the first bird took up its song, and now a thin curtain of mist hovered upon the river. Its current was slow, placid, yet strong. White shapes of swans drifted by like unmanned kayaks. One could be fooled into thinking their serenity was rootless, when really below the surface their feet paddled frantically to go upstream. Much was the same. As people arose from their slumber, preparing for work, they could be pardoned for forgetting what society was based upon. The smooth functioning of transport, energy suppliers and financial transactions could be seen as processes of a healthy, sustainable economy. Yet the underlying foundations were crumbling – frantically paddling on an ever-shrinking body of water. It was all based upon unstable, unsustainable resources, held up by slave labour in other countries. One day it would all fall to ruin, unless a new path of opportunity and sustainability was unlocked…

From the rear of their budget hotel, John and Sarah carried the bags and equipment to the rental car and drove to a parking spot near the river. A solitary strip of cloud fringed the horizon, blocking the sun. Only the passing of a few cars gave any indication that the city was inhabited.

On reaching the tunnel's entrance they took out their disguises and prepped themselves for the upcoming endeavour. Neither of them saw the freshly-sprayed graffiti outside; nor did they see the UV beams that guarded the tunnel's entrance.

'So this is it,' he said. 'No turning back.'

She nodded with a barely-visible expression of excitement.

As they slipped into boiler suits and secured their canvas bags in an alcove, he handed her a spare clip for her gun. 'Chances are, we're not going to fire a single shot '

She took the clip without comment and slipped it into her waist pocket.

Flashlights on, they proceeded down the tunnel in silence, following a trickle of water that made a tremulous song on the slimy walls. In their masks and suits they could have been ghosts, moving relentlessly forward to an undreamt-of destination. It did not take long to reach the ladder. The drain of the casino grounds was directly above, surrounded by a ring of bright light. He climbed up to test that it could still be lifted, then replaced it and climbed down again. 'We'll wait,' he told her, 'until Howie gives the word.'

'What's down there?' she asked, probing the beam of light into the darkness at the other end of the tunnel. Shadows leapt and ran as if alive, crouching in corners and staring back at her stubbornly.

'The tramp didn't say,' John replied. 'I guess it just leads to other parts of the city – probably connects to the trains.'

GOOD INTENTIONS

'That would explain the sound.'

'What sound?'

'Can't you hear it?' she paused. 'Like running trains.' But, standing there, part of her thought it was something else: a whispering, maybe even a *calling*, as subtle as the trickling water, only far more sinister and powerful.

At 8:30 precisely the group of security guards entered the pin code to the cashiers' station. They loaded the waiting cash into six cases, with three men carrying two each and one man to lead them across the floor. A deputy manager brought up the rear. Among the three who carried the cases was Matt.

He had never known so much money to be moved from the cashiers' station to the casino's strong room. Clearly the final tournament night had been a culmination of big-stakes gambling. Millions had been made in the space of a week. Each case carried from £250-£300k and they would have to make a second trip to collect the rest.

Management always chose weekday mornings for these cash moves. It was a time when few people were in the casino, making it easier to monitor and maintain a good level of security. In the near future it would become unnecessary to do this, since they were building a chute to the strong room, relocating the cashiers directly above it.

As they walked across the gaming floor, the lead man scanned around for any potential threats. In a separate room security tracked their progress via cameras. No one paid any attention to the blackjack croupier discreetly texting messages on his mobile phone.

When John received the second message from Howie, he was waiting outside the delivery door with Sarah, having climbed up the ladder in the tunnel and taken an unobserved route through the casino gardens. As soon as they stepped up to enter the access code of the delivery door they would be visible. But even then security would not be immediately alerted of a threat. Their boiler suits and masks gave them the appearance of delivery workers. It would take casino security a few minutes to confirm that there were no deliveries scheduled and by then – God willing – they would be away with the cash.

It was always the same before a heist. A wave of adrenalin flooded their bodies. For Sarah, this was what she found so revitalising, giving her a rush akin to white water rafting or sky diving – two sports they both loved. But in this 'sport' the anticipation (and aftermath) was even more intense. Heartbeats pounded express train rhythms, racing against each other, thrumming out a covert resonance.

He took some deep, slow breaths, stepping up to the door and entering the access code. A mechanism clicked. He turned the knob.

The door opened silently, giving a view of a long corridor with an access point at the end. He stepped in, holding the gun in his right pocket.

Sarah followed.

20

The lead guard was entering the corridor. Someone in the security surveillance room contacted the deputy manager via his radio, informing him of 'the delivery men'. By then it was too late. The four guards were already through the door and the deputy manager looked on helplessly as a gunman stepped into view. Backing away, letting the door slam, he screamed into his radio what security already knew.

* * *

John got the first man onto the floor as Sarah covered the other three guards.

'Spread your arms and lie flat,' he instructed.

Sarah went to get the cash cases. There were more than they expected – two of the six would have to be left behind. As Sarah slid the cases towards the delivery door, one of the guards made a move. She caught him before he could do anything.

'Don't bother,' she said.

With a gun pointing at his head, he could hardly disobey her.

* * *

Matt could not believe what was happening. He had been trained for this sort of situation, but nothing could prepare him for the reality. Lying on the floor with his three colleagues, he did exactly as the robbers said. But to his dismay, Richards – the man closest to him – tried to reach for his radio.

The stupid bastard, he thought, *security already know we're being robbed.*

When the quiet robber spoke, he was even more shocked. A woman's voice. Someone he knew. He could never forget that voice, even if spoken in live-or-die urgency, and the slim figure beneath the disguise was suddenly all too familiar. His mouth moved before he could control it, and he called out her name.

* * *

Turning at the sound of her name, Sarah looked into one of the guard's faces and instantly recognised Matt. Although she knew he worked at the casino, she was not prepared for encountering him in the corridor. She had pushed that possibility to the back of her mind, thinking that if it did arise then her mask would protect her identity. Now it seemed that he had recognised her just by a few spoken words. For a moment, she lowered the gun.

That was enough for the guard closest to her. In one swift movement he knocked the gun from her grip, trying to twist it out of her hand. Her finger slipped. She pulled the trigger.

John jumped at the gun blast and swung around.

Sarah lay on the floor, struggling with a guard who was

trying to get her gun. The others were close to helping. Within seconds the situation would be completely out of control. He rushed forward and pressed his gun against the forehead of the struggling guard. 'Nobody move, you hear? Back on the floor or he's dead!'

Sarah flipped up and trained her gun on the other men.

They both moved towards the delivery door where the cases were. John could see that she limping. She looked protractedly at one of the guards, who held his hands against his stomach. A crimson spot was rapidly spreading around his shirt.

'Come on,' he said, grabbing one of the cash cases. She did the same.

'Don't follow us,' John called back. 'We'll shoot on sight.'

Slipping the gun back into his pocket, he glared at the men sprawled on the floor, then picked up one more case.

Sarah had the delivery door open for him. Before closing it, he put one of the cases down and reached into his pocket. A coin flew from his hand and rolled along the floor, gathering momentum before entering the ever-widening pool of blood.

The last thing he saw, before the door clicked shut, was the golden disk turning red.

Alarms were ringing, strobe lights flashing. The security room was a flurry of activity and armed police were on the way. They had given the order to seal the main gate – whatever happened, the robbers were not getting away. Meanwhile, emergency paramedics were being flown in by helicopter to pick up the bleeding security guard.

On the gaming floors, the punters were told to stay put and not to leave the casino. There was little panic as they did not hear the gunshot in the corridor, and most were too bleary-eyed to react to a false rumour of a bomb threat. After last night's poker tournament, they were overloaded with action.

The delivery door camera tracked the two robbers disappearing into the gardens. One of them was limping. Already the first police vehicles were arriving at the main gate as members of an elite tactical squad surrounded the perimeter. Every route of escape was blocked…

Carlson paced the damp tunnel restlessly. He knew the target had entered the tunnel almost an hour ago, yet he had not returned. The two canvas bags which Carlson found at the entrance remained empty – except for some loose tools and an angle grinder, which he presumed were to be used for opening security cases.

Has Stevens been caught? he wondered. Of course, he realised it could be something else. Betrayal was the obvious alternative; Carlson realised that Stevens might not be working alone, and one of his accomplices could have killed him, or they could have turned him into the police. But no Rat would walk away from big money. Carlson had a vision of Stevens lying dead somewhere back in the tunnel, with his accomplices dead as well, shot simultaneously by silenced pistols. The more he waited and dwelled on that scenario, the more it seemed true. To him it would be fitting: an almost

GOOD INTENTIONS

poetic outcome for collaborators in a species of betrayers.

Yet the last thing he wanted was to venture into the tunnel again to collect cash from a corpse. He also needed to vent his overflowing reserves of anger. If Stevens was dead he would have to go out into the city this very night and find someone else to kill. Oh, how he longed to fly to lands far away, rich and free to do as he pleased! There would be no-one to report to, no one to satisfy…

Abruptly he saw something that wasn't there before: a glowing, shimmering light. He heard something too – running footsteps.

The target was coming.

Retreating into a corner, Carlson crouched in the shadows, withdrawing his gun and grinning.

* * *

They carried the cases through the tunnel, with John stopping every few seconds to wait for Sarah. For her, progress was slow and painful. Her ankle had become twisted again during the struggle with the security guard. Each step led to a stabbing flash of pain, as if someone were jabbing scissors into her heel.

From time to time the flashlight she carried seemed to lose power, dimming to a weak orb of light and then leaping up to full intensity. There was still no sign of the tunnel's entrance. Waves of frigid air swept over her, and despite her rapid pulse she felt an insipid coldness. After a few minutes her flashlight failed, plunging the tunnel into absolute darkness. She cursed and heard a banging of metal against stone as John put his two cash cases down. As he fumbled in his coat pocket, it took a few seconds to locate his flashlight's switch. In that interim of darkness Sarah again felt an unidentifiable presence, creeping unctuously behind her.

'John… what's going on?'

There was no response. She heard the whispering again, the strange fluting noise, but this time it was a distinct voice.

'John…'

Something sharp and glacial touched her shoulder… reaching right inside her, digging past her skin and even her bones, going right to the core of her thoughts. A *Presence* hovered above everything – every memory, every dream, every plan. It probed her. It enveloped her fear. It was so, so cold.

'I know who you are. I know what you're doing. I know where you're going. Everything that you were and will be is within my gaze. You are – '

Suddenly light flared up in front of her. John was pointing his flashlight in her direction.

'You OK? I thought this bloody thing wasn't working either for a moment… here, you take it.'

She grabbed the flashlight and moved swiftly forward, too shaken to speak, least of all look to behind.

Gradually a light began to take form before them as they neared the tunnel entrance. The canvas bags were right where

GOOD INTENTIONS

they left them, and the tools were ready to be used. They threw in their masks and boiler suits and began opening the cash cases. All three were securely locked, but a minute against the blade of the battery-operated angle soon changed that.

John peered into the first case and grinned. Bundle upon bundle of notes were stacked neatly side by side, fitting snug against the silver metal.

Sarah took hold of the grinder and copied John. A fountain of sparks flew up, momentarily painting the shadows in streaks of flashing fire. They were so intent on the job that they never took in every detail of the surroundings. Had they done so, they might have glimpsed the shape crouched in a corner, whose eyes reflected the sparks and glowed in the weird light. A single torch beam would have revealed their patient assassin in deadly contrast.

John began loading the notes into a canvas bag. There was no time to do a proper check of dye packs or tracking devices: he just had to put faith in Howie's assurance that there were none.

As Sarah opened her own case, her mind was numb to a flood of emotions. The shock and guilt of accidentally shooting Matt mixed with a sense of awe and triumph at seeing the cash. But she was also fearful and confused. Had John heard her name being called in the casino? And what really happened back there in the tunnel? Such questions were shoved to the back of her mind as she moved the money into one of the bags.

For John, all other concerns were relegated for future consideration. He did not brood on what had happened in the casino, nor on Sarah's strange behaviour. All that mattered was getting away to a safe location with the money. For although the tunnel was unknown to police, it wouldn't stay that way for long. Such worries were paramount to his thoughts.

When the last case had been opened, Sarah came over to help him transfer the cash. They were both bent over when a booming voice resounded in the darkness.

21

'Freeze!'

A man appeared from a patch of deepest shadow. In his hand was the unmistakable glint of a silencer-fitted gun. John and Sarah were too shocked to react; they just stared. He was tall and imposing, but other than that there was nothing to make him stand out.

'Place your hands on your heads, real slow, and kneel down.' They did as he asked.

He gestured towards the two canvas bags. 'Is that all the money?' John nodded.

'Is that a yes?' the man said aggressively.

This was no police ambush, they realized. It was a robbery, a hold- up, a repeat of what they had enacted barely a few minutes ago. And it was terrifying. They had no idea who this man was or what he would do once he got the money. They only hoped that he would follow the same code as they did, a code they had recently broken: leave no casualties, cause no unnecessary harm. Yet no one could know the thoughts of an anonymous gunman. For the first time in their lives, they experienced the very same fear that they themselves had inflicted countless times on tellers, clerks and security guards. It stung badly. Simultaneously a conflagration of doubt spread through their minds – a doubt over the righteousness of *the mission*, the worthiness of the Organisation. Within that doubt arose the head of guilt, and within guilt there was regret.

Understanding comes at the most unexpected of times.

* * *

Carlson was overjoyed. His fingers itched to spray lead, but he wanted to savour the moment a little longer. The money was right there for the taking, and Stevens was there ready to be killed, along with his blonde girlfriend. Carlson buzzed with the power. Part of him admired them, which only made them worthy of quick elimination. He was also thinking of saving the blonde for another kind of *release*… killing her immediately seemed such a waste.

'Just the two of you?' he asked.

'No one else,' Stevens replied, practically whispering.

Carlson trained the gun on his forehead, making a pinpoint of laser light between the target's sorry eyes. Then he realised that it would be best to get their guns first – that was standard procedure in all neutralisation orders whenever two or more targets were 'captured'. This method reduced the risk of getting shot in the unlikely event he missed a vital organ. Few people could match Carlson's reaction times, but he wasn't going to give the target and his girlfriend a chance to up the tally. 'All right, listen carefully. One at a time, using your left hands, get out your guns and slide them over here.

GOOD INTENTIONS

Starting with you, Miss, slow as a snail.'

The woman did exactly as she was instructed. Even kneeling on the floor, shivering with fear, she moved with such grace and beauty. Her hair made it seem as if she had a faint halo of gold. Watching her, Carlson felt himself harden.

'Now you,' he commanded, turning to Stevens.

No problems with him. Kicking away the guns, he re-centred the laser beam on Stevens's head, returning to the spot his mentor had called 'cognito'. Then his finger pressed lightly against the trigger.

'Bastard!'

An insane voice broke behind.

Crashing down unguarded, something smashed against Carlson's head. His body swayed as his finger completed its relentless pressure, a single bullet exploding through the air. Another man might have fallen unconscious or even died. But Carlson swung around, fighting back the curtain of blackness that shrouded his vision, feeling warm blood trickle down his right ear, and looked into the face of his attacker.

The shock was even greater than the pain. He couldn't believe it.

The object was making another arc towards his head, and he only just managed to block it, using his forearm as a shield. The beggar – yes, Carlson had no doubt about it now – let forth a spray of spittle, crying out in rage.

'You bastard!'

Yes, this was the man Carlson had drugged and killed, who called himself Neil. In the darkness it seemed he had also become someone else.

Carlson still had the gun in his hand. He raised it, intending to fire into the beggar's torso, only to feel a jolt of pain in his balls. The beggar kicked out viciously, causing Carlson to collapse. A curtain of blackness once again rimmed his vision, interspersed with bursting white supernovas. He kept it at bay. All pain was masked by a sudden flood of adrenalin, giving him the strength to fight back. He grabbed the beggar's legs and pulled him down, rolling over to avoid being squashed beneath him.

Unbelievably, the beggar rolled too. The bearded, smelly man got on top of him… and he still had the object. It looked like a piece of driftwood, lined with rusting nails. Carlson saw it rise into the air, seconds away from crashing down into his forehead.

Lightning fast, he shot up his arms and grabbed the beggar's wrists. It was part of a manoeuvre which he had perfected after many years of training. Few, if any, could extricate themselves from it. Already the heavy piece of driftwood had fallen from the beggar's hands. Carlson would crush his wrist tendons with animal force, rendering him defenceless with pain. The fight was over.

* * *

GOOD INTENTIONS

John and Sarah had been watching the silhouette in the entrance of the tunnel before he pounced. Now he was lying on the ground, fighting with the gunman. They were struggling madly, and it seemed the gunman had gained the upper hand. John was not going to wait any longer. He lunged forward and swept up his Glock.

* * *

Carlson saw the target move, saw the gun that was pointed at his torso. He quickly released his grip on the beggar's wrists and rolled around, whipping out his right leg. It caught the target on the ankle, unbalancing him and sending him crashing to the ground. Something hard bounced into Carlson's chest: the target's gun. He wasted no time in snatching it up.

Triumphant laughter almost burst from his lips as he rolled around to eliminate the primary threat – the one who should never have interrupted his plans. Neil would be the first to go in an inevitable explosion of blood and cartilage, and oh how Carlson relished the look of quizzical surprise on the beggar's face.

'Goodbye, Rat,' he said, pulling the trigger and then taking aim at Stevens. But something was wrong. There had been no recoil, no flash of light, no 'pop' of sound. In horror he looked down at the gun, suddenly realising that Stevens still had the safety on.

A red mist of light flashed across his right eye. He blinked, quickly flicking back the safety catch on the Glock. And then he saw. The beggar was there, standing up, holding Carlson's own gun, the laser slicing into his forehead.

'Goodbye,' Neil said.

As the first bullet slammed into Carlson's skull, his last thought was not one of shock or sorrow. It was a sudden realization. The voice in the tunnel had not said 'line' or 'thine'.

It had said *mine*.

As Carlson rushed away into an incomprehensible vastness, that word was being whispered, over and over again, like a spider-web constantly being re-spun: *mine, mine, mine...*

* * *

Blood streaked Neil's clothes and beard as he got up. The crimson rivulets were interspersed with white-grey debris as they ran down his neck and disappeared beneath his bulky coat. Inside, deep inside, there was a strange emptiness, a hollow vacuum that didn't make any sense.

He had killed a man.

For over a week he had searched the city for Tony, the one who had tried to end his life, who had taken away his last chance by tricking him to drink. Neil may have escaped the tunnel that night, along with the Presence that dwelled there, but he had not escaped his addiction. Tony became an idol

GOOD INTENTIONS

of every disappointment, injustice, hardship and disaster. A hatred arose for this man, who Neil had come to think of as *the bad man,* and the need for some kind of vengeance consumed him. With every subsequent drink he dreamt of settling the balance, effectively ending the bad man's life. Now that ambition was finally fulfilled, Neil felt no satisfaction. Only emptiness.

Had it been Fate? he wondered. An hour ago he was determined to end it all by jumping into the river. He had been walking along the embankment near the tunnel when he heard a strange mechanical sound. He crept down to investigate, and that was when he heard the bad man's voice. There was no doubt in his mind: Tony was right there, talking. In alcohol-fuelled confidence, Neil had retrieved a plank of wood by the river bank and crept up behind the bad man until he was close enough to use it. From there Fate, or Destiny (or just pure chance) had taken its sinuous path. Relentless, bloody, yet somehow *Just.*

Standing there, looking at the man and woman on the floor, he wasn't sure what to do. He still had the bad man's gun in his hand, slick with blood, and the metal felt more than warm… it felt good.

'I know you,' he said, looking at John. 'Yes.'

'I know you too,' he said to Sarah.

She didn't reply. Neil's eyes sparkled with something that made her uncomfortable. He walked over to the bags, keeping one eye on her. He nudged the money that was in the last cash case, then knelt down. His face was strangely blank, yet his eyes still had that eerie iridescence. Using the gun, he caressed a bundle of notes, turning it over to look at the one below.

Sarah was tempted to reach for her gun, which was a metre away from her foot, but John shook his head. *'Don't,'* he whispered.

Neil got up, holding the cash case in his left hand. Carlson's gun was still in his right one.

Then he whistled.

At first the notes were distorted and tuneless, but soon he had a smooth, melodic flow. It was a vaguely familiar tune, something you occasionally heard emanating from city scaffolding, or from an anonymous rush hour worker. The dark tunnel echoed with strange subterranean pitch, seeming to provide a counterpart to every note. It sounded as though someone else was in the darkness, whistling back.

As if going to board a departing train, Neil walked away – not outside, but *into* the tunnel. Into the dark. He had no light, but he kept on walking. He walked until there was nothing but the click-clack of his footsteps.

Seconds later, they heard a clatter of metal on stone. Silence.

John called into the darkness. 'We won't follow you, Nail, you can have that money.'

There was no response. He raised himself up and gave Sarah his hand. 'Let's get out of here.'

GOOD INTENTIONS

The two canvas bags of cash were untouched. Neil had only taken the remainder in the last cash case – about £140,000.

'What just happened?' Sarah asked, still unable to take her eyes away from the tunnel.

'No time,' he said.

They walked outside into the blinding sunlight. In the distance were sirens.

22

Morning moved to afternoon as the sun declared its supremacy in a cerulean sky. Robes of heat were thrown down onto the sweltering city, moving to a capering plethora of rhythms. The parks were crowded with students who half-heartedly perused textbooks and drank soda. Families strolled by the riverside, throwing bread crumbs to the swans and searching out the stores for sun tan lotion and wide-brimmed hats.

Activity along Newport Parade was an intense shuffling of police investigators, centred around the Crown Casino. They scoured the gardens looking for clues but it would still be hours before they discovered the tunnel. Far below, in those passages of perpetual night, something stirred. It was as far removed from the world above as the dark side of the moon. Yet it was trapped here. Its callings for release would never be heeded – not until the Earth's plates shifted and the wind blew where it had never blown before.

Now there was another companion to join the lamentations; to haunt the passages with a shared yearning, lingering where only the lost dared tread. Ever-drifting in the shadows where he had been shot, an imprint of the one known as Carlson remained. Trapped.

"The Crown Casino has been robbed" echoed from abode

GOOD INTENTIONS

to abode, from the slum tower blocks to the boardrooms of skyscrapers. If the casino management ever thought the publicity over the poker tournament would be over, they were profoundly wrong. The robbery had made headline news. Reports were still vague and lacking in consistency, but most correctly summarised the robbers as a man and a woman, which in itself was exceptional. They had left 'with up to a million pounds' and had fired a gun at a security guard. His condition was described as 'critical, but stable.'

Sarah felt a wave of relief engulf her as she read this on her laptop. Matt was still alive. This did not, however, detract from her guilt. Over

£650,000 was spread out on the bed behind her, but neither of them could surrender to celebration.

John's worries were on getting the money hidden and filtered into the Organisation. The pressing need to discover exactly what happened at the casino and afterwards would have to wait. Some pieces of the puzzle were already fitting together: that the man who followed him in Bath was the same man in the tunnel. But who he was, and how the guard in the casino had known Sarah's name, still needed to be answered.

He looked over at Sarah and frowned. 'When you've finished looking at that computer, can you help me sort out this cash?'

'I thought you've done it already,' she replied. 'So did I.'

She came over to the bed and began marking up the so-called 'poverty pool' – the ten percent of loot that they gave directly to homeless people and national charities. The other eighty percent would go to BlueBridge. Only the remainder did they keep for themselves; usually spent on travel and accommodation costs.

'John,' she began. 'Yes?'

She had thought of telling him a lie about what happened at the casino, saying that Matt had known her name from the last time she was there. Instead, the words clogged her throat before she could get them out. She only just managed to save herself by referring to the news coverage. 'You should take a look at what they're saying about us,' she said, moving a bundle of fifties into a brown envelope.

'In a minute,' he replied.

It actually took him around ten minutes until he removed his latex gloves and went over to the laptop. Sarah had set the browser on the most recent report:

> Police are hunting a 'Bonnie and Clyde' pair of robbers who entered the Crown Casino on Newport Parade at 8:45 this morning, surprising security guards and making off with an undisclosed sum of money. One casino employee was shot and taken by emergency air ambulance to King's Hospital. He is said to be in a critical condition.
>
> It is believed that the person who shot him is the same woman who fired a weapon at a security guard a week ago. In that incident, on 28th May, she was found in

GOOD INTENTIONS

an elevator shaft and was confronted outside the main entrance of the casino. She escaped in a taxi, holding the driver at gunpoint and forcing him to drive at reckless speeds through rush hour traffic.

Detective Marc Davis is conducting the investigation and has described her appearance as 20-25 years old, 5ft 8" with blonde hair. She was wearing a blue sequinned dress and sunglasses on the night of the 28th May. In the robbery this morning she wore a beige workman's suit with the label 'FitNFix'. The male who accompanied her is estimated at 20-30 years old, 6ft, of medium build. Both were wearing masks and carried firearms.

The report ended with details of who to contact should anyone have information, and it appeared there was already a reward of £50,000 for "information leading to an arrest". Accompanying it was a close-up of Sarah in the casino on the 28th May, and a photo-fit of himself. The images sent his heartbeat rocketing.

Police wouldn't take long to see the significance of the 'calling card' that he left behind. It would allow them to connect this casino heist to all the other robberies he had done before. They would realise that it was not a man acting along with a friend or two, but *a man and a woman acting together*. Nevertheless, leaving the coin behind was agreed by both of them from the start. That's how it always was. Despite the risks, it was a necessity – a means of sending a message that they were different, not just ordinary criminals.

Indeed, the coin was a symbol of their mission, for although they had taken hundreds of thousands, and now millions, it was no amount to those they stole from. To those banks and corporations a million was the equivalent of one pound – a sorry object for every act of exploitation and oppression that paved the road of capitalist riches. In this way the coin was what they *owed* these billion-dollar businesses, their debt being re-paid.

He reflected on this, sealing away the guilt and regret he had felt earlier. But lurking in the shadowy recess of his thoughts was a daunting awareness; a realisation that all debts, in the end, had interest.

That was often what made them unpayable.

* * *

The situation had just escalated to a whole new level. The Mafiosa had been stunned by the casino robbery, but when the Theta secondary surveillance team reported that the culprits could only be Mr Stevens and his female accomplice they were positively astounded. There were also hints that there was more to this than a well-planned robbery. The surveillance team had heard references to others. One comment suggested that someone had been shot and killed. All this was relayed to the highest echelons.

The Mafiosa quickly used their influence to get one of

their 'police plants' on the case, a detective by the name of Dawry. He was a seasoned DI who had been under their hook ever since a nasty incident with a prostitute and a kilo of hash. His unhealthy appetite for illicit substances and high living guaranteed his co-operation. They kept him on a tight leash, instructing him to report every finding, every bit of information, and every clue.

Meanwhile, a new high level Mafiosa investigation was underway on Mr Stevens – revitalising his accounts and financial affairs, scrutinising his past in meticulous detail. Within a few hours they found out about the orders for casino chips from his print shop. They also looked in detail at the companies he had chosen to invest in, seeing potentially massive dividends over the horizon. Things started adding up. Facing the possibility that this individual could be a threat to their operations, a neutralisation team was assembled. Then, as if things couldn't get any more complicated, DI Dawry reported back with a disquieting find.

Late in the afternoon, an old man had been walking with his dog along the river. The animal was unleashed and had shot off down the embankment – giving the man no choice but to follow. He had found the dog peering into a broken drain grate, whining and sniffing. Venturing into the dark, he stumbled across the body of a man. Police forensics had arrived soon after, taking fingerprints and collecting DNA. Bullets had been found, along with two cash cases and a silencer-equipped pistol further into the sewer. There was also a plank of wood, tinged rusty-red with blood. Tracing the tunnel back to the casino storm drain, it was realised that this was the getaway route of the robbers.

As soon as the corpse was identified as Tony Carlson, the Mafiosa began to put things together. Somewhere along the line he had found out about Stevens's plan, neglecting to report it, and had chosen to go freelance. That was a capital offence in their organisation. The fact that Carlson was dead did not placate their anger. DI Dawry indicated that the police investigation was taking routes that could become highly dangerous. The silencer-equipped pistol, which was a special model known only to professionals, brought new agencies into the arena – those known as SOCA, Trident, and the NCO. Some Mafiosa tiers were getting tetchy.

Dawry told them something else. The security guard who was shot in the robbery had provided a vital lead. It seemed he had known the female robber, and he told police about having her phone number. Now they were in the process of tracing it, triangulating the location to somewhere in the city. For the quickest positioning, all they had to do was call.

* * *

When John deposited the bags in a secure locker, it was almost night. They had counted the money to £672,000, a total that was still incomprehensible to him. He wanted to celebrate, to go out on the streets and shout in triumph at the sky; to find the nearest homeless person and drop them a wad of cash. But there was still much to do.

Travelling back to the hotel on the Underground, he went over the plans in his head once again: move the cash to the office in Bath, distribute it through WinImplex, BlueBridge and the print shop, then get a flight to Mumbai with Sarah. There they would begin the next phase of the organisation. Before he did all that, there was also the bank: 'The Last Heist'. It was too good to neglect, even given their latest victory. Moreover, two heists on two consecutive days would be an unprecedented announcement of fearlessness; one last ring of glory for their retirement away from robbery. Everything was already in place and the bank was in a completely different part of the city, away from the police hordes who still scoured the casino area for clues. Moreover, the casino heist had been Sarah's brainchild and now he had the opportunity to claim some shared pride with the bank. Even if the loot would be smaller, he felt certain it would go *much* smoother – not to mention safely. There would be no mad street wanderers taking their cash, no assassins crouching in the shadows.

He shivered, thinking about what happened. *Who was that gunman?*

Did Sarah know him?

Someone brushed past him, edging towards the pair of sliding doors.

She has a lot to answer, John thought, listening to the train begin to slow as it stopped at another station.

'*Earl's Court*', the signs and tannoy announcements declared. A handful of people got off and an equal number boarded. For a moment he thought he saw Nail standing amidst the crowd of commuters on the platform, his beard brushed by a subterranean breeze. The crowd soon enveloped him and the train rushed off again, recalling John to thoughts of Sarah.

* * *

Dark clouds gathered all evening as the sticky humidity of the day reached its height. The first jagged rope of lightning was but a prick in the sky, followed by a timorous roll of thunder. From the large window of the budget hotel, Sarah watched the cloud's set aflame by the disappearing sun. Like streaks of blood and swollen bruises of purple, the approaching storm was a painting of her emotions. Its power and beauty reflected her image in the glass. The trembling thunder, growing in strength, echoed her unstable thoughts. There was an irony out there, a subtle reminder of *the mission*, seeing all that energy being channelled to the tallest skyscrapers in bolts of burning blue – a resemblance to the flow of human wealth.

John will understand, she told herself. *The thing with Matt was just a one night stand – a means to an end. If he can justify our robberies in the same way, I can do the same with Matt.*

Perhaps it was not the act of betrayal that so concerned

her, but the way she had achieved nothing from it. The information Matt had given her on their night of passion had turned out to be completely useless. In fact, it was detrimental. Had she not slept with Matt, she would not have tried planning an ambush on the casino elevators. She would never have injured her ankle. It was only through her fling with Matt that he was able to recognise her in the corridor, subsequently getting shot. Thinking along these lines, she realised that there was something else she had done – an unforgivable error. But the more she tried to remember it, the faster it receded. A thunder clap brought her back to the crux of the matter: how she had endangered the whole operation by putting her determination for *the mission* before John. Now she risked losing him as well.

Few statements are as sad as 'what could have been'. It is a sentence that underlines every sentiment of despair. Every could have, would have and should have are great blocks on a road to howling ruin. They are dark clouds covering the light of hope and optimism, far deeper and foreboding than the storm Sarah watched outside. Only love could heal the pain she was feeling; the fear of losing her soul mate, coupled with the guilt of shooting – and almost killing – a man. Part of her knew these feelings of guilt did not only stem from hurting a person, but someone she had feelings for; someone she had shared not just passion with, but also a measure of love. It was not as strong as her relationship with John, but it was there nonetheless. Thinking of Matt, part of her wanted to call King's Hospital and check he was OK. Then that memory of a forgotten mistake almost came to her – something she could still do to avoid total disaster, something so simple and so tantalisingly close, a moth dancing before her eyes.

There was just too much to think about to catch it. The man in the tunnel. The tramp. The feelings of there being someone (or *something*) else down there… touching her, probing her, seeing into the heart of her fears. If questions could be melded from clay, and fired in a kiln of emotion, she would be standing in the centre of a terracotta army.

23

No group or organisation always acts with complete harmony. There would always be disagreements and differences of opinion. For larger groups it is normal to have subgroups and 'cliques', just as society itself is differentiated into separate communities and individuals. The Mafiosa was no different. It was full of egocentric powerbrokers who sought to uphold their will, whether for the greater good of the organisation or not.

No final decision had been reached on the Stevens case. The neutralisation team were still on standby. But one individual – an old man whose power stemmed from his connection to the family – decided to take things into his own hands. He foresaw Stevens and his unknown female companion becoming a big threat. He thought there was a possibility that Carlson had contacted Stevens, revealing the Mafiosa's operations and doing some kind of deal that ended up going bad.

The old man had tremendous local power, with interests in the Crown Casino, amongst other things. All it took was a simple phone call to despatch his personal security 'assistant' to take care of Stevens. The old man had used him before as a lone assassin and had never regretted putting faith in his skills. Tonight he was certain the threat Stevens posed would be over.

The tagging team relayed target 10112's location with no questions asked. Within minutes the man chosen for his neutralisation skills was en-route to the hotel. His codename was 'T-man', derived from his first name, Trev. He rode on a motorbike through the sparse traffic, ignoring the heavy thunder and crashing lightning of the overhead storm. He was at the prime of life and peak of fitness, 25 years old with six years' experience in the SAS. In his waist pocket was a silencer-equipped 9mm pistol of fully-automatic capabilities, with a smaller backup gun concealed on his right ankle. He wore no helmet, just a pair of wraparound shades. Beneath his leather jacket he had an armoured vest, having been told that both targets were armed and had already killed an investigator.

Trev didn't know Tony Carlson personally, but he knew *of* him – a skilled assassin, if rumour was true, although he was never trusted enough to be allocated a place on a neutralisation team. (For good reason, if the stories about him were half accurate.)

Unlike Carlson, Trev didn't enjoy killing. He did the job for two reasons: because he was good at it, and because it paid well. *Like* Carlson, he had plans for early retirement, but not by incurring his employer's wrath. He looked to settling down and living a quiet life – meeting a woman, getting married, having kids. In that respect Trev was the same as a great many other people. He could love, care, show compassion… only his line of work was different. If he had

GOOD INTENTIONS

ever heard the adage that a man should be judged by his work he would have deemed it a falsehood.

As he parked the bike outside the hotel, thick drops of rain began to plummet from the sky. He strode into the entrance and stood under the portico, checking his phone. Two pictures of the targets were shown, with brief biographical details. A man and a woman. Both armed robbers and murderers. Room 112.

* * *

In an operations room in a building off Denmark Hill a group of police electronic surveillance experts had finally confirmed the location of the female robber's mobile phone. The Beta territorial support group (TSG) were convened, briefed on what to expect, and despatched to the suspect's location. They would have it fully surrounded within ten minutes, poised to storm into the premises and authorised to use lethal force as an alternative to capture.

* * *

By the time John got back to the room, the storm had wrapped itself around the hotel. Rain thudded intermittently against the window, its long streaming threads lit up suddenly by concertinaing flakes of electric fire. The ruminating thunder seemed to be loosening the building's very foundations.

He could no longer delay asking Sarah about what happened at the casino, just as she could no longer bear keeping her secret from him. With a suitcase on the bed, she was already packing for their departure in the morning. The plans for the bank heist were spread on a table next to the laptop. He lifted up the first sheet of paper, checking the blueprints, then sat down on a chair.

'The money's safe,' he told her as she continued packing. 'Sarah?' 'Yes?'

'That man at the casino. The one who spoke your name. What was that about?'

She stopped packing and turned to look at him. After meeting his eyes she glanced back at the folded clothes.

Then she told him.

The storm rushed over the horizon, driven back by the pressure that flooded John's mind. His mouth moved, but no words came out. Sarah came over and put her hand on his shoulder, but he pushed it away.

How could she?

In their two years of being together, he had never betrayed her. He had never given in to the temptation of sleeping with another woman.

Why did she?

Lightning tinged the room momentarily white, shaping new contours from shadows. It was nothing to the crackling tension that now surged within him.

How many other men has she slept with?

GOOD INTENTIONS

A sudden wave of anger swept over him, coinciding with a tremendous crash of thunder. Before he knew it, he was on his feet, scattering the papers onto the floor, kicking away the chair.

He looked at her. Pain burned in his eyes. 'You... how... why did you do it?' he stammered.

Tears trickled down her cheeks. 'To get more information, John, to further our aims. For us...'

'You slept with this guy 'for us'? You conceited, faithless bitch!'

A ringing sound filled the room. It emanated from her phone on the bed. He lunged for it, intending to smash the phone against the wall, but answered it instead.

'What the fuck?' he shouted at the silence. 'Is this another of Sarah's boyfriends?'

Quietly, Sarah said something. Her words seemed entirely alien, distorted, as if coming from a great distance.

She remembered what she had forgotten earlier. That phone it had the same number she gave to Matt. If he'd told the police about...

As if to herald this insight, thunder crashed again in the night outside.

* * *

The TSG surrounded the building and showed the receptionist photos of the suspects. Unfortunately, she didn't recognise them. The Commander did not want to wait for her to contact other staff members. He wanted an arrest as soon as possible. The only way to quickly find out the suspects' precise location was to call the woman's phone – that way they could lock onto the signal with remote equipment, using the hotel's blueprints to determine the floor and room. It would also allow the negotiator to speak. The Commander would prefer to surprise them, as with a normal operation, but the Superintendent had specifically instructed him to give the suspects a chance to surrender. It rarely happened that way, but perhaps there they could be convinced fighting or running was pointless. If the woman was on her own she would be told that co-operation would be 'looked on favourably in a court of law'. As it turned out, a man answered the woman's phone. The male suspect, no doubt. Within three seconds the exact location was acquired.

The police negotiator began speaking as the TSG rushed up the stairs.

* * *

Striding along the corridor, Trev withdrew the pistol from his pocket. His shades were bright oval reflections of the lights, and behind them he could see only different tinges of grey. It helped him focus, as well as providing a subtle disguise. He stood outside the targets' room and went over his plan. It was simple and effective: knock politely on the door and then open fire through it, blasting away whoever was on the other side when they went to disengage the lock. Then he would enter, ducking low and sweeping the area with a fatal barrage of gunfire. His ammunition would cut through the hotel's doors and even the walls like hail stones through tissue paper. The pistol had an extended magazine that enabled effective automatic fire, almost giving him the same security that matched his old HK91.

He glanced to both sides of the corridor and confirmed there was still no one around. Then he raised his left hand to the door and knocked. Once, twice, three times.
Had he added a fourth knock, it would have echoed the opening sequence of Beethoven's 5th Symphony – otherwise known as 'Fate'.

24

As John held the phone against his ear Sarah shouted belatedly for him not to answer it. A man's voice resonated on the other end, speaking with a tone of authority.

'This is the police. The building is surrounded.'

Lightning flared against the window, briefly dimming the lights. 'Don't hang up,' the voice said, 'my name is -'

John cut the connection before he could continue. 'Quickly!' he shouted. 'Pack up!'

A ricocheting roll of thunder beat itself in tumbling crescendos from floor to ceiling.

'It's too late,' Sarah cried, 'they'll be here any moment. It was Matt… I gave him my number. God, I'm so sorry…'

John wasn't listening. He opened a window and threw a black object outside, which trailed wires down the glass as it fell. The laptop was no more. 'We can't let them identify us!' he shouted. 'Take anything they can use – papers, passports, whatever, and destroy it. Quickly!'

Sarah rushed to do as he said. Another thunder beat came from nowhere.

Neither of them heard the knocking on the door.

* * *

GOOD INTENTIONS

Standing in the corridor, Trev realised that the storm had blocked the sound of his knocking. He could hear angry voices in the room, confirming that the targets were both there. They seemed to be upset about something, although he couldn't distinguish their words.

Next time he knocked it was harder – not so loud as to frighten them, but strong enough for them to hear above the rumbling noise of thunder.

* * *

This time Sarah heard the three knocks on the door. She ran up to John.

'The police are here,' she said, 'at the door.'

He turned and looked. There was only silence. Then, as if to shatter all uncertainty, there were four loud raps.

He pulled out his gun and she got hers. Yes, *this* would be their last stand, going out like Bonnie and Clyde in a deadly blaze of glory. Somehow they always knew it would happen, a secret acknowledgement that only grew with time.

She turned to look at him. 'I'm sorry'. A solitary tear caressed her left cheek.

All his anger evaporated as he looked into her eyes, his heart bursting with sorrow. 'Me too,' he whispered, kissing her.

As their lips touched in shared warmth and love, a flash of lightning turned them into silhouetted statues, two lovers frozen by fate on the cruel sands of time. In that moment they found something of the eternal, lasting more than a few seconds or minutes, going beyond both time and space. They remembered everything... their walks in the African wilderness; their lovemaking beneath the glittering stars; their shared secrets, hopes and dreams. Everything. Because at that moment it *was* everything – their love was all that mattered, all that existed.

With expectations of impending death, they breathed as One and united their heartbeats in perfect devotion. Before the door crashed open they would raise their guns together, staring into each other's' eyes as the bullets tore into their bodies.

* * *

Trev was beginning to suspect that something was wrong when a noise at the end of the corridor startled him. It was the fire escape door, which he had just come through, being thrown open.

He fell to the floor and took aim at the first man. Others were in the background, dressed in black, wearing helmets with the word 'Police' clearly marked above their visors. All carrying assault rifles. He knew immediately who they were: the TSG – a civilian version of the SAS. There was no way Trev was going to let himself be arrested.

With little thought and no hesitation, he opened fire.

* * *

GOOD INTENTIONS

Pressed together at the window, John and Sarah jolted at the sound of gunfire, expecting to be killed by a volley of bullets. A few moments passed before they realised that the shots were coming from outside the room – out in the corridor. It sounded like two opposing armies had clashed.

'What's happening?' Sarah asked.

Whatever it was, they could not leave via the door. John glanced out the window, trying to ascertain if they could exit from that way, but only darkness greeted him. The window opening was too small to allow him to lean out, although he could see the sides of the hotel shrouded in shadow. He was about to turn back to the door when a flash of lightning illuminated something he had not seen before: a ladder, creeping up the brickwork. But it was too far to reach. Had they booked a room three doors away it would have been a different story.

The gunfire in the corridor paused. In its wake came a jumping wire of bursting light, blinding them with power. A herd of ebony horses seemed to pursue it, drumming hoof beats across the ceiling and down the walls. John looked down at the small ledge beneath the window. It was only about six inches wide. 'Where there's a will,' he whispered, turning to Sarah.

She looked at him, finishing the sentence off for him, '… there's a way. What are you thinking?'

Another burst of gunfire echoed outside in the corridor. Brief this time. Like a death throe.

John stepped away from the window and motioned Sarah to do the same.

Both safely away, he fired at the glass.

* * *

The TSG were not expecting to encounter resistance in the hotel's corridor. They were told the suspects would be in their room. Down on the first floor, the Commander heard the frantic reports coming through on the radio.

'He was in the corridor,' the team's leader told him, 'quick as a bloody cat. I had no choice but to order a retreat. The fire door was too closely covered. He's got an automatic weapon, looks military issue.'

Who are *these people*? the Commander asked himself, and not for the first time. 'Where's the other one – the woman?'

'Didn't see her… but if she's got the same type of weapon, and can handle herself like her partner, we're going to need another entry point. And we'll need to use gas.'

The Commander agreed. He also thought they would need reinforcements. There was no reason to put any more of his men at risk. Within minutes the Alpha team were on their way. The storm prevented India 99 units from being dispatched, but it would soon pass. One way or another, the suspects would either be in custody or confirmed dead. After what had just happened, either option was acceptable.

* * *

GOOD INTENTIONS

Trev was still lying on the floor, covering the fire door, when he heard the shots from within the targets room. At first he thought they were firing through the door, but then he felt a sudden change in temperature. The sound of shattering glass told him that they were trying to make an escape from a window.

There was still no sign of the police at the end of the corridor. Nevertheless, he rolled over to the other wall, slotting into the adjacent recess, and fired through the gap in the fire door. Then he fired through the targets' door, blowing away the lock and smashing it open.

A cool breeze enveloped him as he entered the room, crouching low and darting to the right. His suspicion was correct. The big window had been shattered. Jagged glass lay sprinkled on the carpet. The targets, he realised, could still be here, hiding somewhere to make him think they went out the window, and then shooting him when he turned his back. He needed to be very, *very* careful.

There was a bathroom door that he shot to pieces. He reached into his jacket to jam another clip into his pistol before going further.

No bodies were beyond the threshold, and no spots of blood stained the astringent white tiles. There were still a few hiding places to check – under the bed, in the closet – but they too were deserted. He was very aware of the demolished door behind him, the one through which police would eventually come. The targets had gone out the window –

there was no doubt about that now. That route was the only way to complete his assignment, something he always did no matter what the obstacles, and it would also allow him to evade police.

Framing the night, the window was a portal to a world of storms. The driving rain and shuddering sky were but inches away, leaping and frothing with violent energy. He peered out, his brow lashed by icy shards of water and glanced from side to side, up and down. When a vein of lightning zig-zagged onto the opposite building he almost staggered back onto the glass-strewn floor. Another gigantic flash followed immediately afterwards, plunging the room into permanent darkness.

As the heavy thunder made Trev's jaw quiver, he glimpsed something clasped to the side of the building. With fleeting realization he came to his senses and saw it was not some monster, not some mutated creature, but a person out there in the storm, standing on the window ledge of the room to the left. He gazed in amazement and saw it was not just one person but two. The targets.

* * *

No situation could compare to the one they were currently in. Standing on a tiny ledge half-way up a ten storey building would be terrifying in any circumstance. Add to that being in the middle of a thunderstorm, with deadly enemies at your back, and it reached an entirely new dimension.

GOOD INTENTIONS

When the last flash of light and crescendo of rolling thunder jumped up behind them, Sarah felt herself freeze to the stone. She forced herself on, following John along the ledge that ran between the windows of each room. On the windows themselves she could keep most of her feet on the stone, but between them the ledge halved in width. It became a mere perch on which even a pigeon would find hard to nest. One slight lean backwards and she would fall to her death. If not for the stone blocks that provided cracks to lodge her fingertips, that was undoubtedly what would have happened. She imagined the cracks as an invisible rope hanging above a tight wire – the only thing to keep her stable. The injury in her ankle was hardly noticeable as she shimmied along the building's side.

As John reached the second window ledge he glanced back at Sarah, whose face was set in a rigour of concentration and perseverance. Looking past her, his own expression darkened, for someone was following… a black figure, just like the one in the tunnel.

25

Although the hotel was plunged into darkness by the last lightning strike, an emergency backup generator started a minute later, powering the neon green exit signs, the lifts, and a few lights. Other guests had heard the gun fire, but two ventured out of their rooms. They were young tourists from Holland who had come to see the Poker Tournament. All their belongings were packed into brown and orange suitcases. They had discussed moving to another hotel last night after banging noises had kept them awake. For them, the gunfire had been the last straw. A phone call made by police to all rooms, telling guests to remain where they were, had missed them by seconds.

They now stood in the corridor of the fifth floor, waiting for the lift to arrive. The man noticed something sparkle on the carpet and bent down to pick it up. 'Hmmm,' he said, moving a hand through along the bullet cartridge and then through his short brown hair.

Once the lift doors slid open the couple were pleased to see nobody was inside. 'Push the button, Suzann,' the man said in Dutch.

With a chime the lift began its descent.

* * *

GOOD INTENTIONS

Down in the lobby, the Beta TSG watched as the display above the elevator doors began to change.

5…

'They're coming down!' a man shouted as others took up position.

4…

The Commander quickly considered ordering the elevator mechanism to be shut down, trapping the suspects within, but letting them walk into the lobby seemed a better option.

3…

The hotel blueprints provided all access points, including the ones in the elevator shaft, and he had men waiting there too.

2…

Twenty assault weapons were trained on the elevator doors as the lift reached the lobby.

1…

When the display read '0' and a chiming sound declared the elevator's arrival, every man (and two women) had index fingers on triggers. The big metal doors slowly slid open.

The Commander wasn't sure if his heart was rushing in triumph, expectation, or fear. The couple inside the elevator matched the description of the suspects. It seemed they had finally decided to surrender.

'Armed police! Don't move!'

The man and woman stood unmoving.

'Get on the floor! Drop the bags!'

Then the unbelievable happened. The man went to reach for his pocket.

A shot rang out.

That single blast of sound precipitated the rest of them unleashing a deafening volley. Bullets slammed against the walls, shredding into metal, cutting right through the couple in the lift. They were thrown back by the force, their blood whipping away in waves and coiling threads against the sides of the lift.

'Cease fire!' the Commander called.

Two of the team ran ahead, checking the suspects were dead. Others stepped forward and relaxed when the 'clear' signal was given. The Commander hurried into the lift, trying to avoid the pool of red which was swiftly widening from beneath the corpses. He looked at the blood-streaked, bullet-torn faces and felt his muscles tense. The male's hand was still clasped around a rectangular object. Prizing the fingers away and wiping away a film of blood, the Commander looked at the emblem before him: a Dutch passport. A deep, vibrating note of thunder beat itself into tremulous silence. In the wake of the rumbling his shouted curse was barely audible.

* * *

Clamped to the side of the building, Trev felt more vulnerable than ever before. He could not use his weapon, nor could he retreat into the hotel. He was trapped between

GOOD INTENTIONS

two great unconquerable forces: the crashing storm and the approaching police. When he heard the faint sound of gunfire he assumed it was them storming onto the corridor.

The targets heard it too. Pausing barely ten metres away, the woman glanced back and met his eyes. He had removed his shades since stepping outside. *Doesn't look like a killer,* he thought, *or even a robber.*

But then, who does? The worst kind of wolves were those who blended with the lambs. The most fearful monsters hid behind pleasant- looking exteriors. Oppressors survived long if they could portray themselves as protectors. The list went on, and for each example Trev realised one long-quoted adage: *never to judge a book by its cover.*

* * *

They had to keep moving no matter what.

The storm had reached its peak and the pursuer behind was drawing closer. John was moving along the glass of the third window when he found himself looking at a pale face. It was a boy, who looked to be only around seven years old. He was fearless, standing there behind the glass, gazing at John as if he was spider man. The flashing sky made strange patterns in his wide eyes, like miniature projections of another reality.

John shuffled on. The ladder was only a few feet away now. All he had to do was stretch out, grip one of the rungs, then swing himself over.

Going down was a shortcut to a prison cell; he had seen the police vehicles around the hotel a long time ago. The only way was up.

As Sarah followed John she too saw the little boy, and found herself smiling.

He waved at her.

Aware of the man pursuing them, she tried to tell the child to get away. He just stared. She had no choice but to keep going, reaching the ladder a minute after John, who was climbing up. Her ankle screamed with pain as she followed. Only now did shuffling along the ledge seem easy. Each metal rung of the ladder was cold and slippery, like trying to grasp an uncoiling snake. It also wobbled precariously, sending out protesting creaks and groans. It was old, eaten away by flaking rust, and it streaked her wet palms with a gritty red. Some of the flakes impaled her skin, briefly dulling the pain in her ankle. Lightning and thunder was still being unleashed from the unforgiving sky, but at least the rain was relenting. The flashes and crashes were slowly becoming further apart. But although the storm was receding, another threat was rapidly approaching. After taking only five steps up, Sarah felt the ladder shudder violently.

The unknown pursuer had climbed on.

Glancing back, she could see his eyes were still fixed on her. Their depths spoke of one thing only, and it was something that could never be bartered with, reasoned with, or tricked.

GOOD INTENTIONS

Death.

John had finally reached the top of the building. He wiped a hand across his rain-soaked brow and looked down at Sarah. The figure behind her was closing fast.

'You're almost there,' he shouted to her, 'a few more steps and you'll be at the top.'

But she wasn't going to make it. The man was barely a few inches behind her.

John lifted his voice above a growl of thunder. 'Whoever you are, go back!'

Echoes spiralled down into the flashing streets below. 'This is your last chance!'

The man paused. He looked up, and John was surprised to hear his voice. 'Okay!'

Sarah reached the ledge of the roof a minute later. He grasped her hand and pulled her over. There was no sign of the unknown pursuer. Glancing around, John began to consider the next problem: they had nowhere else to go.

26

Trev realised that he had a problem. The male target had reached the top of the ladder and had told him to go no further. If he wanted to, he could have reached up and grabbed the woman's ankle. But what would that accomplish? The male target would soon be able to get a clear shot of him, and no amount of skill or training could reverse their situations. The target was above, with both hands free, and he was below, clinging to a ladder. Trev might have been able to shoot with one hand, but he would be at a severe disadvantage. So he decided to make the target think he was giving up.

The only chance he had was to get off the ladder and find another way to the top. There was one floor left, and the same sort of ledge ran along the side of the building, connecting one window to another.

Trev gripped the side of the ladder. He withdrew his weapon and fired into the closest window, inadvertently timing this with a rumble of thunder. The window shattered completely and the glass was blown inward by the driving rain. In one movement he leapt off the ladder, spring-boarding off the ledge and into the unknown darkness beyond. Few would have landed on two feet after completing such a manoeuvre, but Trev's training served him well. Not bothering if the room was occupied or not, he headed straight to the door,

GOOD INTENTIONS

his shoes trailing a glittering path of broken glass along the carpet.

In the corridor, he swept his gun in both directions, seeking out any sign of movement. As he side-stepped towards the fire door at the end, he wasn't sure what to expect. He just hoped the TSG were concentrated on the fifth floor.

Pausing in front of the heavy metal door, he listened. Only the murmurings of the storm resonated beyond. He pushed down on the bar which opened the door, slowly and gently, and leant back against the wall to avoid any blast of gunfire. Satisfied that no one was waiting behind it, he eased the door open a crack.

This floor, it seemed, was deserted. For now. The parroting bleeps and chattering of radios from the floors below told him it wouldn't stay that way for long.

* * *

On the roof of the hotel John and Sarah re-considered their options. Looking over the sides of the building, they could clearly see the flashing blue lights of an extensive police cordon.

'How are we going to get out of this one, John?'

He was stumped. The roof was flat, spotted with air conditioning vents as well as a raised doorway marked 'Fire Escape'. He briefly thought of going down that way, but realised police would have it covered. The only other structure on the roof was what looked like a shed, no bigger than the average gardening tool shed or paint store.

There were buildings close to the hotel on three sides. Two were much taller, but one was approximately the same height, and it had a flat roof. Sarah could see what John was thinking, but she knew that jumping across was an impossibility. The gap was just too great – it would be a 50/50 shot even for John, who didn't have an injured ankle.

A sudden gust of wind leapt up from the embers of a distant lightning flash, lifting up the corrugated metal coverings of the shed and slamming them back down. She had an idea.

* * *

The Commander could not accept what had just taken place. The two bloody corpses his men had shot to pieces in the lift were *not* the suspects. They were still up there somewhere in the hotel. Calls to Room 112 remained unanswered, and every other guest co-operated in staying in their rooms. But there was one who had some very interesting information – a father who claimed his son saw three people creep outside their window, three doors down from Room 112.

It could only be the suspects. *But three?* The commander had not counted on there being more than two. It was a disturbing thought.

Luckily, reinforcements had arrived. He only had to give the order and both Beta and Alpha teams would storm the

GOOD INTENTIONS

hotel, coming in through exits and lift shafts, sweeping every floor from bottom to top. The lobby was a flurry of activity as men from various agencies began to arrive. He had got here first, and had been charged with apprehending the suspects, and he'd be damned if anyone had the audacity to take over. Twice he had to remind a DCI in the Flying Squad that his was the only authority with the necessary firepower to deal with the situation. Not even the death of two tourists could change that.

Outside, the media was pressing for information. A cordon had been set up around both the hotel and the immediate area, but somehow press reports always managed to filter through. The situation needed to be dissolved soon.

'Are your units ready?' he asked the Alpha team leader.
'Yes, Sir, standing by.'
'We believe the suspects are outside the hotel. Beta have secured the building's perimeter, so they can't get away.'
'Did you say *outside*, Commander?'
He was fed up with people questioning him. 'Yes, outside the hotel! Or rather, *on* it. They were seen creeping past a guest's window on the fifth floor. And there's three of them.'
Groaning thunder briefly shook the lobby.
'In this weather, Sir? They've got to be pretty desperate.'
'And deadly,' the Commander added, 'armed with fully automatic weapons. My bet is they've gone to the roof, or are holed up in some room. Any word on India 99?'
'Negative, Sir,' the man replied, 'they are still waiting for

the storm to pass. Maybe we should wait until it clears – it can't be much longer.'

The Commander told him about the two dead tourists. 'We can't risk any more unnecessary casualties, and I don't want more of these Press vultures gathering. If your units are in place, give them the go ahead.'

The Alpha team leader nodded grimly. 'Very well.'

* * *

Looking at the shed, Sarah told John about her idea. It had come to her like one of the storm's flashes: use the corrugated metal sheets on the roof of the shed to provide a bridge to the other building. 'We can lay one on top of the other,' she said.

'Will it be strong enough though?' John asked. 'There's only one way to find out. Come on!'

The door to the shed was unlocked, and they went inside, trying to see through the cloak of darkness. Due to the power cut, the light switch did not work. John went back outside and clambered onto the roof. He began trying to loosen the corrugated metal, using the handle of his gun as a makeshift hammer. The harsh rap and scratch of opposing metals briefly drowned out the drumming rain. Doing damage to the gun was the least of his worries.

'It's no use!' he cried, 'it will take hours like this!'

The receding storm declared its presence in a series of distant flashes across the city. They danced across the horizon,

GOOD INTENTIONS

illuminating the thick mammatus cloud that hovered above. The formations were the fattened scales on a beast of black iron – an ultimatum of endings, a wasteland of chaos.

Something was happening to the city. Light was blooming on the other buildings. A giant sign with the hotel's name clicked on at one side of the roof, and within the shed a bulb lit up. Sarah rushed back in. She could now see a large work table, with a fire hose and various carpentry tools housed in a glass cabinet. Looking up at the underside of the roof, she could also see where the metal was screwed onto beams of wood. Some of the screws had already broken free along the edges. It was not that, however, which interested her.

Laying crossways along the floor and stacked neatly were six beams of wood, about ten feet long. She called John.

'We'll use these as the bridge,' she told him triumphantly. He almost allowed himself to smile.

Together they manoeuvred one of the beams out the shed, carrying it to the other side of the building. Sarah's ankle burned fiercely with each step, but she could not surrender to the pain.

'All right,' John said, 'we're going to need all our strength.'

Placing the wood along the edge of the roof, they crouched at one end of the beam and began swinging the other end out towards the other building. The weight strained at their wrists as the beam slowly rotated, like the arc of a great wobbling pendulum. And it wasn't going to hold. John could already feel their side lifting upwards as the other side was pulled relentlessly down. 'Stand on it, Sarah!' he cried, sweat breaking along his brow. She quickly did so, using her weight to snap back the wedge of air that had formed between wood and stone.

As John heaved against her stabilising weight, slowly rotating the beam within a metre of the other building, it began to bend. Hands turning purple, etched with splinters, his muscles trembled with the strain. He lent out over the building and pushed on the beam closer to its centre. You bastard! he thought, blinking away a beck of sweat.

Because the other roof was slightly lower, the beam was able to bend and still meet the other side. Moreover, there was about a foot to spare. John's doubts had proven ungrounded. Now all they had to do was cross.

Sarah let the beam tilt into its full angle. At one stage it had seemed to be lifting *her* off the building's ledge, and she was pleased to be getting down again.

'You alright?' John asked.

'Yeah… or I will be when we get across.'

John tested his weight on the beam and grimaced as it bent with his first step. 'We need another one,' he said. 'But I think it should take your weight.' He knew there was little time left.

'No,' Sarah said, 'I'm not crossing without you.'

Before he could argue further, a noise sprang up behind them.

* * *

GOOD INTENTIONS

Trev was edging carefully up the staircase, keeping his body close to the wall, when he heard a thundering sound. At first he thought that's what it was, but as he listened it began to separate into different tones – the unmistakable echoes of many boots ascending steps. He quickly turned and raced up to the fire door. There was no time to be cautious – he took it like a bullet, exploding into the night air.

* * *

John and Sarah turned around and looked in the direction of the noise, towards the fire exit.

No-one.

'Let's go,' John said, 'I'll follow afterwards.' 'But -'

'Go!'

Carefully she placed both feet onto the wood, feeling it move slightly and then stabilise. It was only about a foot in width, which made it necessary to walk like a tightrope acrobat. Distant lightning crackled across the sky, curving down from brooding clouds. Remembering a piece of advice given to climbers (*'never look down'*), she kept her eyes on the edge of the other building. Not even the insidious bending of the wood beneath her feet could force her to shift focus.

To her surprise, she found herself nearing the other side quicker than she thought. The make-shift bridge had only bent slightly under her weight, and it didn't move much at all. The distant thunder no longer seemed menacing. She had done it!

Feet firmly planted on stone, she looked back at John. 'Come on!' she cried, 'it should take your weight!'

He didn't think it would. He weighed around 80kg and if it could bend with Sarah's weight (who weighed about 40kg), it would surely snap with his.

But he was going to try. There was a strong feeling that someone was close by, watching and ready to pounce; a feeling that could not be ignored. Indeed, he felt as if some monster was breathing down his neck, exhaling a meconium wrath. Above, the thinning storm clouds scudded over a sickle of silver light – the moon, their confederate – which sketched the wooden bridge before him.

After only one step he wanted to go back. There would be at least another twelve if he kept going. Although not a superstitious person, the thought of taking thirteen steps between two ten-storey buildings only added to his fear.

* * *

Trev hid behind the tool shed, waiting for the male target to cross the plank of wood. He didn't want to shoot him. Not yet. He needed to cross as well, and if the target fell it might destabilise the plank enough to make it fall. There was also the female target to consider, who was standing on the roof of the other building. Far better to shoot them as soon as they were both across. They would never even see it coming.

GOOD INTENTIONS

The distance was well within his weapon's range.

Part of him admired the ingenuity of the targets, but he did not allow himself to start feeling any warmth towards them. *Cold, merciless killers,* he thought, without any sense of irony. *And the male is taking his sweet time... slower than a baby ballerina, or a —*

His thoughts were interrupted by a subtle clicking coming from the fire door opposite him. He didn't have to see the miniature mirror peeping through the gap to know it was the TSG.

He ran around to the other side of the shed. From his jacket he withdrew an object the size of a ping-pong ball. It was an explosive device – small but powerful – used in the same way as a standard grenade. As the mirror took in a little more of the rooftop scenery, Trev sent the ball rolling towards the door. He timed it perfectly.

The first wave of men rushed onto the roof a second later, sweeping their rifles from right to left. A sphere of flame engulfed them as the device exploded. It killed them instantly, blasting the fire door off its hinges in a shattering shockwave.

Trev waited a few seconds before peering around the shed, his gun trained on the thick smoke. No shapes moved, no guns raged.

He trusted that the explosion had given him enough time to complete his assignment and make good his escape.

* * *

John was half-way across the bridge when he heard the explosion. It jolted the beam, making the wood quiver like the string of a harp. That was enough to make him lose his balance. Wheeling his arms, tilting forward, he found himself falling…

'No!!' Sarah shouted.

She had seen the men in black step onto the roof of the hotel, and the subsequent explosion had been even more shocking. But all this was nothing compared to the sight of John falling to his death.

Her world reeled and span. A roulette wheel… a horizon of heartless storms… a pool of flaming oil… all these images inexplicably flashed through her consciousness. She blinked.

She blinked again.

Suddenly hope sprang phoenix-like from the ashes of her despair.

On the beam of wood, lying flat, beautifully alive, was John!

Her joy was so great that she didn't notice the figure standing on the roof of the hotel until the last moment. She didn't even hear the pop of sound that emanated from the gaping mouth of his gun, the bullet flashing through the night like a hungry barracuda.

But she felt it hit her.

27

When John fell he managed to lean forward, crashing face-first onto the beam. It bent and moaned, seeming for a moment to split under his weight. Then it bounced up a little, making him grasp it with his hands. This time the sound of splitting timber was all too clear.

Unbelievably, it still held. He was about to reassure Sarah that he was all right when he saw the look on her face: one of utter shock and dreadful anticipation. He knew without turning that the man – the one who had pursued them along the window ledge – was standing on the roof of the hotel. He went to reach for his gun... and then realized he had dropped it when he fell.

Drawing his breath in, shouting at the top of his voice, as if to implore God to intervene, he screamed. '*ST-*'

'*OP!*'

The voice startled Trev. It echoed eerily in the space between the two buildings, seeming to come from the sky itself. He stood a few metres from the edge of the building, unable to see the lower end of the wooden plank, totally focused on the female target. His finger was already on the trigger, but his aim shifted a little by the mysterious call to 'Stop.'

Nevertheless, the female target crumpled onto the roof of

the opposite building – either dead or mortally wounded. He realised that the voice might have come from a police helicopter, which had managed to hover in stealth mode directly above him, but that wasn't the case. Nor was there anyone behind him.

He looked at the smoke surrounding the fire door, which veiled whatever forces had gathered beyond. They would return, he knew. Very soon.

Trev guessed that the male target had fallen in the explosion – either that or he had managed to reach the other building. In either case, Trev needed to cross their bridge.

* * *

Sarah withdrew her gun, trying to ignore the waves of pain that emanated from her core. She didn't understand what happened, other than that the man had shot her. Lying on the cold stone roof, she brought her gun up and aimed at where he had been standing. John was still on the beam of wood, shuffling towards her. With each movement the beam groaned and bumped. She wanted to help him, but she knew that would lead to them both getting shot.

The man had shifted from his last position. He could now see John. His wicked-looking gun was being angled down. Focusing on him, Sarah clenched her jaws, thinking not of the recoil that would slam into her injured body but of the accuracy of her aim.

GOOD INTENTIONS

Three times the gun coughed. Three times the blasts resounded between the two buildings. They spiralled down to the alley below like a rearguard of the storm's thunder.

The first bullet hit Trev's right shoulder. The second missed him. The third, had it been an inch to the left, would have dropped him dead. As it was, the impact pulverised his ear. He went to return fire but found the act of rising the gun impossible. A tendon snapped in his shoulder joint. Facing the prospect of more bullets, he ducked and ran for cover.

By the shed again, he removed his jacket and ripped away his shirt- sleeves. He did his best tying make-shift bandages around his shoulder and ear, stemming the flow of warm blood that trickled down his neck and arm. Then he saw movement. Black shapes were streaming ant-like from the blown-away fire door, apparently not seeing him crouching beside the shed. They were moving fast, right towards him.

He gripped the gun in his left arm, targeting the nearest man, and fired.

Popopop.

The TSG reacted immediately. They shot randomly in all directions, most of their firepower unnervingly focused on his position. Dodging bullets, feeling one or two slam into the back of his Kevlar vest, he took new cover behind one of the air conditioning vents.

* * *

As John crawled across the splitting beam, he heard the police storm onto the hotel's roof, guns stamping out their authority. He just hoped the unknown man would keep them busy. On the other building, Sarah was doing her best to stabilise the beam. He could now reach out and touch her hand. The coldness in it frightened him.

After pulling himself onto the other building he kicked away the beam and watched it twist and turn like a broken sycamore seed into the alley below. He was careful not to stand up, which would immediately betray his position to the police and make an easier target for the unknown man – if he was still alive.

Sarah was lying still. He could see blood stains on her clothes. Something clogged his throat as she raised her head and smiled at him. 'You've been shot,' he stammered.

'It's OK,' she replied, almost whispering.

He had to get her out of here. Fast.

He was not sure what sort of building they were on, but he could see a small swimming pool and a garden. The flowers and potted trees were colourless here, and he suspected the same would be true even if the sun was shining. How could there be beauty when the love of his life lay bleeding?

There was a door on the other side of the pool, similar to the fire exit on the hotel's roof. 'Keep low and follow me,' he told Sarah, helping her up. 'Can you walk?'

'Yes,' she said, 'as long as you're helping me.'

A new sound was in the air – the chopping blades of a

GOOD INTENTIONS

helicopter. Ignoring the chaos erupting around them, they crept along the side of the pool, stopping intermittently to rest and use the small trees as cover. They reached the door just as a bright oval of artificial light reflected from the rippling water.

* * *

Trev crouched behind the air conditioning vent as bullets whipped into the plastic and ricocheted off stone. The silencer was useless given that they already knew his position, so he removed it in order to take better aim. Although he could use the gun with his left hand, it wasn't half as effective as his right. He found himself firing without bothering to pick a target, allowing him to keep cover and not expose himself.

When the helicopter arrived he knew the odds against him were colossal. It wisely stayed out of his range, but all it took was one bullet from a snipers' rifle and he'd be dead. That was an ending he welcomed. Like his targets, he would rather die than be captured by police. It was just a shame he had not killed them. That way he could leave the Earth having served his duty and completed his assignments, with no exceptions whatsoever.

Sitting there, he wondered if that really mattered. He would never marry, never have children, and never fulfil the dreams he still had left. It was over. In a flash of understanding, he knew what to do.

He removed his Kevlar vest, feeling the air touch his bare chest and back. He breathed it in, tasting the freshness that the passing storm had left behind. With a deep sorrow that only the courageous could know, he leapt up from his hiding place, raising both his hands to the sky and crying out a wordless sound of pain and freedom. The gun was still in his left hand.

Within seconds he fell, dead.

Far in the distance, the groaning storm declared itself in a series of rumbling lamentations. All the humidity had been cleared, but up on the roof all they could smell was smoke, cordite, and blood. Three more men were down. The Commander would have a lot of questions to answer. He had ordered the Alpha team leader to proceed from the fire exit after the explosion, despite his protest that they should wait for the helicopter.

There were two innocent foreign nationals shot dead in the lobby. That made a total of eight fatalities. On top of all this, the two Crown Casino suspects had still not been located. It would take another hour to do a complete sweep of every room in the hotel, which opened the door to a higher body count – if they put up as much resistance as the man on the roof, that was.

The Commander came up to see the carnage. He went over to see the unidentified gun-man, who lay spread-eagled behind an air conditioning duct, his body half-naked and covered with bullet wounds.

GOOD INTENTIONS

The helicopter still hovered above, using its infrared cameras to scan the hotel. Another was on the way.

On the streets below, countless flashing vehicles had gathered; ambulances, fire engines, police vans, all competing for priority. Despite the cordon, or probably because of it, the media were pressing in, demanding information. Soon he would have to relate a formal statement about what happened. The Dutch embassy would need to be contacted. But for now these concerns faded against the need to apprehend the two suspects. One way or another, he would have them arrested or confirmed dead within an hour.

* * *

John removed his coat and wrapped it round Sarah. A rose of blood had spread from her stomach area, forming petals right to her waist. Her breathing was shallow and weak. They were standing in a stairway similar to the one in the hotel, except in this one there were potted plants placed on each landing. When John opened one of the doors he saw a richly-carpeted corridor with apartment numbers on each side.

They continued walking down the stairs until they reached the ground floor. All the time he supported Sarah, with her arm draped behind his neck. Occasionally she made sharp intakes of breath – a painful but reassuring reminder that she was still fighting for life.

A buzz of voices echoed behind the last door. John had

hoped there would be a clear run to the outside, allowing them to get away practically unseen, but finding another way out now would be futile. With Sarah critically wounded, speed was essential.

He opened the door a crack and found himself peering into a noisy crowd. Immediately a twenty-ish man in a blue shirt turned around, his eyes wide.

'Bloody hell, didn't see you there, mate!'

At this remark three others turned around to face them. Holding Sarah, John came out of the door, trying to act normal.

'You both look drunker than we are,' Blue Shirt laughed.

The others continued talking amongst themselves, apparently not thinking anything was unusual.

'Yeah,' John said casually, 'we've just had a real dive.' He looked around, trying to see who else was standing in the lobby.

Blue Shirt was still interested in talking, and began mentioning the results of a football game, speaking in a slurred, almost comical monologue.

Satisfied that there were no police, John excused himself and carried Sarah across the lobby to a seating area. There were a few glances in their direction as they manoeuvred through the crowd, along with a few hushed murmurings about 'weird strangers', which John thought was unavoidable.

Leaving Sarah slumped on a red sofa, he went to one of the large windows, which gave an expansive view of the street. The sporadic blue-red lights of police vehicles swept through the night, skimming a throng of people who had gathered around a barrier. Looking to the right, he saw the black uniform of a police officer, who seemed to be standing sentry. At the end of the street was a row of police vehicles, blocking traffic.

'Madness, ain't it?' a middle-aged man said, appearing by John's side. He was holding a half-full glass of frothy liquid.

'Yeah,' John said, trying not to betray his anxiety. 'What's going on?' The man tilted a little to the side. 'I've been trying to find out for the last twenty hours,' he slurred, 'all I know is something's happening in the Plaza Hotel, right by. I think it's a bomb!'

'Are they letting people leave the area?'

The man shook his head slowly and shrugged. 'Told us stay… and not 'grout. But that ain't stopped them reporters.' He gestured to the group of people outside, burped, then turned and pointed to the crowd in the lobby. 'We were going out… to a birthday party, you know, and then decided to have it right here! They stopped us from leaving. The youngsters ain't happy… they want loud music, a bar, more women… they've been…'

It was possible to become inebriated simply by inhaling the man's breath. He suddenly tilted an inch forward and looked at Sarah. 'She yours?'

John felt his fists clench. 'Yes. What were you saying about the others here?'

'Oh, you're a lucky guy, yes you are, hahaha!'

Now the man was really getting on John's nerves. He made

one final attempt at conversation, repeating his previous question.

All the man said in reply was a senseless song. 'They wanna get out, o they wanna get out! Let us out, o they won't let us out!'

To John's relief, he veered away and fell into a dense group of people whilst singing his song. 'Yes,' someone said, pushing him away, 'now get a grip on yerself, Unc's… we're going out when the police bug off. It can't be much longer.'
Another cried out. 'I say we go out right now!
We've waited long enough!'

This comment seemed to inflame the conversation in other groups, and John could hear them debating on whether to leave or not. The situation, he realised, could provide an opportunity. He went over to Sarah.

She was still slumped on the sofa, her head tilted backwards. 'Sarah! Don't you go asleep on me now!' He shook her lightly until she opened her eyes.

'John… where are we?'

'In the lobby of the other building. We're getting out of here. I need you to stay awake, OK?'

'Alright,' she whispered, reaching up to touch his cheek.

He kissed her gently, meeting the love that swam in her eyes. Yet the coldness in her lips chilled him more than any wedge of ice. The grains of Time's hour glass were slipping through a pinched apex of ruin; he could feel the seconds fall as Sarah drifted further away. He wanted to grasp them,

GOOD INTENTIONS

squeeze them, stop them from passing.

Standing up, driven by a ruthless determination, he raised his voice above the crowd. 'You guys want to go to a party?!'

They all looked in his direction. There was a uniform response of nods and 'yeahs'.

'We want to leave too!' he shouted, 'if we go out together, they can't stop us!'

'Yeah, he's right!' a young man replied.

'That's what I've been trying to tell you,' another chipped in. 'Let's go already!' a girl shouted.

Soon the crowd of party-goers were pressing at the door of the lobby. John bent over Sarah, relieved to see her eyes had not shut. She was gazing off to a far-away place, but then looked at him and made a faint smile. 'We've got to go now,' he said, reaching for her hand. Helping her up and supporting her with his arm, he weaved a way into the centre of the crowd, ignoring a spatter of questions that flew in his direction. The door was already open, and at least half a dozen people were streaming outside.

But someone was blocking the way out: the police officer. He was commanding the party-goers to go back inside, making threats of arrest. Here was the penultimate test of rebellion: the moment when the masses confronted the figures of authority. In most situations they wavered, thinking there would be no way to win or to overcome those who had always seemed stronger.

For a moment the crowd seemed to pause in suspended

animation, walking a ridge between obedience and defiance. Then someone shouted something. John didn't hear exactly what it was, but it drove the crowd forward. The ones in the front could not resist the flow. They ignored the police officer and formed together, yelling what they thought of the law. One young woman was laughing and singing 'No one can stop me from dancing!' which the rest soon took up.

Within seconds he was going to walk straight past the police officer. He turned to Sarah. 'Try to smile and pretend you're having a good time'. Holding her closer, he did the same – laughing as if the very air was nitrous oxide.

The vexed police officer bent over his radio, scowling. He had given up his attempt at blocking them.

Still keeping with the party-goers, they headed up the road towards the line of police vehicles. Beyond was the traffic of another street – the only route to freedom. If they didn't get past, John wasn't sure what to do. He could get Sarah an ambulance, but that would lead to imprisonment for both of them. It was a scenario which they had always agreed to avoid, opting for death before capture, but now that Sarah's life was threatened he thought that *anything* was preferable to losing her completely.

A few police officers were standing by the cars, holding weapons. Their fluorescent jackets grinned vainly beneath the orange glare of street lights.

The party-goers kept going, continuing to sing their song about dancing. John tried to keep within their centre.

GOOD INTENTIONS

He never saw what happened next. Someone nudged him, and there was a banging sound, like a car door being slammed. The young people around were walking much faster, changing direction. Within seconds he found himself sliding past a parked police car, and Sarah lost her grip on his shoulder. He grabbed her before she fell, but by then the party-goers had sprinted ahead. To his left and right were the police.

'Sir!' one of them called.

He couldn't run – not without Sarah.

28

The concrete was covered in a wet sheen that could have been a replica of the world above. One thing was for certain: it could offer no escape.

Police surrounded them. The chase was over. Sarah was still slumped over John's shoulders, appearing not to know what was happening. One of the policemen stepped forward and reached behind his back.'

John didn't trust himself to speak.

'Miss?' the policeman said. 'Are you all right? Do you know who you're with?'

Hopes of getting away plummeted with each second of Sarah's silence. *Say something*, John silently urged her. *Please!*

'Miss!'

A slurred voice rose from her silence. 'Yeah... I've drunk too much.

He's my fiance.'

'All right,' the policeman frowned. An urgent chatter abruptly came from the radio behind his jacket, prompting him to pause. There were sounds of smashing glass from the Plaza Hotel.

Come on, John thought, *get it over with.*

'All right,' the policeman repeated, looking at John. 'Take her home. Next time, listen when you're told to stay in a building. And don't drink so much.'

John nodded, still unable to speak. He staggered away, holding on to Sarah, trying to quieten his pounding heart. The noise of the city streets soon enveloped the chattering of police radios. Never in all his life had traffic seemed so comforting.

He kept walking until the line of police vehicles disappeared around the edge of a clothing store. Then he stood at the curb, frantically waving down every taxi that passed. It didn't take long before one arrived. As he helped Sarah get in, he asked if she was okay.

'Yes,' she replied, 'and I've got money to pay the driver in my back pocket.'

Her voice was stronger, her eyes clearer, but he didn't fool himself that she was getting better.

'Where to, fella?' the taxi driver asked.

John gave the name and address of the Nuacorn Clinic. 'Wait,' Sarah whispered, 'we can't go there, it's too risky…' 'You need help,' he protested. 'Where else can we go?'

What she said next was barely audible, and yet John would have been able to understand it simply by watching the movement of her lips. He couldn't deny the reason behind her choice, even if it was somewhere he dreaded returning to. As he told the taxi driver their new destination, he prepared himself – for the second time – to face the prospect of arrest.

* * *

The search had gone quicker than expected. There were only a few rooms remaining. Other parts of the hotel – from the kitchens to the laundry shafts – had been cleared, and the Commander concentrated his men in searching the last rooms, praying the suspects would be hiding there. But if they weren't...

Just *thinking* about this scenario gave him a migraine. Already the hotel's guests were clamouring to be allowed out. If it came to that, he'd have to organise a way to escort them from the hotel, room by room, and then sweep the hotel again.

The words he most dreaded came over the radio: 'All rooms are clear.'

Hell, he would tear down the walls if he had to. The suspects were here *somewhere*.

Hours later, word of the gun fight at the Plaza Hotel had been leaked to every major Press outlet, and the Dutch were launching their own investigation into the death of the two tourists. Zapped by countless caffeine pills, the TSG Commander had just finished a telephone conversation with 'the top man'.

It had to be the worst night of his life. All responsibility for the casualties had fallen solely on him, along with letting the two suspects get away. Everyone wanted his head. There were threats of prosecution for police misconduct and unlawful killing flying around like poisoned darts.

'Oh well', he sighed, 'in a week I'll be at the villa in

GOOD INTENTIONS

Marbella, falling into bed with one of the locals.'

*　*　*

The flat was a pillar of hope in a landscape of ruin. Its random lights shone out rectangular, standing like a rocket on a necrotic horizon. Glancing towards the tops of skyscrapers, John saw the bulbous shapes of cumulonimbus clouds, their bases lit up by the city. Another storm was approaching.

Somewhere along the ride in the taxi, Sarah had passed out. She was still breathing shallowly, but it was even weaker than before. John had to carry her out, telling the taxi driver that she had drunk too much. He found money in her back pocket and paid the fare.

Red-shaded street lights cast sombre orbs of light on the pavement as he carried her to the front door of the flat. He pressed Howie's intercom number and waited.

He pressed it again.

'Bo,' a croaky voice finally issued from the speaker. 'Howie, it's John. Sarah's with me.'

'Ug.'

The door clicked open and he climbed the stairs, bending under Sarah's weight.

Howie was standing on the fourth landing, frowning down at them. He wore nothing but a pair of shorts and socks. 'What the –' he halted mid-sentence, looking at Sarah. 'What happened?'

'She's been shot,' John said breathlessly.

No further questions were asked. Howie led the way into the flat, swiping away a few magazines from the sofa so that John could lay Sarah down. He bent over her, wrapping his fingers around her wrist and checking her breath. Then he vanished into a doorway. There was talking, a few muttered curses, and then a shout.

'Don't start now, woman!'

'Don't you dare shout at me!' the unmistakable voice of Harriett replied.

The door flew open and Harriett came rocketing out, wearing a bright-red night dress that blended with her wild hair. She ignored John and went over to Sarah, doing the same procedure as Howie. 'Get water, Bo!' she shouted.

'You!' she snapped, looking at John, 'get towels and tissue.'

He went towards the kitchen area. 'Not there, idiot! In the bathroom! It's in the bedroom, over *there!*'

When he returned with what she wanted, Howie had placed a bowl of warm water on the table. Harriett began delicately removing Sarah's coat, telling Howie to fetch some scissors so she could cut away the other clothes. Once this was done, she used the towels and water to dab Sarah's wound.

'Not good,' she muttered, 'the bullet's still in her. I can clean the wound up, but she needs surgery.'

Looking up at Howie with worried eyes, Harriett ordered him to get her triage kit.

GOOD INTENTIONS

For over an hour she worked on Sarah, cleaning the wound and applying disinfectant. She also put bandages to Sarah's hands and arm, which had become cut during the escape from the hotel room. She did the same for John, ignoring his protests that the injuries didn't hurt. All the time he sat there helpless, unable to provide any assistance or ways to prevent Sarah from slipping closer to death. Eventually Howie broke his vigil by tapping him on the shoulder.

'We need a word.'

They walked out the flat, and Howie led him to the flight of stairs. His gaze was hard and cold. 'Now tell me what happened. Don't leave a single thing out. I'll know if you do.'

John took a deep breath and began relating the events of the last 24 hours: their robbery of the casino, the meeting with the unknown assassin in the tunnel, then their hazardous escape from the hotel. Throughout it all Howie was silent, raising his eyes a few times in surprise, then reverting to the same penetrating stare.

'All right. I've heard enough. You've broken your word by getting Sarah involved, and because of it *this* has happened.' His eyes were rimmed with anger. 'You could have done it on your own, damn you!'

Fists clenched, elbows bent, he presented a daunting sight. 'She wouldn't listen,' John said, 'I tried to tell her...'

Quick as a striking cobra, Howie grabbed him by the collar. 'What's wrong with you?! You're a man, aint ya? You're telling me Sarah *forced* you into making her go? Bullshit!'

For a moment John was certain Howie was going to hit him. Maybe even kill. He would not have the strength or will to fight back – not now, not after all that had happened. But Howie let go; stepping back, breathing deeply, muttering inaudible words.

John tried to cool the atmosphere by telling Howie he would still get the money – all £224,00 of it.

'Don't speak!' Howie roared. 'I know you'll get that money… because if you don't, I'll kill you. Rest assured of that. No matter where you run!'

John was incredulous. He felt his own temper rise. 'You'd think I would run from you? From Sarah? After all we've been through? I *love her* – don't you realise that?'

Howie's eyes burned. He was silent for a few seconds. When he spoke next his voice was almost a whisper. 'It's only by virtue of that why I haven't killed you right now.'

John nodded.

'Listen,' Howie continued, speaking up, 'Sarah needs a doctor. We both know that. Harriett's a nurse but can only do so much. I can contact some people tonight, but there's no guarantees that they can get Sarah the help she needs. I presume you have nowhere else to take her?'

'Not really,' John replied. 'There's a hostel down the road though, if that -'

'Forget it,' Howie interrupted, 'I meant a crooked doctor, some private surgeon.'

John briefly considered Nuacorn, but he knew Sarah had

been right. They'd report the bullet wound, and Sarah would find herself waking up not in a hospital but in a prison. John wasn't ready to be the one who decided that for her – not yet. 'In that case,' he said, 'no… I don't know anywhere else to take her.'

Howie sighed. 'I'll call around.' He turned and strode back to the flat.

'We can't let the police know,' John called back.

Howie swung around, anger re-igniting a red light within his pulsing veins. 'You think I'm stupid?!'

John stood there blankly, like a man staring into the face of a bull that is seconds away from charging. A stand-off. He could have sworn that a sound emanated from Howie's throat – some kind of growl or animal snarl.

Before re-entering the flat, Howie swung a fist into the door. The solid bang echoed right along the corridor. He neither grimaced nor cried out.

John followed at a distance, noticing the dent half-way up the door before he entered the flat. He caught a glimpse of Howie vanishing into the bedroom.

There was no respite for the rest of the night. He was left alone with Harriett, since Howie had locked himself away. Her demands and orders were continuous: 'get this', 'get that', 'make me some coffee' – the woman was in a perpetual state of agitation.

No wonder Howie's like he is, John thought. But then he supposed they were probably a good match, suited to one another's nature. Thankfully, Harriett eventually got up and went to the bedroom, telling John to look after Sarah. The room fell silent as he bent over the sofa. He stroked her hair, feeling its velvety texture.

'Don't you dare die. Keep fighting, as you always do. I love you, you hear? God, I love you.'

There was no response. Only the slight brush of her breath – so gentle – against his skin.

He fell into the chair by the sofa, tears streaming down his cheeks.

He was scared. Terrified. If she died…

The thought alone was agonizing. Thinking back to their past – their meeting, their romance, their arguments, their reconciliations – he felt a deep tiredness slip over his eyes.

Surrendering to the darkness, he fell into a better world.

29

City lights dimmed and flickered as night, for the billionth-something time, gave way to day. Many processes and mechanisms had shifted in the interval between dusk and dawn. Babies were born, people died, lightning had brought down a church tower. A major drug shipment had arrived by lorry. A jeweller's had been burgled.

The organisation behind these latter events, and many more, was re- configuring and solidifying its ranks. The solo neutralisation order on Target #10112 had not been authorised. Those responsible for organising the original neutralisation team had informed international co-ordinators, who arranged for a 'message' to be sent to the stubborn old man who thought he could do priority Mafiosa business by himself. One of the co-ordinators was appointed to take control of the situation. He arrived by private jet in the morning.

Reviewing all details on Mr Stevens, along with the reports sourced from police plants and other information, he reached the conclusion that a new tact was warranted. Ordering the neutralisation team to stand down, he contacted a local controller and arranged for Mr Stevens to be intercepted.

* * *

When John awoke, Harriett and Howie were in the room talking. A cold yellow light poured through the flimsy curtain at the window. He yawned and stretched the stiffness out of his body. They both looked at him – one with an expression of repressed malice, the other with disapproval. He went over to the sofa and bent down to check on the most valued person in his life. Yes, she was still breathing. Slowly, and oh so weakly.

'Where's the doctor?'

Howie shook his head. 'There is none. I've been trying all night.' 'Don't worry,' Harriett said. 'I'm going to convince a friend from the hospital to come here. She'll be by Sarah's side before ten.'

'Ten?' John said, looking at his watch. 'Sarah's dying. Even minutes could make the difference. Can't you get a doctor here sooner?'

'We could take her to a hospital right now,' Howie pointed out, 'but you know what that would mean.'

Would I rather see Sarah locked in a prison cell or her name on a plaque? John asked himself once again. *At least she would still be living. But alive? Could anyone be alive when deprived of their freedom – everything that defined a life?* They had discussed this many times, and always reached the same consensus. '*Death*', they vowed, '*before such an existence*'. The mission – the Organisation which they had built – had gone too far. The stakes were too high. If captured, it would mean decades, even a lifetime, in those shadowy places that mankind called jails.

'Look,' Harriett said, interrupting his thoughts, 'the pharmacy down the road should be open now. I've made a list of things that Sarah will need.'

She passed a note over to John. Her eyes seemed to soften when she looked at him, perhaps seeing the distress of his soul. 'The walk will help you, too,' she said.

He was reluctant to leave Sarah.

'Go on, kid. Sarah's not gonna die whilst you're gone. Here, take this money,' Howie said, pressing some notes into his hand.

He could not help feeling that they were trying to get rid of him. Nevertheless, remaining would be a pointless act, so he slipped into his coat and checked he still had Sarah's gun. He didn't feel safe leaving it behind anymore. As he reached the door to the flat, he glanced back at the beautiful body lying on the sofa. Then he left, fighting back the tears and running down the stairs.

A soft drizzle was falling from dull grey clouds when he got outside. In the distance a dog barked, sending out its discordant notes of dismay to all who would listen. It seemed to John that it was speaking directly to him.

Under the horizon the ground was a mirror to every object, holding no capacity for colour. There was nothing bright or good about the world in Sarah's absence; even the trees were ugly skeletons bedecked with ivy cloaks. Every fight for equality and justice counted as nothing in the battle to save Sarah's life. His thoughts were not for the families and children whose lives could be uplifted by the Organisation he had built; they were only on the woman he loved.

The drizzle was changing to a more forceful rain, which performed a tremulous rhythm on his coat and streamed down his neck. Shivering, he glanced across the road to the pharmacy store.

Just as he was about to cross, a car pulled up to the curb. Blacker than a bat from the festering swamps of hell, it blocked him from crossing. A door sprang open.

He jumped back and reached into his pocket for the gun.

A large man sat in the car, wearing a suit. 'We're not police,' he said. 'We want to help.'

Remembering the assassin in the tunnel and the man who had shot Sarah, John still kept his hand on the gun, discreetly pulling back the safety catch, but not yet taking it out to fire.

The man held his hand up, appearing to signal to the driver. 'We know about Sarah,' he said.

Only then did John get in.

The seat was rich leather and the car stank of expensive tobacco. The man sitting next to him looked in his fifties, large but not obese, with a greying moustache and a pair of shades. 'I guess you want to know who I am,' he said, smiling. 'We'll get to that. First of all, I'm going to make you our offer.'

Looking to the front of the car, John noticed two men, both young and wearing suits, with broad shoulders. The rear mirror was centred firmly on his position, and their strong brown eyes gazed at him piercingly.

GOOD INTENTIONS

'We know everything about the robbery,' the man said as the car began moving, 'and about you and Sarah, your organisation... we've been watching you for a long time.'

A tone of what seemed apology entered his voice. 'The man you encountered in the sewer – he was there against our orders. We didn't know he was there. It is good fortune that you killed him. That saved us from doing it. Our congratulations.'

John did not tell him the truth: that it was the tramp who did the killing. He thought it was best to appear more dangerous than he really was. They could be taking him anywhere – and he had the feeling that, once they arrived, more than one journey would be over.

'Last night,' the man continued, 'the other person you met – that was a mistake. Our apologies.'

The man laid his hand on John's shoulder. 'You have proven yourself more capable than we would ever deem possible. Your commitment to your organisation matches my own. I respect that.'

His yellow-toothed smile revealed a history of countless cigars. 'Now, the offer is this. We'll give Sarah the treatment she needs, get you out of the country, leave you alone to continue your operations. Acceptable?'

The man was hiding something. He was either lying or leaving something out. John straightened and looked him in the eye. 'We can already get out of this country without your help. Sarah will get the attention she needs. And I don't need your 'assistance' in my business.'

The man continued to present a thin smile, but it resembled what John had seen from a Nile crocodile. 'Think carefully, my friend. Without us, the police *will* get you. Sooner or later, it will happen. You know this. As for Sarah, are you quite sure you can get her the necessary treatment, even with our mutual friend Howie? Ah, think carefully indeed.'

John was stunned by how much he seemed to know, and the apparent extent of his power ('*mutual*' friend?), but he was right. Considering what to do, John was all too conscious of the clock that was ticking. *'Even minutes could make the difference,'* he had told Harriett. Those same words reflected back on him, forcing him into a decision.

'All right! If you can help Sarah – do it. I will give anything to save her.'

Now the man's smile really did begin to resemble a slight impression of genuineness. 'What we want in return is exactly the same as what's in it for you,' he said smoothly. 'Profit. We want a slice of your pie, Mr Stevens.'

'Money from the casino?'

The man laughed – a deep, throaty sound that ended in a wheeze and a hacking cough.

'You think you can buy us off so easily?' he winked. 'No, no. That's nothing! We want in on your operations. Whether you know it or not, your investment portfolio is about to bloom. And then there's the casino counterfeiting chips… yes, we'll help with that too, share out the profits between us.

GOOD INTENTIONS

Of course, you'll also be expected to process money for us as well, but that won't present any problems.'

'I see,' John said, tempted to ask what exactly he meant by the term 'process'.

'Well?' the man asked, 'do you accept?' All eyes were on him now.

John paused. The world seemed to be gliding on a totally different level. Time itself seemed to wait for his answer. Thinking back to Sarah, who was lying on the sofa in Howie's flat, he spoke with confidence and conviction, saying the two words that could guarantee a new future, whether for good or bad.

'I accept.'

The man held out his hand. John, with resignation, shook it.

As the car continued moving to its unknown destination, stopping at street lights and being passed by traffic, John was told about the organisation that the man worked for. The more he heard, the less he liked.

'We have always been around,' the man said, who introduced himself as Victor, 'working tirelessly behind the shifts and currents of history. As my favourite poet once said: *No man is an Island, entire of itself; every man is a piece of the Continent, a part of the main.* We all make ripples, and the ripples of others in turn affect us. A man is shaped by his country, his upbringing, his time. And we *are* men of our time, Mr Stevens, a time that we are – to some extent – responsible for moulding. Laws, deals, inflation, recession, unemployment… they never happen without us. We're behind them somewhere, working and moving in tandem with others who you never even know exist. People like yourself.'

Victor began to philosophise about the power of ideas. 'Men and their constructions all die out. There is only one thing they can make that lasts: an idea. Your organisation, like ours, is an idea… something that is immortal.'

John listened as Victor made glittering promises of advancement. He saw how his own organisation could grow with the Mafiosa, drawing strength and wealth as a co-operative, even if their interests and intentions were essentially polar opposites.

'There will come a day,' Victor said, 'when we will toast each other's enterprises, looking not at the setting sun but at the rising Earth.'

They dropped him back outside Howie's block of flats. As John got out Victor called: 'We'll be in touch.'

The rain had stopped falling, and the sky was almost clear. Along the pavement a series of puddles reflected a world that was constantly changing, intangible, and uncontrollable.

Before John reached the entrance another vehicle pulled up to the curb, its heavy brakes sending up a wall of spray. Two men wearing paramedic uniforms appeared, carrying a folding stretcher. At first he thought that Howie and Harriett had called them, but then one of them put a hand on John's shoulder.

'We're with Victor.'

GOOD INTENTIONS

It seemed so surreal. He went up with them, trying to think of what to tell Howie.

'It's OK,' John assured him when they reached the flat. 'I've got things sorted out.' There was no time to explain what had taken place, nor mention the momentous contract he had entered into. The men carefully lifted Sarah onto the stretcher, then took her down on the lift, with John and Howie close behind. They got into the back of the ambulance, sitting on a small bench as Sarah was tended by one of the paramedics. Within seconds the siren was blazing, and they were rushing through traffic.

'Is she going to be OK?' John asked.

'I hope so,' the paramedic said, avoiding the question. 'Where are you taking her?' Howie asked.

'Mount Rushmore's. It's a private clinic on the edge of the city.' 'Never heard of it,' Howie frowned.

It could have once been a country estate, with extensive grounds and a mansion serving as the main hospital. The ambulance drew up alongside a row of smaller vehicles marked with 'Medical' and 'Doctor'. Sarah was placed on a gurney and wheeled through a set of doors.

The smell of disinfectant engulfed him immediately as John entered a corridor, passing doors on each side. More people joined the procession as he rushed to keep up.

Eventually a woman stood in front of him as Sarah disappeared into a big swinging door. 'Let me be with her!' he said, struggling briefly to get past the large, blue-capped nurse.

It was Howie who pulled him away. 'Calm down, you idiot!' he said. 'It's an operating room. Only doctors can go in there.'

Grudgingly accepting this, he was shown to a seating area. A man appeared, dressed in the attire of a surgeon. 'Mr Stevens?' he said, stepping up to John.

'Yes... how is Sarah? Can you operate?'

'We can. There's a great deal of blood loss and internal trauma, but the treatment she's already received has improved her chances. May I ask who treated her?'

'My partner,' Howie said. 'She's a nurse.'

'Ah,' the doctor said, 'that would explain it. We are now going to remove the bullet. This will be the most... uncertain time.'

'Can I see her?' John said anxiously.

'Not now, I'm afraid,' the doctor said sympathetically, 'but I will send a nurse to get you if I feel... it's appropriate.'

'I guess you gotta report her injuries, huh doc?' Howie asked.

The doctor raised an eyebrow and spoke flatly. 'How and why she got shot is not my business. My job is to save lives.'

Appearing reassured by this, Howie smiled and put a hand on the doctor's shoulder. 'Do your best, doc, she means a lot to me... to both of us.'

'I will,' he said, walking back to the operating room.

The rest of the morning passed like a whole day as John sat in complete despondency. He ignored Howie, whose attitude had changed to one of concern and sympathy. In the resulting silence Howie spent most of the time pacing,

GOOD INTENTIONS

getting soft drinks and snacks, building towers out of the empty and half-empty cans, then cursing whenever they fell down. John just sat there, planted to the same spot, his head in his hands. Eventually he got up and asked a nurse where the toilet was, but his mind was still hovering in the same place. Howie's curses echoed along the corridor as he tried to build his towers higher and higher, retrieving more empty cans from the bins. They were the only two people in the waiting area, although people were continually passing and using the vending machines, glancing at them with worried expressions.

Finally the doctor returned. John awakened from his stupor as Howie shot up from his seat. The white-clad man spoke words fit for a Royal Coronation or Knighthood, declaring 'She's in the clear.'

Howie clapped him on the back, beaming a wide smile, as John fought back tears of joy. 'When can I see her?'

'Soon,' the doctor said. 'We're taking her to the recovery ward, but she's in a coma. It's not an abnormal thing in these situations, don't worry. It's the body's way of conserving energy, and usually lasts a few days at most.'

Suddenly John's joy had transformed to anxiety. He had read of people who had been in comas for months, even years. Would Sarah wake up as an old woman? Would he be able to keep her safe for all that time, fighting back the threats and changes of a cruel, unrelenting world? Thinking along these lines, he wasn't sure what to feel.

30

In the week that followed, John sat by Sarah night and day. There were two occasions when people from the mysterious organisation visited, when he was given new fingerprints using laser-moulding equipment in one of the hospital's rooms. They also offered him plastic surgery to change his facial appearance, which he refused. As soon as Sarah was well, they assured him, she would be offered the same treatment.

Howie and Harriett visited often, always bringing a bouquet of flowers, which were beginning to turn the room into an exotic conservatory. Howie was getting anxious and impatient to leave the country after all employees at the casino were scheduled interviews with police. He was certain they would be able to make a crucial link. Consequently, John arranged with one of the Mafiosa men for new identities to be provided for Howie and Harriett. They readily agreed, and the next day new passports were waiting in a drawer by Sarah's bed. Meanwhile, John began the process of relocating the robbery money. It went from the secure locker to the safe in the industrial unit on the outskirts of Bath.

When Howie next visited he was given a suitcase with everything he needed to start a new life overseas: £224,000 in cash, along with the passports provided by the Mafiosa.

GOOD INTENTIONS

'Don't think this can repair your mistake,' he warned John. 'I still hold you responsible for what happened to Sarah. Make sure you look after her in future… because I'll be watching.'

He left the room carrying the suitcase – destination unknown.

As the ongoing police investigation took new avenues, John felt a growing need to leave the country, lest one of those avenues eventually converged on him. If not for Sarah he would have left the day after the robbery.

She had been in a coma for almost a week when the investor from Coutts bank contacted him. It turned out that some of the companies he had invested in were beginning to show dividends.

'Shall I sell, Mr Stevens?' Wainruth asked.

'No,' John said firmly. 'Just keep me monitored if there's any changes.'

He was not going to sell this year, or the next, or the one after, whatever happened. The companies in the WinImplex portfolio represented a new road humanity was taking, and soon the Organisation would be a part of building that road – taking the next generation to a bright destination of hope, equality, and opportunity. Yet it was all empty without Sarah. He would still work towards their dream, making it become a reality, for her sake as well as the people he vowed to help. But it would be more like an enforced duty than a willing creation. Indeed, everything in life – from breathing to eating – had become the same. Half of him was a shadow, lost in the place where Sarah had gone, and the other part longed for unity. Without her nothing would be complete.

After concluding the call with Wainruth, he held Sarah's hand, sitting beside the bed. 'You and me have changed the world,' he told her, 'and our dream will never be destroyed. It will last as long as our love forever. Can you hear me, Sarah? Squeeze my hand if you can.'

He waited. The sound of the beeping electrocardiogram was hypnotising, a beacon of hope. But Sarah neither moved nor spoke. She didn't squeeze his hand.

'Where are you?' he whispered. 'Where have you gone?'

Bright rays of sunlight deepened to scarlet-ruby before he left the room.

* * *

In Africa the savannah was silent, but the slums could never rest. Lines of people skimmed garments along the remnants of a river, defying the oily water that no longer sang. In Asia the ruins of a temple echoed with the flute of an orphaned child. In the city her siblings scrambled through garbage, searching for scraps. Sarah had seen this, and now she was seeing it again. In South America a daring teenager stole food from an anchored yacht, and was shot before he reached the beach. These images, and countless more, flashed through her mind. They kept coming until it was just one chain of moving shapes and changing colours: villas, tents, cars, refugee camps, factories,

GOOD INTENTIONS

suits, rotting fruit, severed limbs, champagne, smoking trees, needles, faces… on and on and on, accelerating into total chaos.

Then they stopped. There was… a blinding light; a supernova of pure gold and aqua-flowing turquoise. A new set of images appeared: a landscape of transforming objects, which flowed in and out of being. There were pillars as tall and grand as ancient temple porticos, stairways as strange and twisted as those painted by E. C. Escher. It all gave way….

…to a sparkling cityscape, lit by a rising sun. Those rays touched upon no sight of suffering or poverty. Sweeping as a bird into every alcove and doorway, she saw gardens filled with fruit-bearing trees, people moving with a great purpose and inner peace. Fountains rose up like reaching hands into a clear sky. Music played in plazas of exquisite beauty. Strange vehicles moved silently on open roads. She saw it was a place where everyone was equal, given every opportunity to reach their full, spectacular potential. There was no place for money or borders between rich and poor. Here the aspiration of 'to each according to their needs; from each according to their abilities' was fulfilled. It was a society where everyone shared an equal measure of power, a pantisocracy. It was a place where humanity realised its limits: that the species was one of many, living in a global ecosystem that was both delicate and intricately connected. But these limits had set a new path of discovery and exploration…

Leaving the city, ascending into the air, flying right out of the atmosphere, Sarah saw a moon that was no longer lifeless and barren. There were cities there, too – under globes of glittering glass, in immense caverns, sparkling with countless lights. And beyond... a new-born highway to the stars, pointing away into the vastness of interstellar space, to other worlds.

Revelling at the splendour of this vision, she ventured towards these worlds, passing beyond the solar system. She catapulted past giant Jupiter's moons, glided beyond the multi-textured rings of Saturn, swung away from the green-blue worlds of Uranus and Neptune. Into the coldness, into the dark, where years became as minutes, and centuries as hours, she saw it:

Life. Thought. Intelligence. On distant worlds she glimpsed a wisdom that superseded any that could be found on Earth; an indescribable depth of knowledge that reached to the pulsing core of existence. It was beautiful. There were floating structures that rose out of indigo clouds, sketched by the light of more than one star; moons that had become entire ships; gateways into unexplored dimensions. There seemed no limits.

Something began to happen – a subtle shift. She found herself being pulled... dragged... backwards. The worlds receded, the stars became mere dots. Some gigantic cloud of dust blackened her sight, like a curtain drawn down by invisible hands. A pulsating light probed through the murk, permeating her consciousness with weird sensations. She felt as though she was falling, gaining weight... descending through vapour to yet another world. A shadow loomed, rapidly approaching.

She was suddenly back in the tunnel, near the ladder that led up to the casino storm drain. The shadow was close enough to touch, only that was the last thing she wanted to do. She wanted to run, to get away, but she was frozen. Trapped.

Now the shadow took form. It groaned, whispered, snarled. A face – too terrifying to contemplate – opened its mouth, revealing only darkness. Then it became a person: the gun man who was killed by the tramp. He was screaming. He reached out with charcoal arms.

A light flooded through the tunnel. The shadow, inches away from touching Sarah, shrank back. But not before whispering something that would stay with her for a long time, dragging itself through her deepest fears: 'you... could have been... mine.'

She had been granted a special kind of grace; saved by virtue of what she intended to do. Without the mission that had become her life goal she would never have escaped the tunnel. She knew that. Good intentions had pushed away the darkness, and yet alone they were not enough to keep the shadow at bay.

Light pierced the walls, breaking through bricks. It began flashing, pulsating, until by gradual degrees Sarah became aware it was a sound:-

Beep... beep... beep...

Steady like her pulse. She realised that she was lying down. New feelings rushed towards her, converging as droplets of rain: touch, smell, sound. Her eyelids were clamped shut by some strong glue. It hurt to open them. When she did, the light was blindingly brilliant. It became a spark that ignited a forest of memories. She suddenly recalled what happened: the casino, the tunnel, the rooftop chase, getting shot, being carried by

John. And beside all these memories was a looming shape, the shadow. It towered over her, returning her to the moments she fired the gun. Matt getting shot. The feelings of guilt and regret that had enveloped her whilst being confronted by the man in the tunnel. That's what the shadow is, she realised, not death, not despair, but guilt. It was the cost of her Return. And the only way to escape it was to embrace repentance.

As her eyes adapted to the light, she saw the tubes that connected to her body and the machine that beeped. She smelt the host of flowers that were placed upon a nearby desk. But the most important and most worrying thing was the lack of something, or rather the absence of someone.

She was alone.

* * *

'Do you have any ID?' the woman asked suspiciously.

The question didn't surprise John, given his youthful appearance, but it was still annoying. He handed her a driving licence – one of many.

'Thank you, sir,' she said, slipping the bottle into the plastic bag.

A few more bottles and I'll end up like the tramp, he thought. Something vibrated in his pocket. He answered the mobile as the cashier reached in her till for some change.

'Mr Stevens? This is Doctor Prenticoule.'

Sarah's doctor. Suddenly everything else was forgotten.

GOOD INTENTIONS

The supermarket no longer existed.

'You should come to the clinic as soon as possible,' the doctor said. 'Sir? Your change.'

'What's wrong, Doctor?' he asked, ignoring the woman, 'is Sarah —'

'No, no, she's —', 'Sir! Your change!'

The woman's impatient voice drowned out what the doctor said. John was tempted to shout 'SHUT UP!' but instead walked out of the supermarket, disregarding the shouts behind him.

'Doctor? Sorry, I missed what you said. What's happened to Sarah?'

There was no response. The signal had chosen the most inopportune time of its existence to fade. He jammed the phone back into his pocket, resisting the urge to smash it against the pavement, and headed to the car.

'Hey! Excuse me!' a voice cried out.

The man's shoes made heavy knocks against the pavement as he ran forward. Other pedestrians turned to look. John could either ignore him or wait to be confronted. There was little time before the latter option was thrust upon him.

'That stuff you brought – you want it or not?!' He was almost bald, with two tufts of black hair that rimmed his ears. He looked about forty.

'I don't want it,' John replied, turning away. 'Hey! Don't turn your back on me, mister!'

John wanted to hit him, but he kept walking. It seemed as

though everyone else on the street was still standing there – watching, expecting something to happen. Like they had nothing better to do, like they…

A hand fell on John's shoulder. He saw a glint of metal. No time to reach for the gun.

* * *

'Mr Stevens,' the man said. 'Who are you?' John asked.

'Calm down. My name's Wilfred. I -'

The metal in the man's inner jacket was not a gun. It looked like part of a badge. John slid a hand into his own jacket, but then thought better of it. 'I don't care what your name is! What do you want?'

'Ah, Mr. Stevens! No need to be rude. I was asked to keep an eye out for you, and test you when the opportunity arose. You might have passed the test if it were not for the attitude.'

'I don't believe this. It's not the time for games, whoever you are.'

The man simply grinned – an expression that only fuelled John's anger. 'I'm going to walk away,' he said slowly, 'and if you're still following me…' John didn't finish the sentence. He quickly turned around, before he had a chance to reconsider hitting the man, and walked to the car.

This time, he wasn't followed.

Traffic crawled along in a perpetual line of red lights. It seemed to take hours before he finally drove through the private clinic's gates. Doctor Prenticoule came to the reception desk after the secretary heard John's urgency.

'Hello Mr. Stevens,' he said. 'How is she?'

'Well, there appear to be no problems with her cognitive ability, which was always a possibility, but we will need to do a few more tests.'

'You mean she's awake?' John asked.

'Yes. She's been asking to see you. There was no unexpected complications in her regaining consciousness. The coma has made -'

'Doctor,' John interrupted, 'I'll see her now.' 'Oh, certainly.'

John rushed down the corridor, going straight to Sarah's room. She was sat up in bed, her face pale, but awake – alive! His heart pounded with happiness. 'Oh Sarah! I'm sorry I wasn't here when you woke up, I was… God! It's so good to see you.' He embraced her, unable to be separated for any longer.

'Is it true?' she said. 'What?'

'I've been gone eight days?'

He stroked her long hair and nodded. 'And the police?'

'Don't worry about that. We're safe.'

She was silent, gazing into his eyes with uncertainty. Then she sighed and laid back on the pillow.

He hugged her again. 'John…'

'Yes?'

'I saw it.'

The door opened and a nurse came in, carrying a tray of

food and drink. 'Is everything alright?' she asked, placing the tray on the bedside table.

'Fine,' they said in unison. Smiling, the nurse left the room.

John gestured to the tray, which Sarah barely glanced at. 'Do you need help eating?'

'No. I've got to tell you what I saw.' She closed her eyes, appearing to fall asleep, then she opened them. 'It was the future, John – what could be, if only…'

Her eyes were sliding downwards, and her words floated away to imperceptible syllables.

'Sarah, what were you saying?' he called her back from the edge of unconsciousness.

'So tired…'

This time he let her slip away, fighting back the fear that she would fall into another coma. One more day – even one more hour – without her was unbearable.

There was a knock on the door. It might have been half an hour after Sarah fell asleep.

'Come in,' John called, preparing to hand the tray to the nurse.

He was surprised by who entered. It was Victor, and he was carrying a bunch of flowers. The red roses only served to contradict his appearance.

'So,' he said, 'the princess has awoken. May I sit down?' 'I guess so,' John replied.

Placing the bunch of flowers on Sarah's bed, Victor sat in the chair next to John's. The smell of tobacco smoke followed him like a hidden entourage. 'I understand there was an incident earlier with one of our minders?'

The word 'minder' didn't exactly infuse confidence; it brought associations of police agents and deadly assassins. 'I was of the opinion,' John said, glimpsing a reflection of his own face in Victor's shades, 'that we were partners – that our organisations would work together, not spy on each other.'

Victor took out a cigar. 'Do you mind?' 'Actually, yes.'

'No worries,' he replied, putting it back in his pocket. 'Yes, we're partners. But all partnerships begin with caution. And don't see it as 'spying'. We're merely keeping an eye out for you. We don't want you getting into any trouble, and we wanted to see how you dealt with confrontation – to assess if you could control your temper.'

He leaned forward and lifted up the bunch of flowers. 'A lot of people in our line of business can't.' He picked a leaf from one of the stalks and split it apart, appearing to stare at the network of veins that threaded the green chloroplast.

'It wasn't the time to test me,' John said.

'Yes,' he said, continuing to play with the leaf. 'Policeman always pick the most inappropriate times, don't they?'

John remembered seeing the badge of the man who had accosted him. 'You employ the police?' he asked, amazed.

Victor smiled. 'More than you would care to know. But don't worry. Now that Sarah's recovered from the coma, I expect you want to leave the country for a while. We can help with that.'

'Thank you, but I can make the necessary arrangements. And I can't go anywhere until Sarah is well enough.'

The mangled leaf disappeared into Victor's brown hand as he thrusted it into his pocket. 'Yes, of course. But know that the police are only partly under our control, and they're not going to give up. They've already made some important links. The sooner you depart to India, the better.'

Briefly John wondered how Victor knew that was his destination, but then he remembered the power of the organisation that had supposedly become his ally. 'All right, I'll keep that in mind.'

Victor nodded and got up, leaving the bunch of flowers (minus one leaf) on the chair. 'Any problems, questions, or issues, and you know who to contact.'

No I don't, John almost said.

A wafer of smoke sneaked into the room as Victor departed.

31

After three days Sarah regained her strength and Doctor Prenticoule confirmed that she would experience no permanent damage from her injuries. The operation had meant a kidney transplant (fortunately the clinic already had a compatible organ) and it was functioning without any problems. Only the scar of the wound would stay with her as a reminder of how close she had come to death. It was difficult to convey what she had seen or indeed experienced whilst in the coma: the vision of the world as it could be; humanity without the blemishes of oppression, exploitation and poverty.

'Could it become reality, I wonder?' she asked John as they strolled through the grounds of the clinic.

'Where there's a will…' he began. 'There's a way,' she smiled.

'In any case,' he said, 'we've got to try – especially after what we've already accomplished.'

'I'm just worried about those people,' she replied, 'this organisation you told me about.'

'Why?'

'Because… they're criminals, I guess. They can't be trusted.'

'Well, others might say the same about us,' he reminded her. 'And they'd be right.'

He stopped and looked at her. 'What?'

'All life is precious, John. I've only recently understood what that means. Every individual deserves consideration.'

A bike rushed past them on its way to the clinic. 'I'm confused. What do you mean exactly?'

She took a long breath before replying. 'I guess what I'm trying to say is that I can't do what we did any longer. I can't do any more robberies. Because people got hurt, John, and even when we thought there were no casualties people were still hurting inside. It's not right… even if it's for a higher good.'

He stared at her, seemingly unable to process what she was saying. 'But you wanted your dreams – our dreams – to become reality. No one got hurt until the casino, and neither of us could be blamed for that, really.'

He looked down.

'Are you sure about that, John? What about all the frightened tellers and managers we've left behind us?'

Silence. Either he didn't know what to say or he didn't want to reply. 'Come on,' she said, taking his hand.

Together they walked across the grass to a bench that was beneath an ancient-looking oak. There was children's laughter in the distance, coming from a group of people who had just left the main entrance of the clinic. Still holding his hand, Sarah gazed at him, visually tracing the contours of his brooding brow to his chestnut-coloured eyes. 'You know,' she said quietly, 'that sometimes the best dream can become the worst nightmare. Sometimes we chase a butterfly… and end up tripping over a snake. And the way to our dream is not through harming others, no matter how little it may seem. That's a step that will lead to somewhere entirely different.'

'Sometimes the means justify the end,' he said coldly, repeating what she had once convinced herself to believe.

'Do they? Do they really?'

For minutes they sat in silence, separated by a gulf of bending question marks. A bird uplifted its song high in the branches above, totally oblivious to the turmoil that stirred below.

'I can't take this path any longer. I will never again hold a gun. I will never put others in fear of their lives. And I couldn't. be with anyone who continued to do these things.'

Nor could I enjoy life without you, John thought, though he didn't say this. She had betrayed him. She had lied. She had refused to listen to him, and consequently was responsible for the bloodshed in the casino. But – there was always a *but*. Despite all this, despite all her faults, he still loved her. Was it enough to sacrifice his life's work? Could he break the vow he had made to those families in Africa; to the orphans in Cambodia; to all the Earth's poor, oppressed and exploited?

No. He didn't think so.

Nor could he leave Sarah. And part of him, a splinter of doubt and regret, agreed with her logic. Looking back to the time in the tunnel, when they had been confronted with the gunman, he saw how she was *right*.

By now she had got up. She was walking away.

He sprang up and went to her side. 'Then there will be no

more robberies!'

She stopped walking, but wouldn't say anything.

'We've got enough to keep BlueBridge running,' he continued, 'its operations will become self-sustaining. You know that. There will be no more people getting adversely affected.'

Still she wouldn't speak. 'What more do you want?'

A young couple walked by, their faces deeply tanned and glowing with vitality. He returned their 'hellos' and then turned back to Sarah. The branches above briefly sang to a gentle breeze, a symphony of wooden triangles tingling together. With their song Sarah broke her silence.

'Yes,' she said, 'I love you. I always will.' She spoke as if to herself, as if she was answering her own question. 'I'm just worried about these people. Who is to say what *they* are doing? I don't like the idea of you being partners with them, John. It makes you an accomplice.'

Her use of 'you' instead of 'us' bothered him deeply. 'It's just a business arrangement,' he assured her, 'just as this government indirectly sells arms to outright tyrannies and a minority stock holder can be indirectly responsible for deforestation. Ultimately *everyone's* an accomplice to criminals – on one level or another.'

She sighed, looking at the young couple who had walked past a moment ago. 'Sometimes I just wish we were like them. Sometimes… I just want to forget the world, let it go where it's heading. Then I remember my past – the time in

GOOD INTENTIONS

Africa, all the people who need help. I'd be a selfish bitch to turn my back on them. You're right… a great dream or vision is worth a little dirt. You just have to be careful not to completely obscure it.'

'The road of good intentions doesn't always lead to hell,' he added, 'and if it will make you feel any better, I'm just as concerned with this 'partnership' as you are. As soon as the opportunity arises, I'll sever it.'

'All right,' she replied, 'but don't forget that. Because, as much as I love you, I cannot go on as we did.'

He squeezed her hand gently. 'I understand.'

Beneath the gradually shifting shade, they gazed across the grass with united vision. Tomorrow, they would be halfway around the world.

Distantly drawn to far-way heights, the summer wind caressed the emerald branches above and flew onwards – through the city, across the fields, over the ocean, towards an ever-changing horizon.

Afterword

Dark is the night, dark is the deepest sea, dark the void between stars. But darker than all these is total fear – something that is devoid of hope, of love, of beauty. In this insipid darkness there are things that move; things that, in any light, would not exist. They dig a labyrinth of horrors, entrapping all who stray with the long chains of insanity.

Neil knew this. He knew it very well. For beside the labyrinth of fear's brood is a stagnant swamp that encompasses every kind of addiction and dependence. Alcohol was one. He had swam in its murky waters for a long time, having wandered the hinterlands of the labyrinth.

After the incident in the tunnel, he had spent several days beneath the city streets, venturing forth only for water. He hid the case of money where no one could find it, then decided it was time to re-enter the upper world.

With a few hundred pounds in his pockets, he brought new clothes and got a haircut. He found a cheap hotel and began searching for the right opportunity. Only twice did he return to the hiding place to get more money. By then he had a flat and a job.

After killing *the bad man* he had lost the engine of hidden anger that fuelled his need for alcohol, although the pain and sorrow of the past could never be forgotten. It was like he had performed a life-long duty, which had effectively released him from his life's bane. He was a stronger and a wiser man for the struggles he had endured, refusing to let them become obstacles any longer. Having the case of money made a big difference, along with all the opportunities it opened up, but it was the foresight to use it well that mattered.

Within a year he would have his own house and a successful business. Within two he would be the proud father of a son. And within three…

Who could tell?

Appendix

As a work of fiction, *Good Intentions* should not be regarded as an account of factual events, even though it is based upon real life. Indeed, any writer with aspiration must derive what they write from experience – as well as its sister collaborator, imagination.

Nonetheless, the 'Mafiosa' is a collective term for an entity that does exist. This is not a reference to some obscure criminal organisation, but rather the higher echelons of business. In today's world, where money has become the measure of power and influence, the most dangerous criminals are those who veil themselves in false claims of legitimacy, who are free to change the world to their advantage. The origins of practically every global corporation have grown from exploitation and oppression, just as the roots of modern governments were steeped in bloodshed. The only difference between law-maker and law-breaker is power. That is a consequence of allowing money to dictate life.

It is not unreasonable to suspect that a global 'organisation' exists: a group of super-rich individuals who assemble through mutual interest. Their activities are not restricted to the creation of monopolies, or secretly managing economies, or even propping up political parties. Arms dealing, co-ordinated assassinations, drug enterprises and regime changes are all part of their agenda. As part of a nexus of global power and wealth, this organisation is intrinsically bound to governments. For power blurs the line which separates legitimacy from criminality.

President Eisenhower was not so far off the mark when he described the rise of a 'military-industrial complex' that controlled many aspects of everyday life. Today that same entity has evolved, becoming more powerful and influential. Without straying into the realm of fiction, it is the new Mafiosa.

BV - #0050 - 080222 - C0 - 203/127/15 - PB - 9780993526510 - Gloss Lamination